The Chic Boutique on Baker Street

Rachel Dove

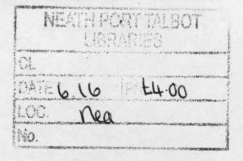

MILLS
BOON

Harlequin MIRA is a registered trademark of Harlequin Enterprises Limited, used under licence.

First Published in Great Britain 2016
By Mills & Boon, an imprint of HarperCollins*Publishers*
1 London Bridge Street, London, SE1 9GF

The Chic Boutique on Baker Street © 2016 Rachel Dove

ISBN 978-0-263-92202-8

09-0416

Our policy is to use papers that are natural, renewable and recyclable products and made from wood grown in sustainable forests. The logging and manufacturing processes conform to the legal environmental regulations of the country of origin.

Printed and bound by
CPI Group (UK) Ltd, Croydon, CR0 4YY

Emily Bronte, the author of my
favourite book, once wrote:
'Whatever our souls are made of,
his and mine are the same.'

I married my soulmate, and my best friend.
Love you Peter.

To my boys, Jayden and Nathan – the two
masterpieces of my life. Mummy loves you,
now go tidy your room.

One

Amanda stared up at the dark wood beam, pondering whether a strip of pale yellow taffeta ribbon would be robust enough as a makeshift noose.

She shook her head, banishing the futile thoughts, and started to clear off the workspace of her new venture when she heard the shutter from next door's shop go up. The metallic clang reminded her that next door had left their advertising board out the night before. She picked it up on her way to the shop front. New Lease of Life had only been open for a week or so, and her next-door neighbour, 'Shampooched', had not been the ideal business colleague. The twenty-something pink-haired rock enthusiast who worked there was not the friendliest person Amanda had ever encountered, but Amanda didn't want to make waves, being new to town and living above the shop and all. She took a deep breath and walked backwards into the shop, clasping the heavy A-board, a blackboard detailing their opening times.

'Hey, Tracy, you seem to have left this out…er again… so…'

Amanda was blocked from walking any further by a wall. Squeaking in surprise, she promptly dropped the A-board onto her own feet, this morning clad in soft green ballet pumps, of all things.

'Owww, son of a b—'

She was tumbling towards the concrete tiled floor, and a bruised bum to boot, when the wall moved and caught her in its grasp. Her words caught in her throat as she gazed up into a pair of steely grey eyes. She found herself smiling despite her embarrassment.

'I am so sorry, are you OK?'

The man was staring at her with a mixture of concern and amusement. Amanda's eyes flitted from his chiselled jaw to his full bow lips, and travelled down to his tanned, muscular neck, and his chest, which was encased in a simple black T-shirt. She loved watching the lips move. The movements stopped and Amanda frowned, disappointed. It was then she realised that the lips were attached to an actual person, a person who was waiting for an answer to whatever question these lips had formed.

What is wrong with you?

A voice, soft and cracking with what Amanda thought

might be suppressed laughter, broke through the awkward silence.

'I said, did you hit your head?' he asked.

Amanda shook her head. 'Er...no, no, just banged it a little. Sorry!'

Looking down at her right shoe, she saw crimson staining the mint green canvas of her pump. He followed her gaze, frowning.

'I'm Ben. Just stay sat there a sec, I'll get a chair and the first aid kit.'

Amanda nodded mutely, feeling a little cheated that the moment had passed, and more than a little embarrassed of her own behaviour. *Seriously, woman, you used to command the attention of courtrooms, a bloke in a shop trips you up, and you lose it!*

Ben returned, bringing with him a black fold-up chair and large green first aid kit. Amanda kept her eyes on the floor, but could just make out his long lithe legs in his smart black jeans and brown Docker boots. He settled her onto the chair, offering himself as a prop to support her as she got up off the floor. Her cheeks flushed as she felt his arm muscles flex under his T-shirt, and her nostrils twitched with the scent of his heavenly cologne. She literally had to stop herself from burying her head into his neck there and then.

'So,' Ben started, as he kneeled before her, opening his kit. 'You just opened next door, right?'

Amanda nodded, grateful for the small talk.

'Er yes, that's right, Amanda Perry. Do you work with Tracy?'

The mention of Tracy reminded Amanda that the goth girl was nowhere to be seen, and Amanda was acutely grateful for her absence. She figured this man couldn't be a customer, as he had no dog in tow, and he seemed to know his way around.

Please don't be her boyfriend, she thought to herself. *Wait, what? You don't care anyway, Amanda, new life, remember? Celibate new life. Men are out of bounds.*

Ben was concentrating intently on Amanda's injury, seemingly unaware of her question. *Yep, definitely her boyfriend then.* Before she knew it, the wound had been cleaned and bandaged up. Amanda was suddenly glad her last pedicure had not been too long ago, and thanked her lucky stars that she had bothered to shave her legs last night. Had this occurred a day earlier, Ben would have been patching up a limb resembling that of a Himalayan yeti.

'All done,' he said cheerily, flashing a smile up at her. He stood and, grasping her hands, pulled her to her feet. The sudden movement startled her and she swayed slightly. He tightened his grip, steadying her.

'Whoa! Are you sure you're OK?' he asked, concern clouding his features.

Amanda stiffened in his grasp and extricated herself from him as gracefully as she could.

'Yes, I'm fine. Thanks for doing that. I just wanted to

bring your board back. I…er…had better get back next door, I left it unlocked and we open soon.'

Ben smiled, and Amanda was once again drawn to his full lips. She mentally gave herself a telling-off, and pursed her lips in a businesslike fashion.

'Well, nice to meet you, Amanda, and if you need anything else, we are just next door.'

Amanda noticed the 'we' in the sentence, and winced.

'Yes, thanks,' she muttered.

'What is it you are doing next door, anyway? Antiques and such? Be nice to have one again, good for the tourists. Since Old Bill died, we have been sadly lacking for the antique market in Westfield.'

'No, nothing like that. Actually it's a boutique. We sell handmade crafts, doorstoppers, shabby chic decorations, upcycled furniture, craft kits, tea cosies, fairy doors. I make a lot of the items myself and run the upcycling service and I am planning to stock some kitchen table businesses' designs too, once my website is up and running. Plus, in the front, I have plans for a small coffee area, so people can shop and get a nice coffee, swap ideas. I am going to expand and sell items online too— handmade goods produced in Westfield. My research showed that people love Yorkshire crafts.'

When she paused to draw breath, exerted from talking excitedly about her new venture, she noticed that Ben was now scowling, and looking quite put out. 'Really? And the town council agreed to all this, did they? Tell them all this, did you?'

Amanda bristled at his abrupt line of questioning. Folding her arms, she suddenly missed her city heels. She drew herself up to her full height, which in flats still meant that she was looking at the bottom of his now up-turned and set jaw.

'Yes, I did tell them, and it was approved. Of course, why I need a town council's permission to set up a shop that I own myself is a little strange, but—'

Ben huffed. 'Strange!' he practically shouted. 'I don't think you quite understand, Amanda. Westfield is a historical Yorkshire village, we have a way of life here, I know you mean well but I just can't see any good coming from any of this.'

Amanda was absolutely dumbstruck. She was about to start apologising and explaining herself when she realised that this was exactly the reason she had left London in the first place.

'Well,' she retorted, poking Ben in his chest with an index finger. Well, not his chest, more like his stomach, from her angle. 'The day I take orders from another man is the day I pack up and quit life, so why don't you just do me a favour, Ben—stay out of my business and keep your bloody board out of my way!' With that, she spun on her heel, not easy in flats, and flounced out of the shop, making sure to bang the door on the way out.

As she was busy storming out, she heard him mutter, 'Bloody Londoners.'

She resisted the urge to go back and slap him, and instead spent the next half-hour pummelling stuffing into her new cushion range, imagining she was inserting things into her stuck-up country boy neighbour.

* * *

Next door, Ben was doing much the same, only he took out his frustrations on an unamused Border collie, who was shampooed and brushed vigorously to within an inch of its doggy life.

Two

Amanda dragged the silver metal shutter down with tired shoulders. The metal clanged into place, and she cursed as she dropped the key twice in her attempts to lock the deadbolts. Sighing, she secured the last bolt and straightened up. She winced as her back popped and clicked back into place. She had always thought that being sat ramrod-straight in court all day, followed by long nights hunched over her desk, would have been detrimental to her health, but after a long day in her shop, she now realised that the city girl in her had actually had it pretty easy compared to her new country bumpkin self.

The one thing she didn't miss was the long commute home. She shuddered as she thought of all those early mornings and late nights crammed on the Tube with sweaty, cranky people and drunks, all trying to get somewhere, anywhere else but the tin can they were entombed in most probably. She remembered the stench, the awkward face thrust into an armpit journeys, the glazed eyes all framed within the condensation of the windows of the trains. To say Amanda had a new-found respect for sardines after all those years would be an understatement. Those fish were the Thors of the oceans, albeit that their journeys were done in the afterlife, but still, kudos.

All Amanda had to do now was pirouette on one foot from the shopfront to her own front door, the flat being directly above her livelihood. The living quarters had been one of the main draws for Amanda, one of the catalysts that had enabled her to even visualise embarking into a new life, far away from her old one.

* * *

She had kept the property listing bookmarked for weeks, occasionally taking time to moon over it in between sending work emails and IMs to Marcus. It was like her porn, property websites and Pinterest. They made her happy, and growing up in the dysfunctional family she had, Amanda had soon realised that happiness had to be grasped where it could.

Being the daughter of two law partners, Amanda's childhood was less My Little Pony and more Mandarin lessons after school and organic vegetables on her dinner plate. Her parents worked hard, played hard and treated their only daughter like a science project, something to be worked on, altered and trotted out to show off at dinner parties. They worked all the time, and Amanda soon found a refuge: Grandma's house. Dad's mum lived alone in a neat bungalow on a leafy street in Muswell Hill not far from the impressive and sterile Highbury house she shared with her parental units. Amanda loved staying with her gran, a woman who despaired at her son's clinical, detached treatment of her only grandchild.

Looking around her new flat, Amanda thought of the happy times she had spent in that house: the smells of cooking, washing on the line, life. That bungalow had more life and joie de vivre within its crooked walls than could be contained, and Amanda learnt everything from her grandmother, Rose. Sewing, cooking, baking: Rose could turn her hand to anything, and showed Amanda another side of life. One where work and money did not rule the world, and where creativity and enjoying life had more value.

She was thirteen when Rose died. She could still remember the bungalow, the smells, the laughter, but now it was tainted, tainted with the memory of her parents picking through Rose's life, selling and discarding her possessions. She could still picture her mother's face, full of disgust at the layer of dust on the surfaces, the baskets of wool around the rooms. Grandma Rose's death affected Amanda deeply, whilst it was barely registered by her own son. After that, Amanda threw herself into schoolwork, working most nights in her room, and when she finished her schooling, she made her escape to university, the promise of a law career already mapped out since her infancy.

She wondered what Grandma Rose would have thought of her actions now; she suspected that she would be watching somewhere, geeing her on. Her parents, however, would not. She shuddered at the thought. Changing her life completely was something they would never understand. She reached out and touched one of the walls of her abode. It was cool to the touch. *Perhaps that bookmark was fate,* she thought to herself. *Maybe it finally brought me home.*

The flat was all high ceilings and bumpy plastering, and it looked to Amanda exactly how she was feeling—a bare shell.

She had pored over the pictures on the estate agent's website all night *that* night—laptop plonked on the bed, Amanda submerged under the duvet, surrounded by sodden tissues and the contents of her household bills box. She had made herself a little island of desperation, her king-size bed floating along on a sea of desperation, isolation and sheer disbelief. She felt like her world had been spun on its very axis, and she couldn't help but think of what her parents would say when they discovered the news. That night, Amanda had cried, wailed, and eventually, at 3 a.m., had emailed the estate agent to not only put her London flat on the market, but to also put in an offer on the shop and flat she had been ogling, far away from the hustle and bustle, in a Yorkshire town called Westfield. Only then, once the email had pinged 'sent', had the sick feeling in the pit of her stomach eased enough for her to drift off. She dreamed that her little divan island had floated away, and she awoke feeling determined and oddly detached from her previous self.

When she came to, with the light from her bedroom window shining on her laptop screen, she winced, wondering what awaited her now the juggernaut of her plan had started the low rumbling of action. She hadn't told anyone yet, but the water cooler gossip at work would be in overdrive this morning when she didn't turn in as normal. What would Marcus tell people? Would he back her up, tell people it was a mistake? Would he even care?

She still had no idea how it had happened herself, so how could she explain it to anyone else?

She remembered how she felt that day, but the reason the contract had gotten so messed up eluded her still. She was always so meticulous. After Marcus's visit to her office, she had knuckled down, eager to get the work done and sent off to Marcus, as he had so rudely requested on his way out to an afternoon at the golf course. Time had escaped her once again, and by the time she had finished printing off the paperwork, a quick glance at her workstation clock told her it was well past office hours. After rubbing her stiff neck, she arranged the papers neatly in the case file, threw her coat on, grabbed her bag and headed to Marcus's office. The office was empty, even the cleaners had gone home. A few side lights lit her path along the sleek corridors. She was just pondering on her pathetic life when she heard a noise coming from Marcus's office. Looking around her, she became all too aware that she was alone and that no one would actually miss her for a while if she were to go missing. Brandishing the file like a weapon, she froze, listening intently. She heard it again—a low grunt, punctuated by the odd squeal. *What the hell was it?* Gripping her bag tight to her side with her elbow, she gently pushed open the door to her boyfriend's office. She jumped as a bang sounded near her, and she realised that she had dropped the file she was holding. The papers exploded from the file, fluttering around her, but she took no notice. What she was looking at was far worse. Marcus was lying across his desk, trousers around his hairy ankles, while a woman was straddled across him, writhing. Both heads snapped towards her at the noise, and they froze. Amanda was trying to form a coherent thought in her head when Marcus jumped up, bouncing the naked woman off him. He jiggled around one-footed on the carpeted floor as he tried to pull his clothing back on. The woman just stared at Amanda, a smug look on her face, and it clicked into place then. Angela, his secretary. The biggest cliché of them all. Shagging her boss in his office after hours.

'Working late again are we, Miss Perry? We needed that Kamimura file by five,' she said, all the while pulling her silky panties back up over her stockings and under her short dress. Amanda nodded, looking at Marcus, who was now heading towards her, red-faced and green around the gills.

'Amanda,' he said, glaring back at Angela, who shrugged and sat down. 'This isn't what you think, I promise.'

Amanda felt as though she would pass out any moment. All those nights, working to make him look good, doing his work, waiting for him to pick her up for dates that never happened. The memories came like stab wounds, thick and fast, realisation dripping like blood from her new wounds. She shook her head slowly, trying to get her brain to connect to her mouth.

She swooped down, picked up what was left of the file and threw it to Marcus.

'All done,' she said and she fled.

Marcus chased her to the elevators, calling her name, but thankfully the steel doors closed on him just as he reached them. Amanda pressed a shaky finger to the lobby button and sank down to the floor, head in her hands. Her phone buzzed in her bag, and, on automatic pilot, she pulled it out.

'Perry,' she said, her words barely flopping for freedom from her numb lips.

'Amanda,' the prim voice said crisply. 'Mummy here, any news for me?'

Amanda stared at the walls of the lift as they took her to the ground floor.

'No, Mother, nothing to report. I'll call you later.'

Clicking off the call before her mother could ask her another question, she threw the phone into her bag, and peeled herself off the floor, quickly rearranging her clothes and hair before the lift doors pinged. Making her way across the marbled floors of the reception area, she smiled goodnight at the security guards and pushed through the front doors, gulping greedily at the fresh night air before hailing a taxi.

Two days later, she had been called into Stokes' office and fired. Gross negligence, they had stated. Amanda had barely taken it in, and before she even thought to ask what she had done, she was standing outside the same doors, a box full of trinkets heavy in her arms.

It was all a colossal mess, and now she was unemployed to boot. She should have been looking for another job, another firm to work for, before the gossip really spread, but she couldn't bring herself to apply anywhere else. What was the point? Her reputation was tarnished—bungling a million pound account did that for your career. The years of hard work and sacrifice would mean nothing. She was the girl who cocked up the huge contract and, now, that's all she would ever be.

She rubbed her gritty eyes, puffy, sore and still caked in last night's mascara, and gingerly reached over. She rolled her fingers over the touch pad and the laptop sprang to life. Squinting at the screen, she refreshed her email inbox. Whilst she had been sleeping, her new life had been forming around her, and when she opened the reply from the estate agent, she smiled to herself. Time to disappear.

* * *

The little Eden she had sunk her life savings into was thankfully not a disappointment, despite the sale being unseen.

There was an exterior entrance on the street, and a staircase within the shop too, which made her feel very safe and self-contained, master of her own realm. She could pretty much spend her life at work and home, all within a few steps. After all the commuting and fast walks in teetering heels, barrelling down corridors and storming into court, it was an appealing thought to Amanda.

Opening the door, she flicked on the light and sighed. After long days of working to make the shop interior what she had envisioned, she had barely made a dent on her new home and it showed. Boxes surrounded the chintzy sofa she had bought from eBay, a buy she intended to upcycle with some new covers, and which at present looked like something from her gran's house. Stepping over them, she passed a dilapidated end table and spied her smartphone. In the city, her phone had been permanently glued to her hand, never leaving her side for longer than a bath. The more time she did without it, the less she missed it, and the people who used it to contact her. Well, maybe her thoughts lingered on one, but she wouldn't allow herself to dwell on that now. Opening the wooden drawer in the front of the table, she scooped up the phone and shoved it in, dusting down her hands as she walked away. Last night's DVD title filled the television screen with colour as it sprang to life. She pressed 'play' and *Pride and Prejudice* began playing again, the embroidered garments flowing across the screen as the title music sounded. She walked to the open-plan kitchen, opened the fridge and pulled out a microwave Thai meal and the remnants of the bottle of rosé from the night before. Spying the washed glass on the draining board, she filled it up and took a swift glug, smiling as the cold chill of the wine hit the back of her throat, warming her through. She sat down on the break-fast bar stool, running her fingers along the bandage on her foot. She pursed her lips as she thought of the di-sastrous encounter, and the feeling that she hadn't been able to shake all afternoon. She had heard him next door, banging about most of the afternoon. He was obviously an arse. Obviously. She just felt sorry for the dogs he had been looking after. She could see him being a dog man though, all jeans, jumpers and ruddy cheeks, skipping over mountain and dale with man's best friend. Her face drew into a frown as she sipped at her wine. Tracy was the polar opposite of him, all mean scowls, and out-there fashion sense. Not a couple you would put together immediately, if at all. She ran her free palm along the side of the cool glass. In fact, they were pretty much the last people she would put together in a relationship. Not that she cared, of course, and his unkind words had stung. *What did he know about her business? Did he really think she hadn't done a little bit of research before she started?* Fair enough, she had sold her London life and skipped town in a heartbroken knee-jerk reaction, but *he* didn't know that, and it wasn't like she hadn't *thought* about doing it before.

She had the bookmark, the ideas, she had a plan. What she didn't need was the sexy—*Sexy? No!*—*annoying* business owner next door causing problems and making her the village pariah. In her last job, she would have taken him on, told him exactly what she thought of him, dragged an apology out of him, but he had rattled her, and the feeling was not familiar or welcome. She resolved to ignore him and his girlfriend, let them get on with it. Plus, they had a regular supply of fresh dog poop at their disposal. Sometimes, a girl has to pick her battles.

She sipped at her drink and rose when the microwave pinged. After setting her food out on a plate, she took both to the couch and wrapped herself up with a blanket left on the arm from last night. As Lizzie Bennet navigated singledom on the screen, Amanda pondered her own fresh start. If her city friends could see her now, huddled under a blanket in a box fort, watching Austen and getting into a tizzy over the first man under seventy she had met this month. Pathetic. And anyway, not only was she over men forever, but Ben wasn't single, he was an opinionated git and his girlfriend owned next door. And one thing was for sure, for the sake of her sanity and her bank balance, Amanda's new life had to work. No, she would stick to Mr Darcy. She would get through this week, spend her nights under this blanket of denial, and then, come the weekend, she would sort her new home, and her new life, out for good. And she wouldn't think about Ben again. She drank a toast to Darcy, smiling through a mouthful of pad thai.

'Just me and thee, Darcy!' she said, in a voice that held more conviction than she felt. Sighing, she took another glug and wondered yet again how life could change so quickly, and how she was ever going to adjust.

* * *

Ben Evans was arm deep in work. Mr Jenkins' prize cow, Gwendolen, to be exact. The poor animal was having a breech delivery. Ben could see the calf's feet pointing up, and Gwendolen was in distress. Not as much distress as Alf was in though. Alf Jenkins, one of the local steadfast farmers in Westfield, was leaning against the head gate, feet shuffling from one to the other. His ever-present roll-up was hanging from his tight lips, and his knuckles were as white as the white plastic apron encasing Ben's body. Ben looked out from the cow's behind, giving Alf a quick flash of his pearly whites.

'Alf, she is in breech, but I can get her out. I need you to get me a bucket of water, and a shot of brandy.'

Alf's impressively bushy eyebrows shot up into his hairline, which was half hidden in his tweed flat cap.

'Brandy?' he asked, incredulous.

'Yes, Alf, a decent shot please, and some water. As fresh as you can, in a bucket. Go now, I have Gwen, don't worry.'

Alf frowned and, looking confused, wandered off towards the farmhouse he shared with his wife of thirty years.

'Annie! Annie, Gwen is nearly there. I need the brandy!'

Ben chuckled softly, his distraction technique working well. Alf loved his cows almost as much as he did his wife, in fact at times it was a close call which he adored the most.

'Come on now, Gwendolen, let's get your baby born.'

Gwen responded with a low, rumbling moo. Ben inserted his hand further into the cavity, pushing the calf back into the uterus as gently as he could. He wondered whether the woman he had met today would be appalled by his job, as Tanya always had been. Did Amanda even like animals? Probably not, she was obviously a ball-breaker, not the type to go all goo-goo-eyed over a puppy.

Tanya sure didn't, unless they came in the form of designer coats and handbags. She had once toyed with the idea of getting a small dog, after seeing celebrities in her coveted fashion magazines being photographed with the latest living handbag accessory. She had even begged Ben to track down a breeder, until he had pointed out that the little pup might, in fact, have to be fed whilst out and about, and might even take a dump in her Louis Vuitton. He still remembered how his wife's lip had curled up in disgust, and half an hour later she was back to her usual online shopping frenzy, the possibility of a pet all but forgotten.

Gwendolen bellowed as he turned the calf around to a birthing position. She banged against the metal gates with her hooves and let out a rumbling low noise. Ben checked the position and, satisfied, he wiped the sweat from his brow onto his shoulder. Just as he was waiting for the next contraction to start, to begin pulling out the calf, Alf appeared, his cheeks red, carrying a large black bucket of ice-cold water and a bottle of brandy, a plastic tumbler perched upside down on top.

'Is she…?' Alf's voice broke with concern.

Ben smiled. 'All turned around, Alf, don't worry. She will be out in a jiffy.'

Alf's shoulders dropped as he visibly relaxed. He set the bucket down and lifted up the brandy. 'And this?'

Ben laughed. 'That is for you, Mr Jenkins, wet the baby's head.'

Alf chuckled as he began to fill the tumbler with the amber liquid. Gwendolen began to bellow again and, after a couple more contractions, Ben hauled the calf from its mother, laying it down on the fresh straw nearby. Alf preened and puffed out his chest, a tear in his eye, as he set the bucket of water down in front of Gwendolen. He planted a brandy-soaked kiss between the prize cow's long lashes.

'Well done, my girl, well done!'

Ben set to work, cleaning out the calf's nose with his fingers, tickling its nostrils with a blade of hay to get the calf breathing and moving about. The calf sneezed and, shaking its head, opened its brown eyes and looked straight up at its deliverer. Ben felt the rush of adrenalin, strong as always, as his job gave him another day to be proud of.

'Welcome to the world, little one,' he whispered softly, as he patted the calf lightly. He pulled his gloves off, reached into his zip pocket for his phone and snapped a picture of the new arrival with his camera phone.

* * *

An hour later, Gwendolen and Ophelia—the latest addition to the Jenkins household—were tucked up in their stall, clean and warm, whilst Alf, Annie and Ben sat around the farmhouse kitchen table, the fire roaring in the hearth. Ben had stripped off his blood-soaked coveralls and was now sat, hay still stuck out of his tussled brown hair, gulping down hot sweet tea and eating a steaming bowl of corned beef hash and Yorkshire puddings, made by the fair Annie. Alf and his wife were eating with him, laughing and joking happily, talking of their new calf and their plans for the upcoming summer county fair. Ben, dressed in a black woollen jumper and dark blue denim jeans, savoured the food and atmosphere. The Jenkinses were such happy folk, and he felt a pang as he thought of driving his jeep home to his own empty cottage.

He lived in the village, next door to his vet practice, and had impressive grounds himself, with space for horses and more, but with running two successful businesses, his dreams of having a little bolt-hole of his own like this had yet to come off as he had hoped. The furthest he had got was to purchase four chickens for his expansive back yard the week before: two black and one white Croad Langshan hens, and a Leghorn cock. He planned to have more animals eventually, but he had held off for some reason, probably due to the time and effort needed to keep them healthy and happy. He had not felt himself lately, and had only taken the chickens on due to another owner becoming unwell. The thought of the chickens being left abandoned had haunted him, so he had galvanised his efforts and stepped in to give them a home. They were still getting used to each other, animal and man, and the notion of how horrified Tanya would have been to share her home with his feathered friends gave him reason to chuckle, which hadn't happened often recently. Lucky for the chickens that Tanya wouldn't be sharing an abode with them, although her departure had been more of an adjustment for their owner than he had envisaged, given the circumstances. Who knew that the wife you are indifferent to, leaving with your best friend, would leave such a hole?

The thought of pulling up his drive to an empty house meant Ben wasn't in any rush to leave, and the Jenkinses were great clients, keeping him in business with their many farm animals and half-dozen dogs. Also, the dogs seemed to be constantly matted from farm life, which meant they often frequented his other establishment, Shampooched. He had bought the dog groomer's a few months after he and Tanya had moved to Westfield when the lady who ran it for many years retired and moved to Spain to crochet away her twilight days from her veranda. He had bought it for Tanya, hoping to get her more involved in village life, but it hadn't worked out quite as he had hoped. In fact, not at all how he had hoped, so now he had Tracy, who was sullen and off kilter to some, but she loved dogs and ran the business well, which took some of the pressure from him. Which reminded him, he had to run to the wholesaler's first thing, as Tracy had left him a list that morning, and he had his regular surgery to attend to as well, so he had an early start.

Having polished off two bowls of hash and enough Yorkshire puddings to fashion a raft on a sea of gravy, he reluctantly said goodbye to the Jenkinses and headed home. On the dark drive, he contemplated two things:

whether his new chickens had started laying yet, and whether he would see Amanda tomorrow. He wondered what she had meant by the 'we' when she spoke about being open soon. Did she mean the normal 'we' as in clients and staff, or did she really mean 'we' as in 'my adorable drop dead gorgeous bodybuilder husband and I'? Ben found himself wondering what sort of bloke she was with. Whoever the poor lad was, he had Ben's sympathies. She looked like a handful, and a bossy one at that. She was cute though…

As he pulled up to his front door, he smiled to himself at the memory of her flouncing off. He felt sure she was going to be a pain in the neck. He just hoped whatever arty-farty stuff she sold didn't drive the regular stream of tourists away. Somehow, he just knew he would have to keep an eye on his new neighbour.

Three

Everyone in the sleepy hill-set village of Westfield knew well enough to let Agatha Mayweather have her own way. The unofficial Lady of the small Yorkshire village was a veritable force of nature, and even the strongest characters in the community cowered under her steely gaze. When *Downton Abbey* had first aired, many villagers, eyes glued to their screens over their latest knitting projects and cups of tea, immediately saw the similarities and soon, unbeknown to her of course, Agatha was nicknamed the Dowager of Westfield. It was unbeknown to her for obvious reasons: she would kill them if she ever found out. It was so obvious to all who knew her though that the name stuck, and even the meekest of the townsfolk had a good titter at the comparison. Agatha had a sharp mind, a mean tongue and a no-nonsense attitude, and had Mr Mayweather not since passed away, he would have guffawed at the notion himself. Agatha and her dear late husband, Henry, were great presences in the community, and since his passing from a long battle with cancer, Agatha had seemed to have coped admirably well, throwing herself even deeper into village life and the many committees and causes she was patron of and involved in.

Their property was on the outskirts of the town, a beautiful, sprawling nine-bedroom Georgian country house that many a Mayweather had resided in over the years. Her gardens were a joy to behold, and she regularly opened them, and indeed her home, to the general public for the summer, donating the proceeds, after the running costs, to various causes in Westfield. As well as this, she also organised most of the events in the village seemingly single-handed (as she often wouldn't let people get much of a look-in). One such event was the summer county fair, held in the village of Westfield annually and a great kick-off to their summer months as a quiet, understated but beautiful tourist attraction. With the lambing season beginning, all talk was of the hard work to be done, both on the village farms and for the big event. Agatha's clipboard was poised, primed and ready to go already and the villagers were all steeling themselves for her firm knock at the doors of their homes and businesses.

As acerbic as Agatha's tongue was, she was dearly loved in the community and had no enemies amongst her kinfolk. She was the type of woman that you were friends with, immediately respected, admired and also, in secret, were a little afraid of.

* * *

Agatha's morning began the same as every morning, with Taylor, her estate manager, gently rousing her with a cup of English breakfast tea. Sebastian Taylor's family had worked as butlers for the Mayweather family for generations. As soon as the current Mrs Mayweather had become the lady of the household, she had done away with many of the old traditions and promoted Taylor, who was in fact her childhood friend from the village, and quite often her playground tormentor, to estate manager. Taylor, being a traditional fellow, was more than a little surprised to gain this new title at the age of forty-five, and a battle of wills had ensued. Agatha had won, of course, much to the amusement of her new husband at the time, but Taylor had managed to get his own way in upholding some traditions, such as bringing them their morning refreshments. These days, however, Agatha was secretly grateful for this small act of kindness every morning.

Losing Henry the year before, after twenty years of blissful marriage, had knocked the wind out of her sails more than she would ever own up to, and quite often, waking alone in the ornate four-poster bed, she was more than happy to see a friendly face as she awoke to seize the day.

'Thank you, Taylor.' She smiled as she took the ornate cup and saucer, embellished with tea roses, from the tray that he proffered.

'Good morning, Mrs Mayweather, I trust you slept well?'

Agatha rolled her dark blue eyes at her manager. 'Taylor, really? After all these years, you can't just call me Agatha?'

Taylor chuckled, ignoring the daily request. 'We have the summer fair to begin planning today, and the council meeting at 3 p.m., to discuss the permits for the beer tents and the marquees. Shall I be driving you?'

Agatha sipped her tea, her eyes closing momentarily as the sweet nectar travelled down her throat, warming her bones and waking her up.

'Yes, please, Taylor, and I have an eleven o'clock in the village for the children.'

Taylor suppressed a smile. 'Of course. I shall get them ready.'

Taylor left the room, and Agatha heard his soft footfalls as he descended the large central staircase. She hauled herself out of bed and padded to the ornate dressing table in her slippers, obviously left there the night before by Taylor. She tutted at his stubborn archaic ways and began to put her face on. Her gaze fell to the silver-framed photo next to her jewellery box. Henry smiled out at her, giggling at something she had said as they stood arm in arm, fresh faces, happy smiles, all decked out in their finery on their wedding day. She smiled and stroked her husband's face through the glass.

'Good morning, Old Boot,' she whispered, using her nickname for him. 'Busy day today, my sweet.' She kissed the tip of her finger and pressed it to the glass. When she had finished applying her make-up, she wandered off to the bathroom to get ready to face the day.

* * *

'Err, gerrof!' Taylor laughed as Buster licked at his head, sticking his wet tongue down his ear canal. Maisie, excited by Taylor's reaction, jumped up at his crouched form and knocked him to the floor. Taylor closed his eyes and tried to cover his face as both dogs continued their slobbery assault on him. He tried to get up, and just got licked all the more. 'Guys, come on now, stop it n—mmmffff!'

Buster took Taylor's open, speaking mouth as an invitation for a kiss and Taylor found his tongue being massaged by that of a huge, rather smelly dog's tongue in return. Horrified, he shut his mouth and began reaching frantically into his trouser pocket for a handkerchief. Just then, a bellow rang out and both dogs stopped, startled, and sat down, contrite at either side of a very wet and dishevelled Taylor.

'Children, stop that immediately!' Agatha was standing on the bottom step of the staircase, looking resplendent in a fitted peach skirt suit, pearly white blouse peeking from beneath, and matching cream cloche, her silvery white curls peeking out from beneath the fabric brim. Her dark blue eyes were shining with anger, and her taut gait made the dogs look to the floor. Taylor chuckled under his breath. Not every day two huge grey Irish wolfhounds looked like scolded children, which of course they were. Agatha, having never been able to have children, had always filled that maternal hole with the biggest, hairiest rescue hounds she could find, and Maisie and Buster definitely took the dog biscuit for being the craziest mutts she had ever given a home to. Agatha called them her children, and treated them as such, and both dogs adored her as much as she did them, although when Henry was alive, he had had to put his foot down and ban them from the bed, which, surprisingly, Agatha hated. She loved to cuddle up with them, but, even now, she honoured her late husband's wish and they slept in two huge plush baskets in the hall of the house, or laid out like two overgrown rugs in front of the ever-present fire in the drawing room. Brandishing the two thick leather leads Taylor hadn't noticed on the crook of her arm, Agatha smiled.

'When you have quite finished, Taylor, let's get into the car. Many, many things to do today, people to see…'

She wandered to the front door, grabbing her cream leather bag from the hall dresser on her way past, dogs in tow, tails wagging excitedly. Taylor groaned good-naturedly, pulling himself to his feet. His suit now looked like a dog blanket. Lucky he kept a lint roller in his glove compartment, he thought to himself, as he wiped the dog drool from his chin. After locking up the huge front doors, he wandered over to the car, whistling as he walked. Agatha eyed him from the back seat as he got comfortable, and he flashed her a cheeky wink. Colouring, she huffed and returned her attention to the dogs. Taylor held back a grin as they pulled away to the village.

* * *

A short drive later, they pulled up at the small parade of shops on Baker Street. Agatha had always loved this little slice of history—the large, ornate mouldings on the shopfronts, the quirky businesses they contained, it was always a favourite place of hers. She remembered running to the sweet shop as a young girl after school for her fix of sweets from Molly's Delights, the little confectioner's that used to be here on this very street. Molly had long since died, and the shop now changed hands, but the feel and look of the shops were still the same. She looked at the newest shop—A New Lease of Life. Rumour was—and Agatha *always* knew the truth—that the new owner was a city dweller, a quiet pale girl, who had recently upped sticks and moved to Westfield alone. The type of shop she had opened perturbed Agatha, and had since she had heard the new business application from the council meeting. Westfield was very much a make do and mend type of village, and an upcycling shop, whilst being a trendy fad to the city folk in today's austere times, was less of a new concept to the villagers. The villagers here never threw out anything without revamping it or repairing it as much as possible, and not many people didn't know how to sew, knit or bake. She did wonder how long this newcomer would stay, as she couldn't see the shop being much of a success, even with the tourist trade. She made a mental note to investigate further. She would pay this girl a visit tomorrow and see what was what. Maybe she could help her integrate into the village, and boost her trade. She was just about to tell Taylor he could open the door to get the dogs out, when something caught her eye in the new shop window. Or rather, someone did. Ben Evans, town vet and owner of the dog groomer's next door, was outside watering the planters at the front of the shop. Or, more accurately, he was drowning them. His arm was holding the green watering can over the poor spluttering plants, but his gaze was firmly on the shop window next door. More accurately, he was focused on the woman within, who was bent over the large wooden table in the centre of the shop, cutting and measuring fabric. She was a pretty thing, Agatha noted, with long brown hair tied in a loose, messy plait, her thin frame covered in a pretty floral dress and matching pastel pink bolero cardigan. Agatha watched as Ben's eyes never left her back. She was the polar opposite of his ex-wife, Tanya, that was evident. Agatha's brow furrowed at the memory of the Day-Glo orange Mrs Evans as was. All labelled clothes, designer perfume, which choked everybody in a one-mile radius, and gaudy talon-like fake nails. Everyone in Westfield had been scandalised when Ben, a native of the village, had returned fresh from university with his new love in tow. She was at such odds to Ben and his quiet, kind ways. Agatha had never taken to the woman, and was not sad when she had left for the bright lights and temptations of city life. She had felt for Ben though; the evil witch had decimated the poor young Evans lad, and he had not been the same since. Agatha's romantic side kicked in immediately, and she was just thinking how wonderful it would be for the two to get together, when the moment was abruptly broken. The nearest plant, bearing the brunt, was half dead, gurgling with the sheer weight of the water, and the terracotta pot, now full, began to overflow and splashed on Ben's denim-clad feet. Startled, Ben jumped back, tripping over the A-board that Tracy always had too close to the shop, and promptly fell over, his legs in the air. Quick as a flash, he jumped up, swinging his limbs widely. Grabbing the A-board for support, he straightened himself up, now damp, and cast a furtive glance at the window to see if the girl had seen. The girl in the shop, however, simply worked on, unaware of the drama outside.

Ben dusted himself down quickly and Taylor took this as his cue to get out of the car, coming round to

Agatha's door. Ben looked horrified, obviously realising that his little trip to the pavement had not gone completely unnoticed. He nodded sheepishly at Taylor and, looking into the car, beamed at Agatha, his grey eyes shining with embarrassment. Agatha grinned back at him before she could stop herself. She had always had a soft spot for the Evans boy, and he had grown into a fine young man.

The dogs loved him too and, as Taylor opened the door, they both made a break for it, Ben only just catching their leads before they barrelled into the shop.

'Good morning, Mrs Mayweather, how are you and your fine charges doing today?'

Agatha smiled. 'Fine, Benjamin, fine, as muddy as always, I am afraid. Buster here still thinks he is a spring chicken. I am afraid he was chasing rabbits again in the far paddock, poor Archibald had to dig him out of the warren!'

Ben chuckled, thinking of the surly gardener, Archie, who had been the Mayweathers' gardener for many years. He had been great friends with Ben's father, Edward, and the only time anyone had ever heard him talk, let alone laugh, was in the Four Feathers on a Saturday evening, whilst thrashing Ben's dad at the weekly darts and dominoes night. Ben's parents had both since passed away, and thinking of Archie gave Ben a pang of loss for his dearly departed mother and father.

Tracy came to the door of the shop and smiled tightly at Agatha.

'Good morning, Mrs Mayweather.'

Agatha smiled tightly in return, trying not to stare at the girl's shocking pink hair, which today was piled on top of her head like a solid structure of candy floss. The youth of today, she thought to herself. Tracy moved closer to Ben, taking the dog leads, attached to the very bouncy Maisie and Buster, from his grasp. Agatha caught a flash of colour from the shop window next door, and discreetly turned her gaze. The girl from the shop was now furtively staring at Ben as he chatted to Taylor, and her gaze flitted from Ben to Tracy, and back again. *Did she think these two were together?* Agatha's interest was peaked. The look on the girl's face was one she had seen before. It was how her husband used to look at her during their courting days, and how the young Evans lad had been looking at the girl only minutes before. The cogs started turning in Agatha's quick mind, and a seed of a plan began to form.

As Taylor said their goodbyes, closing the door near Agatha and moving to his own, he looked at his long-term employer and suppressed a smile. *I know that look*, he thought to himself, *that woman is plotting again...*

Had Agatha noticed Taylor watching her through the rear-view mirror as she straightened her already immaculate suit on the leather upholstery of the back seat, she would have seen his amused look, and another, very different look in his eyes. But Mrs Mayweather was lost in thought, planning her strategy on her next pet project, and, as everyone knew, what Agatha Mayweather wanted, she generally got, sooner rather than later.

Four

Four months earlier
London

Stepping down onto the platform, Amanda juggled her leather briefcase, black wool coat and Grande Caramel Macchiato. She felt grotty, despite the flesh-grating power shower she had subjected her skin to only hours before. The fetid stench of the rat race seemingly clung to her clothes. The memory of the sweaty bloke's armpit she'd travelled pressed up against on the train was still fresh in her memory, and the smell still lingered in her nostrils. She took a gulp of her strong caffeine and sugar fix and fumbled for her ticket, swiping it as she went past the ticket barrier, a single body in the herd of office workers walking stridently towards the various workplaces in the city centre. Feeling a buzz from her handbag, she tapped on her Bluetooth earpiece, barking, 'Perry!' into the busy atmosphere.

'Miss Perry, it's Elaine. I just wanted to go over your schedule for today. You haven't left any time for lunch again. Do you want me to rearrange anything?'

Angela rolled her eyes, almost tipping her coffee over herself as she flicked her wrist to check her watch. 'No, Elaine, it's fine. I will send out for something, and have a working lunch.' She walked out of the station, click-clacking in her high heels along the pavement towards her office, law firm Stokes Partners at Law. She could hear her long-suffering assistant sighing down the line.

'No problem, Miss Perry, shall I ring Antony's?' Antony's was the deli round the corner from the office, and they delivered. Pasta, salads, breads and cheeses to die for. Amanda's stomach growled, betraying the yoghurt and blueberries she had gulped down this morning. Amanda smiled at her assistant's fussy care of her.

'Yes, please, Elaine, my usual. Thanks, I'll be there in ten.'

Elaine said goodbye and the line clicked off. Passing the newsagent stand, Amanda's eye was distracted from her fast walk to the office when she spied the latest craft magazines on the stands. Striding up, she smiled at the stallholder, then picked up half a dozen of her coveted magazines and passed the armful to him.

'Wrap them up please, Terry,' she said, handing over the cash.

'I know, I know, can't have those fancy lawyers knowing about your secret knitting habit, eh?' he teased, as he wrapped up the magazines in brown paper and then sheathed them into a large carrier bag.

Amanda laughed. 'Something like that, Terry.'

Moments later, she entered her office on the fourth floor, coffee still warm in her hand, fired up her computer and walked over to her filing cabinet. Opening the bottom drawer with a small key from her bag, she stashed the package of magazines inside, relocked the cabinet and double-checked it was locked. Relieved to have once again smuggled them in undetected, she walked across the plush grey carpet, her tiny stiletto heels leaving small dents in the thick floor covering. At the large low window, she reached across with a manicured hand and drew back the fabric blinds, letting the early morning London sun dance across her workspace. Amanda loved her office, with its stark white walls, huge cherry-red desk and a small seating area, complete with table and elegant carved chairs. Although the decor was a little too bland for her personal tastes, it was perfect for meeting clients in comfort. She preferred to work this way, rather than using the impersonal and imposing meeting rooms on the first floor. In fact, other than being in court, Amanda would be quite happy to spend all of her working hours in her office. She liked the logical side of the law, seeing through a project from start to finish, undertaking each stage, piece by piece, layering the work needed to be done in neat piles, all in colour-coded trays on top of the large mahogany surface she slaved at. The cut-throat side of the business always left her cold. She was tough, and fierce in the courtroom, but she had no passion for it. She always felt like her mother when she turned on the ball-breaker side of herself, and her grandma's voice would ring in her head: *You are not like them, my little duck, their world is not for you.* She still wondered from time to time whether her grandmother was right. There must be more to life than feeling the need to conceal half of your personality every day. *Did anyone know the real her? Didn't anyone notice how conflicted she was?* She sighed to herself. *They don't know, because you don't show them.* She knew what they thought of her.

Amanda was well liked in the office; in fact she was pretty much considered a maverick in the law firm of Stokes Partners at Law. She was a shark; an organised, keen-eyed, methodical-minded shark and her billable hours were always stellar, month on month. Even when she had been knocked down with the flu, she had worked from her couch, sending in dictation via email to her disbelieving PA Elaine.

The partners were considering a new addition to the partnership in the next few months, as Mr Ford, one of the oldest and most senior members of the firm, was retiring, much to his neglected (and at the moment, very insistent) wife's delight.

Amanda, as oblivious as she was to such things as

office gossip and the buzz around the water cooler, was the clear front-runner, and tipped to be the first ever female partner at the firm. The other contenders were few and far between, and it was widely accepted that the partnership spot was between Amanda and Marcus Beresford, a guy with more years at the firm under his designer belt.

Amanda wasn't even sure how she felt about the partnership. After all, what was the point of more money if you never left the office to spend it? And who would she spend it with? Other than her work colleagues, she didn't even speak to anyone, let alone socialise. Last Saturday night, whilst her colleagues were all with their families, or knocking back overpriced drinks in loud sweaty clubs, she had been sat in her flat, knocking back wine, flicking through Plenty of Fish for a possible date and screening calls from her parents, both eager to give her pep talks about 'the last push for partner'. Her mother had even taken to sending her daily emails, suggesting ways of clinching the partnership, whilst simultaneously disparaging her for not cutting her hair short or returning their calls.

As though summoned by Amanda's mind, Elaine buzzed through.

'Miss Perry, I have your mother on line one.'

Amanda rolled her eyes, groaning.

'Tell her I am in a meeting please, Elaine.'

'Er…' Elaine's hesistant voice came through the

speaker. 'I have told her that excuse the last five times, and she says if you don't speak to her now, she will come to the office.'

Amanda grimaced. 'Well played, Mother,' she said under her breath. 'Fine, put her through please, and hold my calls.' She knew this would take a while, like root canal treatment and about as pleasant.

'Hello, Mother,' she sighed into the line.

'Hello, darling, meeting go well?' She didn't wait for an answer, knowing full well there was no meeting. 'Did you get my email this morning, with the picture?' Amanda fired up her email, putting the phone receiver between her cheek and shoulder.

'Do you see it?' her mother pestered.

'Yes,' Amanda said, looking at the woman clad in an astronaut suit, minus a helmet, that now filled her email screen. 'I like my hair though,' she said, running her fingers through the ends of her hair as though to comfort the strands under threat.

'No, no, it's too girly, too feminine. Think Anne Hathaway in *Interstellar*, elfin like, efficient. Would save you valuable billable time too, dear. How much money must you lose every month just by straightening that mop of yours?'

'Well, if I stopped going to that overpriced muscle gym you made me sign up to, I would save even more,' she retorted like a sulky teen being made to take French for her options against her will.

'The gym is not a waste of time, it's an investment. Trust me, when you get to my age, you will be thanking me for making you exercise. Now, have they made an announcement about the partnership yet? My sources tell me it is due any time. Kimberley is threatening divorce if he doesn't step down soon,' her mother declared, referring to Mr Ford's wife. Sometimes, it felt like Amanda was still at school, getting regular reports from her teachers and having to sit through parents' evenings with her mother and father barraging her poor subject teachers on every aspect of her education. She half expected her mother to check her homework too. Amanda deleted the email and short hair Hathaway disappeared from the screen.

'Look, Mum, I have to go, I am busy,' she said, bringing up her schedule on the screen.

'That's fine, Amanda dear, go get some work done, get this partnership nailed down. Think about the hair, OK?'

Amanda strangled the receiver a little between her fingers, before putting it back to her ear. Marcus sidled into the room and she pointed a finger at him to stay silent. The fact that she was sleeping with her colleague and partnership rival was something for another day. Like the twelfth of never.

'I have thought about it, and the answer is still no. Bye.'

Celine Perry let out an elaborate sigh designed to guilt

trip her spawn, and hung on the line, her disapproval making the phone lines jangle. Amanda put down the receiver like a woman handling a live grenade, staring at it ticking away in its cradle. Marcus cleared his throat, and she jumped at the noise, turning her gaze to her visitor, her demeanour tightening further.

'Marcus, what do you want? I am busy today.'

Marcus Beresford grinned from the corner of Amanda's office, clearly amused by her terse welcome.

'Why, Miss Perry, anyone would think you weren't pleased to see me?'

Amanda's frown deepened as she eyed him from the top of her computer monitor.

'I'm not pleased to see you, and I am busy—what is it?'

Marcus smiled, now appearing contrite. 'Is this about last night?'

Amanda angrily motioned him to come in and shut the door, aware that Elaine was sitting outside, probably earwigging every word.

Marcus stepped in, closing the door behind him, and sat on one of the meeting chairs. Despite herself, Amanda found herself gazing at him. His hair was freshly cut and still slightly damp, and the edges curled slightly at the nape of his neck, showing the grey flecks in his black hair against the dazzling white of his shirt. He was dressed impeccably as always—crisp dark grey suit, cream striped tie and polished-to-perfection black loafers.

Even his hands were immaculate, with manicured short nails, and wisps of coarse dark hair peeked from his cuffs, licking around his designer watch. Amanda turned her admiring gaze swiftly back into a glare and she returned to the commercial lease she had been poring over for the last two days. She felt his eyes on her. Sighing, she met his eyes, anger fuelling the feeling in her gut.

'Marcus, I have said this before, our personal life does not come into this office, ever! I don't want to talk about last night. You stood me up, *again*. Remember Saturday? You are a git. End of conversation. Now, I am busy, so, please, close the door after you.'

Marcus stood up, walked over to the side of the desk and knelt down beside her. Amanda flushed at his proximity, and willed her cheeks not to betray the fluttering in her chest. 'Marcus…'

'Amanda, I am so sorry. It just got too late to call, we had the Japanese clients fly in unexpectedly, I couldn't just blow them off. I am so sorry! It was a late one and, when I did get a chance to call, your phone was off. And I explained about Saturday, my mother was in town. Did you really want me to not see my mother when she had come to London to see me?'

Amanda paused. She liked how attentive to his mother he was, always on the phone to her, spending time with her when she came into town. Last night she was furious, but she did turn her phone off in anger before she went to bed, having waited for two hours, dressed up to go to a dinner that never happened. Again. Softening slightly, she nodded slowly.

'OK, fair point, but I have a busy life too, Marcus. A call or even a text earlier would have been nice. I could have worked late.'

Marcus stuck his bottom lip out, pouting like a child at the girl he was dating.

'I know, pookie, I am sorry.'

Amanda rolled her eyes. 'Don't call me "pookie", I am not a bimbo. Now let me get to work, I have lots to do today and you dribbling on my desk is counter-productive.'

Marcus grinned then, bouncing back upright. 'Thanks, babe, I mean Amanda. I will make it up to you, I prom-ise.'

Amanda raised her eyebrows at him and pointed to the door, before returning to her work, feeling slightly better about her morning. Marcus swaggered to the door and paused with the handle in his hand, a gap showing the offices outside.

'Oh and, Miss Perry, I emailed you a contract to look over, for the Kamimura account. Would you give it a look?'

Amanda's fingers stilled on her keyboard. She had a busy workload, and that account was not hers to work on, it was his!

'Why can't you attend to that, Mr Beresford? It is *your* account,' she retorted, trying to keep the indignation out of her voice, aware that they once again had an audience. Marcus pursed his lips sheepishly.

'Ah, well, the clients have booked a golf session for this afternoon, so I am leaving the office now till tomorrow.'

Amanda's jaw dropped, and her mouth flapped as she struggled to form coherent words. Sighing, she gritted her teeth and nodded.

'Fine, Mr Beresford, I will take a look. *If* I get time.' Marcus winked at her, smirking.

'Why, thank you, Miss Perry. I will need it by five.' Before she could answer, he swiftly pulled the door to and she heard Elaine gushing over his attentions outside her office. She ran her hands over her tight ponytail and then pushed away from her desk sharply, swivel chair barrelling in the wall behind her. She reached into her bag and pulled out her little key. She then buzzed her secretary, who could be heard outside giggling.

'Elaine, I am not to be disturbed for the next hour, hold all calls, and get me the Kamimura files. Please,' she added as an afterthought.

She locked her office door and opened the bottom drawer of the filing cabinet. Running her fingers along the brown paper, her stress started to melt away. She selected a magazine and sat behind her desk, pulling her legs up on the chair. After pulling up her Pinterest account, she started to read the magazine, adding ideas to boards as she went along, sighing contentedly, whilst outside her sanctuary, the legal world forged on. At least in here, she could be herself. If the week went on like this, she would be spending her free time making voo-doo dolls to stick pins into.

Five

Amanda awoke on Thursday morning to the sound of birdsong coming in through her open bedroom window. As always, it took her a little while to adjust to where she was, and resist the urge to dive out of bed and check her emails from work. Smiling, she thumbed through her hangers, settling on a pleated cream skirt that swished as she walked, and a thin cream camisole with embroidered flowers around the dipped neckline. She looked down at her shoes, all lined up in the bottom of the wardrobe, spying her green suede pumps with dismay. She hadn't been able to get the blood out, yet she couldn't bring herself to throw them away either. They sat there, among her other footwear, a little reminder of the day she had met Ben. Not the best memory, it had to be said, but she left the shoes sitting with their buddies all the same. Cringing at her own sentimentality, she picked up a similar pair, this time in a light grey colour, and slipped them onto her bare feet.

A quick brush of her hair, a slick of dusty pink lip gloss, and she was dressed. Looking into her cheval mirror—another junk shop find with her magic worked on it—she did a double-take of the girl staring back at her. Her brown hair loosely framed her face, which now looked well rested and less drawn than in recent weeks. Her outfit was pretty, casual and summery, and matched the weather streaming through the muslin voiles, which framed her large bay bedroom window. She smiled at her reflection and headed for the stairs to the shop, hoping to everything holy that she had a good day. Amanda was realistic—she had never thought that she would open to an instant success, but now, with no income, and her life savings all literally in one basket, the business had to work, as for the first time in her life, she didn't know what direction her life was heading towards.

Still, she had three working days left till Sunday, her day off. She could come up with some ideas. She had seen a flyer for the summer fair—maybe she could set up a stall, showcase her goods and services, get the word of mouth out. She made a mental note to find out more.

She unlocked the front door to open the window shutter, and was faced with a mesmerising pair of grey eyes.

'Oh, sorry! We have to stop doing this,' a deep voice gently said.

Amanda flustered, panicked at his words, till she realised he was talking about bumping into each other. She mentally brushed off the sinking feeling she had, and smiled thinly.

'Sorry, Ben, I was just opening up.'

He smiled back, matching her wary half-smile, and reached out and took the shutter key from her. A spark zinged up her fingers as his brushed hers, and she shivered. Looking at Ben, she saw his slightly shocked expression, mirroring hers, before he turned away. *Man, he has nice eyes*, she thought to herself. Ben turned away from her, deftly unlocking and lifting the shutters, and she found herself watching him. His muscles twitched as he pushed up on the cold steel, and she idly wondered what was under his white cotton shirt. His buttons were open at the neck, showing off a tanned throat with a sprinkling of dark hair peeking out from underneath. She bit her lip as she imagined running her hand over his bare chest, his curls twitching around her fingers as…

'You OK?'

Amanda's lip sprang abruptly from between her teeth as she realised that Ben was speaking again. His amused grin was evident, and she flushed at being caught acting like a gormless idiot, yet again. *What was it about this man that made her want to jump into his arms whenever she saw him? He was awful! Get a grip, you know no good comes from attractive and haughty men. The guy hates you.*

'Sorry,' she said sheepishly. 'Did you say something?'

Ben chuckled, his grey eyes sparkling with mirth. 'I just wanted to say sorry for yesterday. I realise I came across as a bit nasty, but I just care about this community.'

'Yes, you were,' Amanda said, setting her jaw and warning her eyes not to wander. She didn't accept his apology, he noticed. He was obviously right on the money—she was another city girl, here to make her mark. Well, Westfield didn't need change, and he wasn't about to let it happen either.

Amanda glanced behind her. Tracy was working in the shop, obliviously washing a Great Dane. She turned back to Ben and wiped her clammy palms down the sides of her skirt, her body zinging with nervous anger. She bit the bullet, swallowing.

'So, you and Tracy, have you lived here all your lives?'

Ben's brows knitted together, a confused expression coming over his face. He opened his mouth to speak, when a car pulled up behind him. Ben looked irritated, and turned to greet the man coming out of the driver's side towards them.

'Mr Taylor, have the dogs been hunting again?'

Taylor laughed, wiping his brow. After glancing between the two of them, he turned to open the rear door. 'No, my dear Ben, a whole different kind of hunt is going on around here, I think.'

Amanda looked at Ben, intrigued, and he glanced across at her, his expression saying 'get ready'. He turned to stand next to her, and she followed his gaze and saw Taylor help a rather well-dressed woman out of the car. Her cream shoes kissed the pavement daintily, and, after smiling thanks at her helper, she smoothed down her already immaculate clothes and levelled her gaze at Amanda and Ben. The atmosphere was palpable, and Amanda felt like she had been caught kissing behind the bike sheds by a strict teacher. She smiled at the lady politely and skipped into her business mode, offering what she hoped was a firm, steady hand.

'Hi, I'm Amanda Perry, pleased to meet you, Mrs...?'

'Agatha, dear, call me Agatha.'

Taylor's surprised expression, caught by Amanda's shrewd eye, told her that this woman didn't offer her first name lightly, which comforted her some. *Who was she? Maybe Ben had called her, maybe she was here to run her out of town.* Agatha stepped forward and wrapped Amanda's hand within her own. They were strong, belying her age, soft and warm, and Amanda relaxed at the gentle gesture.

'Pleased to meet you, Agatha.' She smiled. The woman spoke well, forthright but friendly, and Amanda instantly took a liking to her.

'Now, dear, I have come to officially welcome you to Westfield. I think we are long overdue for a meeting. I am the committee head of a number of things here, and I would like to introduce your new venture, if it would please you, of course.'

The words came out as a statement rather than a question, and Amanda guessed that the woman before her generally didn't ask, but rather expected. She was a doer. Her liking to her grew all the more, and she grinned happily. Ben tutted loudly next to her, and she clenched her fists by her sides, ignoring him.

'Agatha, I would be delighted. Would you like a drink?' She motioned to the shop doorway. Agatha smiled, a little shake of her head making her tight bun catch the light, shooting off glints of grey into the sunshine.

'I'm afraid I can't today, but I appreciate the offer, thank you. I was thinking Tuesday? I could get Taylor here to pick you up perhaps, bring you to my house for a light supper?'

Taylor sniggered at the side of her, and Agatha shot him a fearsome glare. He coughed, covering his tracks feebly, and straightened up, clasping his hands in front of him. Amanda shot a quick look towards Ben, and saw he was watching the exchange with wide-eyed interest. *Put that in your pipe and smoke it, poodle primper.* Amanda quickly looked back at Agatha.

'That would be wonderful, thank you. I close at five, is that OK?'

Agatha smiled warmly, her eyes flicking to her companion once more.

'That's fine, Amanda—' she said it 'A-marn-da' '—I shall send the car for half past six.'

Taylor nodded once, eyes cast to the floor. Amanda also nodded and Agatha smiled again, seemingly satisfied. She then turned her attention to Ben.

'Now, Benjamin, Miss Perry here is new to the area, and being a native like myself, I would venture that you could be of some assistance, don't you?'

Ben didn't get a chance to reply before she went on. 'Amanda, you are closed on Sunday, do you have plans?'

How did she know that? Amanda thought of her impending day off. *My day off? Oh, hours of being sat in PJs probably, scouring Pinterest on the laptop, checking my bank balance and crying intermittently.* This didn't seem like the thing to say, so she just whispered feebly, 'Er no, not really.'

Agatha bristled with pleasure, not seeing Taylor's eyeroll to Ben.

'That's settled then. Benjamin, you have a day off too. Why don't you take the girl on a tour, show her the sights of our lovely village?'

Ben cleared his throat, turning to Amanda, an embarrassed look on his face. 'Er, well, I have a lot on at the moment, I will have to check my...'

Amanda looked up at him and waited a second till her heart stopped doing jumping jacks in her stomach. *A day with him! No chance!*

'Benjamin Evans,' Agatha said, her best scolding voice in full flow. 'You have better manners than that.'

Ben visibly sagged, his shoulders drooping. Turning to Amanda with a 'she is making me do this' face, he said glibly, 'Of course, I would be delighted to take you on a tour.'

Amanda wanted the ground to swallow her up. She dare not even try to get out of it now. Agatha and her mother would get on like a house on fire.

'Er, yes, well that would be lovely.' She paused. 'If you and Tracy are not too busy, of course.'

Amanda couldn't think of anything to get out of it. A day with Ben would be bad enough, but watching the couple being all loved up while he sat there plotting her grisly death seemed a lot less appealing.

My Lord, Agatha thought to herself, *I could bang this pair's heads together! Don't young people talk any more? There was a lot to be said about Facebook statuses, that was for sure. Even an old fogey like me knows that. The two of them had enough tension to implode the universe. She half expected them to start pulling each other's hair.*

Agatha spoke up, cutting through the miscommunications. 'Tracy?' she said, trying hard not to yelp in frustration at the duo. 'Well, Tracy will be busy, dear, with her *boyfriend*. But I am sure that Benjamin here can manage the tour on his own.'

Taylor sniggered again, louder this time, and Agatha jabbed him with a pointy elbow. He made an 'ooof' sound as she connected with his torso, and he spluttered twice before turning to the rear door. Agatha stared at the couple before her as though nothing had happened. *They are like moody teenagers*, she thought to herself.

'So, shall we say 10 o'clock, Ben, for you to pick Amanda up?'

She turned to the door, seemingly thinking all was arranged, got in and looked expectantly through her open window as Taylor returned to his seat, red-faced.

Ben muttered quickly, 'Yes, that would be fine. Amanda?'

Amanda looked into his eyes and nodded.

Agatha nodded back, a smile of accomplishment lighting up her features. 'All settled then, and I shall see you next week, Amanda. Drive on, Taylor,' she said in a clipped tone, obviously still ticked off with her driver. Taylor shrugged good-naturedly at her as he pulled away, but Amanda and Ben were oblivious to all, as they still stood, staring at each other.

Ben eventually broke the silence, his voice cracking as he spoke. 'Wear something warm, OK?' he said gruffly.

Amanda nodded, turning to her doorway. Male chauvinist pig, he probably thought she would turn up in heels and a ball gown, like some feckless damsel. She would show him.

She felt a warm, manly hand grab hers and she turned back to him in question.

'Sorry,' Ben said, his grip easing slightly. 'I just wanted to ask, do you like chickens?'

Six

The next couple of days went by in a blur. Amanda worked hard at the shop, finishing her projects and cutting out fabric for cushions and scented drawer liners, the items she was hoping to sell to the tourist trade. At night, the TV stood quiet, Mr Darcy left unwatched, as she frantically put together her flat into some semblance of the home she wanted. All but three of the packing boxes were now crushed and sat by the door for recycling, her sheets were all unpacked and put away. She had even been to the local grocer's and filled her fridge with some proper food, things that required more than the pricking of plastic and the ping of the microwave. The shop had even made some sales, not enough for her to relax, but she had noticed a small trickle of townsfolk and was cautiously optimistic about things picking up once word had got around.

And here she was, Sunday morning, the date of her tour with Ben. *It wasn't a date*, she reminded herself. She hadn't slept well the night before, mentally and literally scanning her wardrobe for the appropriate outfit. *Dress warm*, he had said, so eventually she had decided on her favourite pair of faded blue jeans, a nice top and a slick of lipstick. She had even bought a pair of walking boots for the occasion, although she had needed to go back to the shop for a pair of thick socks, realising that her Betty Boop trainer ones wouldn't quite fit the occasion. In the city, she had never really worn socks, other than for the gym, and she much preferred to be barefoot or wear simple pumps or heels. Now her feet felt heavy, encased in thick wool and hard rubber. She had been clumping around the flat since she got up, just to wear them in. She felt like a spaceman, but she was going to show the Cockapoo shampooer next door that she was not just some city slicker, and she had a right to be here.

The trill of the doorbell downstairs made her jump. He was right on time. Amanda headed for the buzzer, flicking her gaze to the mirror as she went past. She looked like a giddy schoolgirl, all flushed cheeks and shiny eyes. *This is not a date. Be cool. Aloof.*

She pressed the buzzer and opened the door. Ben was halfway up the stairs, and she resisted the urge to meet him halfway.

'Hi,' he said, smiling. 'Ready to go?'

Amanda smiled, her small rucksack—also new—

hanging from one shoulder. 'Yep,' she said, grabbing her warm parka from the hook on the way down. Locking the door downstairs, she was very aware of Ben's gaze on her, and she willed her arms to work the key into the lock. Ben now stood by the side of a dark blue jeep, and he opened the passenger side for her. She settled into the seat, as Ben took her bag from her and put it into the boot without being asked. *Country manners,* Amanda scoffed.

Ben slid into his leather seat at the side of her and started the engine. 'So, I thought we could maybe have a picnic on the fell? I just need to call at my place first, to make lunch. That OK with you?'

Her head whipped around in suspicion. 'A picnic? Just us?'

Ben kept his eyes on the road, his cheeks colouring. 'Yes, well, Agatha thought it might be a good idea.'

She nodded slowly. She felt a pang of embarrassment. This was like a pity date, she realised. Take the poor lonely girl out and feed her. She folded her arms tight across her chest. Fine, she would play along. It was just one afternoon, then he was out of her life. She could avoid him easily enough.

Thank the Lord for the nice weather, Amanda thought to herself. It was slightly cold, but the sun was warm and the sky clear. 'Sounds lovely,' she said, throwing him an over-the-top smile. 'Do we need to shop first? I didn't bring any food.'

Ben shook his head, pulling away from Baker Street in one smooth movement of the wheel. 'No, I have that covered.'

* * *

A short drive later and they pulled into the drive of a large house. The shopfront next door said Evans Animal Practice, and was painted in green and white. After flicking a button on the dashboard, an impressive wrought iron set of gates slowly rumbled closed behind them.

Amanda looked around. *Was this his parents' house? An arranged date and meeting the parents? What was next? Shotgun wedding?*

Ben got out and dashed to her door before she could even reach for the door handle. Giving her his hand, he helped her out and then led her down the cobbled driveway. Amanda tried not to notice the jolt she felt when his fingers once again wrapped around hers momentarily. After opening the front door, he led her through to a large farmhouse kitchen. An Aga gave the room a nice warmth, and Amanda was immediately drawn to the huge pile of food amassed on the wooden table, and the small woman cutting doorstop slices of bread on a wooden chopping board. She looked like Ma Larkin, complete with pinny and ruddy cheeks. Ben dropped a kiss onto the woman's cheek and motioned for Amanda to take a seat at the table. *Was this his mother? Did he live with his parents?*

Amanda sat down and smiled at the lady, who was quite possibly the happiest woman she had ever seen.

'Amanda Perry, this is Dotty. Dotty, Amanda Perry.'

Dotty wiped her hands on her apron and held one out to Amanda. 'Pleased to meet you, dear, I work with Ben. I'm just here to give him a hand with lunch. Do you have any preferences for sandwich fillings? Ben said you might like sushi, but we don't get much call for that around here. Pickled herring is probably the best you will get,' she chuckled, her belly rocking with mirth.

Amanda laughed too, throwing a quick dirty look Ben's way. His eyebrows shot up in surprise, but he said nothing. 'Oh thanks, but I am not one for sushi anyway. I'm not fussy with sandwiches, this all looks lovely though.' The table was groaning with bread, cheeses, fruits, a potato salad and a huge pork pie. Amanda's stomach rumbled, and she put a hand on her tummy, embarrassed.

Dotty smiled at her. 'Did you not have any breakfast, dear? I can make you some toast if you like?'

Amanda opened her mouth to say no, but Dotty had already picked up some bread slices and moved over to the toaster on the worktop. Amanda looked at Ben, who was staring out of the kitchen window. He looked back at her, a funny look on his face.

'So, you never answered my question, about liking chickens?'

Amanda looked at Ben. 'To eat?'

Dotty laughed, setting a kettle of water onto the stove. 'Show her, Ben, go on, I'll put the coffee on.'

Ben grinned and, motioning for Amanda to follow him, moved to the back door. He clicked the stable doors together and opened the door to the outside. Birdsong and sunlight infiltrated the kitchen. Amanda stood up and walked out to the garden. 'Garden' was an understatement of course. Beyond Ben's back door was a huge field, complete with patio and garden furniture. A large gas barbecue stood covered in one corner, and one side of the garden was home to a huge hen house. Ben opened the door to the house, and Amanda gasped as four chickens tentatively popped their heads out. He stifled a chuckle. He had a feeling that coming face to face with some animals would freak her out.

'Wow, you meant real chickens then, huh?'

Ben sat down on the grass. 'Yep, not had them long. They were going to lose their home, so I took them in. Come, sit. They are quite friendly.' He tapped the ground beside him, challenging her.

Amanda, well aware of what he was doing, defiantly strode over and took a seat next to Ben, careful to sit far enough apart from him to feel comfortable, and to resist the urge to jump into his lap. *What was it about this man that made her want to run her fingers through his hair? Why were the wrong ones always so cute?* The chickens strode over to them, pecking at the green grass around them.

'So, do they have names?'

Ben shook his head. 'No. They were kept for their eggs, not as pets, so the owner never got around to naming them. I have three hens and a cockerel. Here he is, look.'

Amanda looked to the hen house and saw a larger, brighter chicken strut his stuff on the lawn. The hens ignored him for the most part, and he snuck the occasional glance at them before sticking his beak back high in the air. He reminded her of something, and she laughed out loud. Ben smiled, curiosity written all over his face.

'What? You thought of a name?'

Amanda giggled. 'Darcy. He reminds me of Mr Darcy, all haughty and proud. It's daft.' She shook her head, embarrassed that she had shown herself in all her book geekiness. Ben chuckled, stroking the head of one hen that came to him, looking for food.

* * *

'Darcy, I like it. It suits him. So that would make the hens what? Jane, Lizzie and Lydia?'

Amanda's jaw dropped. 'You know Austen?'

Ben nodded, standing up to grab a bucket of corn from the back door.

'My mum did,' he said, stroking the back of his neck with his free hand. 'I am afraid to say, I was pretty much force-fed it when I was a kid.' *Smooth, Ben, smooth! Why don't you just don a cardi and recite Keats*

to her! You are not here to impress her, you donkey.
'Er, I guess some of it stuck.'

* * *

Amanda smiled broadly. 'Smart woman.' For a second
her mind flashed to an image of Marcus. His idea of
reading had been perusing the sports pages on the toilet. With the door open. Yuk. He had always mocked
her for her love of reading, berated her for her flat full
of books. She looked again at Ben, who was now talking to the hens, feeding them from his hand.

'You want to give it a try? I think Lydia is getting
impatient.'

Amanda stood up and scooped a handful of yellow
corn from the bucket.

'You're not really going to call them that, are you?'

Ben looked down at her. 'Yes, why not? I think that
they suit them, don't you?'

Amanda nodded happily, and for a moment their eyes
locked on to each other.

Ben looked like he was going to speak, and Amanda
found herself willing those lips to move, but the moment
was broken when the back door opened. They jumped
apart from each other.

'Coffee and toast is ready, my dears. I have packed
your lunch too.'

They both looked to Dotty, and then back to each
other. After dispersing the rest of the corn, they walked
back to the house, a sizeable gap between them.

* * *

The toast was the best that Amanda had ever tasted. The bread was thick and crunchy, and the butter was melting into the slices. It was heaven. She devoured the contents of her plate, resisting the urge to lick her fingers clean. Dotty smiled, passing her a napkin. Ben had excused himself to pack up the car.

'So, Amanda, how are you liking the village life so far?'

Amanda smiled at the friendly woman. 'I like it so far—everyone seems calmer here. The pace is a lot slower than London, it was quite a shock to the system.'

Dotty's face dropped slightly. 'So, you are a city girl born and bred? Don't you miss the bright lights?' Amanda noted the concern in her voice, unsure why this question seemed so loaded.

'Bright lights are all well and good, but it also comes with long hours, stress and drunks peeing in the street. I am enjoying the change of pace to be honest.'

Whatever test Dotty had just thrown at her, she had seemingly passed it. Dotty's shoulders had notably relaxed, and her returning smile was genuine.

'Oh good, we are often worried that newcomers will leave after the novelty has worn off. Us natives, we never get far. Ben went away and came back, and we are glad he did.'

Amanda was intrigued. *He left? Why all the pompos-*

ity then? He had gone full-on League of Gentlemen on her when they first met.

'Oh really, why did he leave?'

Dotty sat back, sipping at her mug of coffee. 'He went to university, and then came back when he graduated. It was a difficult time—he had not been in a new job long, when his parents passed.'

Amanda's heart plummeted. *He had lost his parents, together?*

Dotty saw the question on her face and smiled kindly. She looked to the hallway, as though checking Ben was out of earshot.

'Ben was working in a practice in London, when his parents died. They got into a car crash, up on the main road. Some boy racer passing through the village, thinking our roads are racetracks. They never suffered, bless their hearts, it was very quick.' Dotty grimaced at some memory playing in her head. 'Ben came home straightaway of course, and took over the family business. Once he came back, he never left. He is a country boy, through and through. It's just a shame that Tanya didn't see it that way, but that's a whole other story.'

Amanda frowned, taking a gulp of her own brew. *Tanya? Practice? Is Ben a vet? Why is he running a dog groomer's then, if he is a vet?*

Dotty's hand patted her own across the table. 'I'm glad he met you, dear, he needs some company.'

Amanda didn't answer. *Nemesis, more like.*

Dotty stood up, taking her cup over to the sink. She started humming to herself as she set to work. Amanda glugged the rest of her coffee down, unsure what to make of the last two minutes. Ben strode into the kitchen at that moment, checked blanket in hand.

'Amanda, are you ready?'

For what she was supposed to be ready for, she had no idea.

* * *

The jeep moved along the country lane leading to the Westfield Fells. Ben had put the radio on low, and the music and chatter helped to diffuse the static in the air between them. Ben was aware that Amanda had not spoken since they said goodbye to Dotty, and he had the feeling that he was in for a long day. Her reaction to the chickens had surprised him; he had half expected her to run for the hills. Peeking across at her, his suspicions only deepened. Amanda was staring out of the window, brows furrowed, lip being nibbled ferociously between her teeth.

He wished he knew what was going on in that head of hers. What made a city girl move to a small town and open up a craft shop? She must have bigger plans, he felt sure of it. Those types of folk always did.

'You OK?' he asked tentatively. Amanda's lip sprang from between her teeth, her face smoothing out. She looked at him, smiling weakly.

'Yes, I'm fine, thanks.' Silence again. Music, chatter, static.

Ben tried again. 'You feeling OK?'

Amanda nodded. 'Fine, thanks.' Music, chatter, static.

Ben sighed. Bracing himself, he looked at her.

'Amanda, do you want to go home?'

Amanda's neck snapped round, her eyes locking on to his.

'No! I mean, er…no…' *Smooth, Amanda, cool operator.*

'Well, what is it then? Something is bothering you. I know neither of us planned this, but we should make the best of it, for today at least. We do have to work alongside each other,' Ben stated, exasperated.

Amanda ran her hand through her hair, distracting him momentarily from even remembering he had asked a question. He got a whiff of coconut, probably her shampoo, and he stifled the urge to sniff her hair. *Where did that come from?*

'Sorry, Ben, I am just a bit confused. Are you a vet?'

Ben flinched, as though she had poked him. 'Er, yes, I am the village vet. Did you not know that?' He mentally slapped himself. *You forget, idiot, she is not from here, she doesn't automatically know your business!*

He sighed softly, smiling a little. Amanda continued to wait for an answer.

'Sorry, Amanda, when you have lived here as long as I have, you forget that people don't automatically know your life story. Yes, I am the village vet, my practice is next to my house, which you have seen. Dotty is my receptionist, and was my father's before that. My parents died, and I took over the practice.'

Amanda nodded, tallying it with what Dotty had told her. 'So, the dog groomer's?'

Ben winced. 'It was my wife's. I opened it for her, and now Tracy runs it for me. I just do stock and fix stuff there really. Tracy manages it and it gives me time to work.'

Amanda put the pieces together. 'Tanya, is that your wife?'

Ben's face was a picture. 'Dotty got a lot of chat in with that coffee, didn't she? Yes, Tanya was…is my ex-wife. She lives in London now. She left a while ago, so now it's just me, Darcy and the Bennet sisters.'

Amanda laughed, and Ben thought how wonderful the sound was, like the static in the car danced and bounced around him. She seemed to relax slightly and she reached for the radio knob. Kings of Leon sang out in the car, and Ben did a double-take.

'I like this song.' Amanda smiled.

'You like Kings of Leon? Check this out!' He pressed the CD eject button and Amanda gasped as she saw the album of the band pop out. She laughed again, and Ben gripped the steering wheel a little tighter as a frisson of excitement gripped him, low in his gut. She pushed the disc gently with one finger and the CD started to play.

Looking at him mischievously, she lowered her window and gazed out on the deserted road they were on. 'Get ready to lose your cool, Ben Evans.' She cranked up the stereo. They both laughed together, singing loudly to the words and taking it in turns to play drums and air guitar as they headed to the fell, all bad feeling forgotten in that moment.

Lose my cool, thought Ben to himself. *I am in danger of losing more than that.*

Seven

Amanda's breath caught in her throat as she looked down over the fell. 'It's beautiful up here,' she sighed. Ben came to stand at the side of her.

'I know, right? Look over there, that's Baker Street.'

Amanda followed his finger to the small street where she now lived. 'Oh yes!' She frowned. 'My shop looks a little bland compared to the others. All decked out in flowers, do they do this every year?'

Ben nodded, turning to flick out the blanket under his arm. His jeep was parked nearby on the grassy hill-top. 'Oh yes, the women in Westfield get pretty competitive. You see there?' He pointed to a large mansion, with huge, beautiful landscaped grounds. 'That there is Westfield Hall, Agatha Mayweather's home. Archie, her gardener, prides himself on the best, and the women go green with envy and turn themselves inside out trying to beat him.'

Amanda smiled. A far cry from the bland flat she had in London, with the pitiful pot plant she had buried in the landfill in the sky before she left.

'I can't keep anything alive, I definitely don't have a green thumb.'

Ben sniggered. 'Speak to Dotty, she will help you, she loves all that. We can get your shop looking like a little oasis of Eden in no time. If you are staying, that is.'

Amanda didn't answer. She had a faraway look about her as she gazed down at Baker Street. Not for the first time that day either, Ben noted.

'Shall we eat?' he asked softly, the fact she hadn't answered his tentative question about staying playing on his mind.

Amanda nodded, and walked to the car with him.

A short time later, the food was all laid out. He shrugged at her gruffly. 'Dotty packed this, I apologise.'

Ben reached into the bottom of the huge cooler and pulled out a bottle chiller. Inside were two tumblers and a cool bottle of rosé wine. 'While it's here, you might as well have it. Would you like a glass?'

Does a bear do its business in the woods? 'Yes, lovely, thanks. You having one?'

Ben nodded. 'Just the one, driving and all.'

Amanda smiled as he poured the wine. He was so responsible, a breath of fresh air from past dates. *Was this a date? It was starting to feel like one, with the wine, the food, the romantic intonations of their solitary outdoor picnic.*

They began eating in companionable silence. Thinking back, Amanda couldn't remember ever sharing a nice meal with Marcus, let alone a romantic picnic on a fell. Post-coital takeout in bed didn't count, she was pretty sure. She found herself wondering again whether this was a date, and squashed the vastly conflicting feelings it caused down into her gut. She sipped at her wine and then tucked into a second sandwich—thick white bread, slathered in butter, with meaty slices of ham. Dotty really knew how to put a picnic together.

'So, Amanda, what made you come to Westfield?' Ben asked tentatively. She finished chewing the bite of sandwich, formulating a vague answer that would satisfy him without having to go into the sordid details.

'A change of scene, I guess. I was feeling a little stifled in London, so I took a chance.' It sounded hollow to her ears, but she hoped that Ben would be satisfied with the answer, because she couldn't bring herself to talk about it. Or think about it. Or put it into words for that matter.

He nodded, and Amanda puffed out the breath she didn't know she had been holding.

He turned his head to her. 'And is it everything you hoped? Are you happy, I mean?'

Amanda gave a small nod, pursing her lips in thought.

'Yes, so far. Ask me again in six months. Once I turn Westfield into the hulking metropolis I want it to be.'

Ben stared at her, horror-struck, before he noticed her sly smile.

'That's not funny,' he said, laughing awkwardly.

Amanda raised her eyebrows at him. 'Only saying what you are thinking.'

Ben offered her a strawberry, choosing to change the subject.

'So, what did you do, before I mean?'

Amanda bit into the huge juicy red fruit. 'I worked in commercial law, for a big firm.'

Ben frowned. 'A lawyer?' Seeing her nod, his frown deepened. 'So, completely new life for you?'

Amanda caught a weird look on his face. *Disappointed? She should have known, he didn't like city girls. She bet that Tanya had been a Westfieldian too, all rosy cheeks, apple pie baking and child-bearing hips. OK, she was clutching at stereotypes now, and Dotty had already told her that she had hotfooted it to London, but seriously, why did she care what he thought of her. Why did that bother her, anyway?*

She realised she had not answered his question and he was looking at her expectantly. 'Yes, I needed a change. The rat race isn't everything it's cracked up to be.'

Ben seemed relieved at her words, his face brightening. 'Their loss, our gain, huh?'

Amanda chuckled. 'Hopefully, once the shop gets established.'

Ben saw her face fall again, and wished, not for the first time, that he could read what was going on in her head. 'Don't you miss it?'

Amanda looked out over the fell, her face a mask as she thought of the pain and stress of the last few weeks in London. She whispered, 'No, not much.'

Ben looked at her, one eyebrow raised. 'I know I went on a bit the other day, but I meant what I said. People don't like change around here, what we have works, and people have tried and failed before to come in and introduce new things. We just like things how they are. I was warning you. It's all well and good to come in and set up shop, but then when things go wrong and you go back to your life, we villagers end up picking up the pieces. I was warning you for your own good.'

Amanda bristled at his tone. 'Warning me for my own good? You sound like my father.'

Ben shook his head. 'I am not trying to be a jerk. I can just see how things are going to go, and the people around here are sick of it. With the cuts to community services, people are fed up.'

Amanda drained the wine in her glass. 'You left and came back, did they petition against you doing that?'

Ben scoffed. 'I was born here, I bought an existing

business from a retiree, I didn't come in trying to change things.'

Amanda put her glass down in a strop. 'I have bought a business selling crafts, I am hardly Donald Trump. What the hell is your problem?'

Ben did not reply, and, when she looked at him, she could see that she had annoyed him. *Good*, she thought. *Who the hell did he think he was!*

He spoke quietly, breaking the silence. 'Are you ready to go? I have some things to take care of this afternoon.' Amanda felt like someone had thrown ice water over her. She tried not to tear up and started to put the food away, nodding once.

'Fine, I have seen and heard quite enough anyway. I have a business to run.'

* * *

Ben could have kicked himself. He had gone and done it again. He had wanted to end the day better than this. He had known all along what Agatha and Dotty were up to, trying to push them together, but they had backed the wrong horse on this one. He was better off alone, despite the silver set of the village trying to marry him off to every eligible woman below forty. He drove the jeep slowly back to Baker Street, willing the journey to end.

Amanda had not spoken since they set off, and he kept sneaking glances at her, but her head was firmly turned towards the passenger window. He resisted the urge to reach for her hands, which were tightly knotted together on her lap, to apologise, but he stayed silent. All too soon, they were at New Lease of Life. Ben clicked on the handbrake and turned off the engine. He silently wished that she would invite him in for coffee, a chance to chat again—it couldn't end on this sour note—but he was stubborn. Amanda took off her seat belt and put her hands on her thighs. Ben did the same, and they each sat there, not willing to break the silence. Ben opened the door slowly, turning to look at his enchanting and annoying passenger.

'Do you want me to get your bag?'

Amanda snapped into life suddenly, opening her door. Ben rushed to meet her. She looked at him in question, seemingly surprised by his closeness. He smiled ruefully at her, taking her hand to help her down from the jeep. She didn't look at him; her gaze was focused on their hands. A frown was fixed across her face, and Ben wanted to smooth the lines out with his fingers. She closed her warm hand around his after a beat, and he felt the familiar jolt once again. *Would this always happen when he was near her? Why did his body not feel the same as his brain?* She broke the spell by moving away towards the jeep, dropping his hand from hers. He followed her, and passed her bag to her from the back of the vehicle.

'Amanda, I…'

'Don't bother, OK? You have said quite enough.
Thanks for the tour.'

She took her bag from him and turned to the door.
When she opened her door and turned back, he was
gone.

Eight

Amanda was drowning. Sinking in layers of taffeta and paper. She was dressed in her nightclothes, and gasping for breath. The layers of fabric and sheets of typed legalese constricted around her body, strips of lace gripping around her wrists, her ankles, pulling her down further. She pulled against them, but they only tightened further. She couldn't breathe, and panic set in. She fought harder, looking up through the mesh of material to see a chink of light at the top. A chink she swam to, kicking out her limbs with gusto. She was just about to break through the surface, taste that first gulp of air, when something solid gripped her ankle. Screaming silently, she thrashed and turned to the terror that held her. She saw Marcus's face, laughing, calling to her, his lip curled in a menacing sneer. She kicked out at him, fighting for her life now, her right to live. He released his grip, and she kicked and aimed for the light, her lungs full, burning. She almost broke through to the surface, when she woke up. Her bed sheets were wrapped tightly around her, and she was slick with sweat.

Her heart pumping, she ran to the bathroom, dragging her sheet with her. She splashed water onto her face, ignoring the shocked pale expression of the girl that stared back at her from the mirror. Two in as many nights. Fab. She had thought that these dreams were finally over, but they had come back Sunday night. She would have blamed the wine or cheese, or something else she would normally eat on an evening, but the fact was that the last few days she had not touched a drop, and her appetite was as non-existent as her profits.

She returned to her bedroom and dragged herself over to her wardrobe, resolving to get dressed and go down to the shop, get some work done. At least her creative side hadn't deserted her; in fact, she had made some lovely things in the last few days, and was building up a nice stock for the shop. She needed to kick these dreams, get rid of the feeling that her old life was going to come and encroach on her new one. It hadn't been the best start, granted, but before her day with Ben she had felt happy, hopeful even. The ending of the day with him had deflated her more than she thought it would, and she couldn't help thinking about him. She had no reason to feel like this, after just a couple of meetings, but she couldn't help poring over the day, wondering what she had said or done that rankled him so much. *Maybe we are just too different,* she thought to herself. *I am a city girl, after all, trying to fit in with a new community. An outsider*, she realised. Maybe she would never fit in around here. But, if she didn't fit in here, where did she fit?

The day passed like the others, a few straggling tourists coming in, not buying much, and Amanda kept herself busy, trying not to hover over them. She was a little worried that her desperation came off her in waves, and was terrified that she would end up chasing the customers down the street before too long, screaming, 'Buy my wares, buy my wares!'

She was just closing the shutters when a car pulled up behind her. Her heart caught, betraying the thought she hoped it was Ben. She turned to see Taylor smiling at her from Agatha's car.

'Hi, Amanda, are you ready for this?'

Amanda laughed, putting her keys in her bag. 'As ready as I'll ever be, Mr Taylor.'

He opened the door for her. *Definitely country folk manners then*, she thought, thinking of how Ben had opened the doors for her.

'Please, Amanda, call me Sebastian. Mr Taylor was my father.'

Amanda nodded. 'So, Sebastian, how long have you worked for Mrs Mayweather?'

Taylor pulled away from Baker Street. 'My family has

worked for the Mayweathers for many generations. My father was butler for Mr Mayweather and, when Mrs Mayweather moved in, she changed the game a little. So now I am estate manager, and I help Agatha as much as she will allow me to.'

Amanda smiled, thinking of the matriarch that he worked for. 'I bet that is pretty hard some days. She seems like she runs a pretty tight ship.'

Taylor laughed as he drove through the village. 'Yep, she sure does. She is not that scary though, a teddy bear when you get to know her. And she seems to have taken a shine to you. Tonight should be fun.' Taylor cranked up the radio and they drove along. Passing the vet's surgery, Amanda looked out at the surgery and Ben's house. His jeep was parked outside, and she looked for signs of life at the windows. The lights were all out, but there was a small light on in the surgery. Taylor saw her looking and she turned her eyes away quickly, embarrassed.

She was just about to start a conversation up when they turned into the long drive of Mayweather Hall, and the words dried up in her throat. She thought Baker Street was pretty, but this place was spectacular. The shale drive was long and windy, lined each side with majestic trees, full with colourful blossoms. After turning the corner, they drove up the left side of a looped drive. The centre of the loop was filled with a water feature—a bronze girl whispering into a boy's ear whilst he looked down at the water. Taylor pulled up and gazed up at the mansion. 'Beautiful, isn't it? Still takes my breath away, every time.'

'It's lovely,' Amanda agreed. 'Like it jumped from the pages of a book. And those statues are so adorable.'

Taylor opened her door and helped her out. 'I always used to tease Mrs Mayweather when we were children that these two were us.'

Amanda looked at the statues again. The two statues seemed so happy with each other, full of life. 'You knew Mrs Mayweather when you were kids?'

Taylor walked up the driveway to the front doors. 'Yep, we went to school together. We all know each other around here.' Taylor caught the upset look on her face. 'You will too, soon enough. You'll see. People are pretty friendly.'

He opened the front door and was immediately thrown back by two huge grey flashes. Amanda jumped and opened her mouth to scream, when a huge beast jumped on her too, knocking her to the floor. Whatever it was, it seemed to be trying to eat her face. She scrambled to stand back up, winded from hitting the floor. The beast let up and licked again once at her face, tickling her nose. She could see Taylor, laughing as he pulled back the two dogs. 'Dogs' was a slight understatement though, Amanda could see as she got to her feet and brushed herself down. These two were like huge, shaggy grey donkeys.

'Meet Maisie and Buster, Mrs Mayweather's pride and joys. Come on in.'

Amanda picked off a bit of dog hair from her clothes as she followed him in, keeping a slight distance from the dogs to avoid being jet washed with drool again. They were cute though. The dogs, once released by Taylor, went to the fire and sprawled out on the huge hearth rug, sighing and snuffing loudly as they settled down. Amanda took a minute to look around the impressive hallway, before Agatha's voice rang out from behind her.

'Hello, dear, so glad you could come. Sorry about my children, they are a little excitable at times.'

Amanda laughed. 'No problem, they are lovely.'

Agatha motioned for her to come to a large doorway. 'I have prepared a light supper in here, with some of the ladies of the town. I hope that's OK?'

Amanda swallowed hard. 'Er…yes, that's fine.' She found herself wondering whether Tanya would be sitting there, waiting for her. Or the local firing squad. Was this a last supper before they rode her out of town on the next hay cart?

They moved into the room. It was as beautiful as the hallway—all high ceilings, ornate mouldings and comfy overstuffed couches and chairs. Along one wall ran a large table, complete with tablecloths, groaning with food and tea and coffee. It looked more like a wedding buffet than a 'light supper'. Four ladies sat in various chairs and sofas, around a large coffee table, drinking

tea and eating, chatting away. They all stopped talking and gazed at Amanda as she walked in. Dotty was
the first to get up and walked towards Amanda. Obviously sensing her embarrassment, she guided her to a
wing-backed chair next to hers. 'Hello, Amanda dear,
how are you?'

Amanda smiled, grateful for the kind gesture. 'I am
fine, thanks, lovely to be here.'

Agatha waved her away, taking a seat herself. 'Oh
pish posh, we don't stand on ceremony here, my darling. Please get something to eat, just help yourself.'
Amanda smiled warmly at Agatha, and she continued
on. 'You have met Dotty, she runs the vet's with Benjamin, then there is Hetty, she runs the greengrocer's,
Grace, she runs the health centre, and this is Marlene.
She is retired now, and helps me to run various events
and organisations.'

All four ladies smiled and murmured hellos. Marlene
in particular was staring at Amanda with great interest, till Agatha leaned over and closed her mouth for her
gently. Grace giggled, her tight silver French pleat not
moving an inch. All the ladies were dressed elegantly,
and she noticed Grace was knitting, and balancing a
cup and saucer of tea on her lap. Agatha picked up her
own cup and took a sip, one finger in the air. 'So, how
did the tour go on Sunday?'

Amanda cleared her throat. 'It was nice, thanks. Ben
had to leave early though, he had a busy day.' She no-

ticed the look pass between the ladies. *Did they know she was lying?* Her cheeks flushed.

Dotty coughed. 'He was really busy, running the vet's and the dog groomer's, and lambing season is upon us too. I am sure he was sad to have to go.'

The ladies all nodded, Grace's cup jiggling with her movement. Amanda needed to change the subject and fast. 'Grace, what a lovely piece of knitting. Is it for anything special?'

Grace preened at the praise. 'My neighbour, dear. She is due to have her first child soon, so I thought I would make her a nice baby shawl. She isn't finding out the sex, but luckily I had some yellow wool so the little cherub will be happy either way.'

Amanda wanted to reach out and touch the pretty patterned garment. It was beautiful, and the wool looked so soft. Grace wasn't even watching her needles, more looking around the room and pausing to sip at her tea. Amanda was grateful that the subject had been averted, but still felt a little sick to her stomach at the thought of Ben. She hadn't heard from him since Sunday, not that she expected to. She hadn't seen him next door since. In fact, other than customers, she hadn't seen anyone, and she once again considered getting a cat. Agatha must have picked up on her pensive thoughts, and she asked her how business was going. Amanda sensed the women all listening intently as she spoke about her shop. All that could be heard in the expanse of the room were the click of needles, an occasional chink of a cup on saucer and the odd snuffle from one of the sleeping dogs nearby. Agatha was listening intently, hands placed primly on her lap.

'The truth is, ladies, that I am new to all this, and it's proving more difficult than I originally thought.' *You didn't think though, did you? You ran, jumped ship, upped sticks, and now you are screwed.* Her inner monologue was proving mardier and mardier by the day.

Grace was the first to break the silence.

'Thing is, dear, Westfield is a bit more "make do and mend" than other places, we all tend to do our own renovations and repairs.'

Amanda's heart sank. This was just what she was starting to fear.

'But,' Grace continued, 'what we do lack is a meeting place.'

Agatha smiled broadly and Amanda suddenly got the impression that this meeting wasn't a mere friendly supper, but more an intervention. *Were they trying to oust her? Maybe they had been planning to use the shop themselves, before she had swooped in with her late night desperation bid.*

'A meeting place?' Amanda asked, her voice coming out as a mere whisper.

Grace, her hands never stopping from making her needles fly, nodded, glancing at each lady in turn before speaking again.

'The community centre in the village is under threat. With all the recent austerity cuts, the council is struggling to keep it open, and the fact it has a leaky roof has sealed its fate cost wise. The council doesn't want to close it, but the money has to be saved somewhere, and the fact is that the roof just won't last another winter. Even with the years of patch-up jobs, it's in a sorry state, which is a travesty as it is so important to the people who live here. It's normally booked up with mums and tots, yoga, t'ai chi, and the local book clubs, not to mention the many events of the Westfield Historical Society.'

Marlene rolled her eyes dramatically at this, and Amanda wondered whether she had reasons for disliking this part in particular.

'So,' Grace added, 'we have been making plans to save it. What we need, Amanda, is a place to meet. The employees are behind us, but they can't be seen to be actively helping us. Marlene here runs the tea bar there, so we have an inside woman.' At this, she looked across at Marlene, who winked at Amanda and tapped the side of her nose in a James Bond style. 'Agatha here tells us that your shop is quite big, and has a large table and chairs in it.'

The words came out as more of a statement than a question, and Amanda marvelled at Mrs Mayweather's ability to case a joint without even setting foot inside. She nodded, intrigued at where this was going.

Marlene piped up. 'What we propose is paying you

for a meeting place, we could then have somewhere to meet, you get some money in your till, and everyone is happy. We can say that we are running a craft club, that way no one will know what we are up to, and Mr Beecham won't be breathing down our necks either.'

The women collectively snorted and growled at the mention of Mr Beecham. Amanda looked to Agatha in confusion.

'Mr Beecham?' Amanda asked tentatively, picturing a man in a flash suit stroking a white cat in her mind. 'Who is Mr Beecham?'

Grace answered in a flash, not tearing her gaze from her needles once. 'He is the enemy, dear. He is on the council, and is the one man who actually wants the community centre to close. He is not from here, and he sees things in pounds and pence, not people.'

Amanda nodded. She knew the type.

Hetty, more nervous than the rest, spoke up then. 'And Andrew at the Four Feathers has one of those new-fangled coffee machines for sale too. So we could even contribute more by paying for drinks. I loved the lattes they did there, but the pub gang are more pies and pints, so Andy took them off the menu.'

She looked crestfallen at the loss of her new-found love of milky coffees, and Amanda's brain started to whirr with the possibilities. It would be nice to have a regular income, and company. Plus, an empty shop always makes people want to pass by; if it was a hub of activity, the tourists were more likely to venture in and then she could hopefully make more sales. Plus, having an income to bolster her heavily bleeding bank account would save a lot of stress, and give her more time to concentrate on projects, instead of eating Chunky Monkey by the carton every night and crying over her failed life. Plus, if she helped the ladies save the community centre, she would certainly be painted in a good light to the villagers, and to a rather opinionated and moody animal whisperer. Not that she cared what he thought. Looking at the ladies' hopeful faces, Amanda made a decision.

'Well, ladies, looks like we have a deal. When do we start?'

Nine

Ben had already seen three patients before 10 a.m.: a dog with a bad cough, a parrot suffering from a bald patch and Mrs Burdock's tabby cat, Sinatra, who was suffering from chronic flatulence. All patched up and sent home with their happy owners—apart from Mrs Burdock, who was given a ticking-off for feeding poor Sinatra spicy sausage—Ben was now staring at the back of the door, thinking about the catastrophic day he had spent with a certain bossy shop owner. She was constantly on his mind, and he hadn't seen her since their date on Sunday. Dotty had seen her a few days ago at the Mayweather mansion, but was keeping pretty coy about the details for some reason. He was just wiping down his table when the consulting room door opened. Dotty, beaming from ear to ear, shuffled through the door. 'Ben dear, you have someone to see you. Shall I send them in?'

Ben, intrigued, nodded, putting the wipes he had used into the bin. Turning around as the door opened again, he saw Amanda standing there. She looked beautiful, dressed in simple grey slacks, black pumps and a white cami top. Ben took in a sharp breath as he looked at her.

'Hi, Ben,' she said nervously.

'Hi, Amanda,' he replied. 'Something wrong?'

She shook her head, her hair loose around her shoulders. 'I was talking to Dotty the other day about getting a pet and she suggested I speak to you. I…er…was thinking of getting a cat? I thought you might know of the best place to get a kitten?'

Ben was nonplussed. Not what he was expecting. He realised she was looking at him questioningly, and he was staring back at her open-mouthed like an imbecile.

'That's great!' he said, aware that she was making the effort, so he should too. 'I do actually. Mr Jenkins' cat has just had a litter of kittens, and they are ready. He was going to advertise them in the vet's this week. I can take you there if you like, to have a look?'

* * *

Amanda grinned, relieved he hadn't turfed her out of the door as soon as look at her. She was determined to make him see that she wasn't here to cause trouble. *No, you are running away from it,* her brain chelped back at her.

'That would be great, thanks. I have never had a cat

before, but I think the company might be nice.' *Way to go, Amanda, you came here and went full on crazy cat lady on him. Sexy.*

Ben reached into his desk drawer and pulled out a pamphlet. 'I have some tips here on kittens, and I can help you if you like, no problem. Shall I pick you up this evening?'

Amanda took the pamphlet from him, her fingers brushing against his briefly. 'If you have the time, I would appreciate it. Thanks, Ben.'

Ben shook her thanks away. 'It's my pleasure. Shall we say six? I'll come get you then.'

Amanda nodded, making a hasty retreat before she opened her mouth again. She didn't want him as an enemy, but she wasn't about to make friends with him either.

* * *

Dotty looked on, amused. Ben blushed as she winked at him, and called his next patient.

* * *

Promptly at six, the buzzer to the flat went. Amanda jumped. *Here we go.* She pressed the intercom button and managed a breathy 'Hello?' Ben's deep tones came over the waves.

'Amanda, it's Ben. Are you ready?'

She was about to say that she would be right down, but got the unexpected urge to invite him up.

'Nearly, would you like to come in for a moment?'

Ben's surprised reply came back. She buzzed him in, quickly racing to her bedroom to check that she had not left any big berthas on show, and then opened the flat door. Ben was just walking up the stairs, dressed smartly in a blue sweater and indigo denim jeans. *Yum*, Amanda thought to herself, before pushing the thought away. She moved back to allow him entry. 'Come on in, I am just going to grab my jacket.'

Ben walked into the room. Her flat suddenly felt smaller as his six foot two body filled the space. Amanda was suddenly glad that she had worn boots with a heel, but she still felt like Thumbelina in his proximity. She closed the door behind him and went for her jacket, which she had laid on her bed. When she came back into the open plan living area, she stopped short in the doorway. Ben was looking at the photo frames on her mantelpiece. Pictures of her in her graduation gown, standing with her parents; a Christmas she had spent with friends skiing; sitting with her grandmother Rose; her first day at her new job, all fresh faced, before the jading from the job had set in.

Amanda cleared her throat, and Ben whirled around, a guilty look on his face.

'Sorry, I was just looking.'

Amanda smiled. 'It's fine.'

Ben pointed to one of the photos. 'That your parents?'

Amanda came closer to the photo, catching a faint whiff of Ben's aftershave as she stepped near to him.

'Yep, that's them. They live in London. They work in law too.'

Ben nodded. 'What do they think of your new life?'

Amanda looked at the faces of her parents. When they found out what she was doing, she guessed they would be pretty angry. Truth was, she hadn't told them. They thought she was on vacation, or they had a few weeks ago, when she had sent them a quick email before dashing off into the hills of Yorkshire. She wasn't about to tell Mr Judgy that though.

'You ready to go?' she said, cutting off his questioning by heading for the door. Ben said nothing and followed her to the jeep.

The drive to the Jenkinses' farm was comfortable, Ben filling the silence by telling her all about the Jenkins couple. He didn't ask any more questions about her life, and Amanda was grateful.

'I delivered Ophelia myself, and she is getting big now. Alf will no doubt want to show her off, I hope you won't mind.'

Amanda shook her head. 'Ben, I like animals. You don't have to apologise whenever we come across one.'

Ben's lips quivered with a suppressed grin.

The Jenkinses really rolled out the red carpet for them. Ophelia was huge now, and happily tucked up with her mother Gwendolen. Amanda found it surprising how graceful they were for their size, and listened intently as Alf told the dramatic breech birth story to them. Ben was modest and obviously very embarrassed by the praise, but Amanda found it quite charming.

Mrs Jenkins was keen to hear about her guest too, and, as she settled in the front room, the men went to get the kittens from the barn while she grilled Amanda.

'So, Amanda dear, how are things? I hear that the ladies have a new meeting place for their craft club, thanks to you. I go sometimes, when I am not busy here.'

Amanda nodded, looking at the many handmade things around the room, from the cross-stitched cushion covers to the knitted tea cosy on the teapot. 'Yes, the ladies are coming from next week. I am looking forward to it actually. It will be nice to have the company.'

'If it's company you want,' Alf boomed, walking in with a wicker basket full of fluff, Ben just behind him, 'then one of these little guys is just the ticket! Now none of these have homes yet. Young Ben here begged me to let you have first pick!'

Ben flushed as Amanda smirked at him. *Maybe he wasn't such an ogre.* Alf set the basket down, and Ben and Amanda sat on the hearthrug at the same time. So much at the same time that they nearly sat on each other. Giggling nervously, they moved to sit side by side, a safe distance from each other, as the little kittens peered out of the basket at them. Mr and Mrs Jenkins sat together on the settee, simpering at each other as they watched the scene before them.

'Awwww, wow, they are sooo cute!' Amanda's gaze

was immediately caught by a very fluffy grey kitten that was stepping on his brothers and sisters to get out of the basket to her. Ben reached in and pushed the kitten's hair back momentarily at the back end, then placed the young cat on Amanda's lap. 'This one's a girl,' he said.

Amanda reached out and stroked the adorable bundle, laughing as it pawed at her hand, moving closer to the attention. Looking back in the basket, Amanda noticed a little white cat, with grey socks on, which was curled into the bottom of the basket, not moving around like the others. She frowned. 'What's wrong with the white one?'

Ben reached into the basket and lifted it out then gently cradled the smallest kitten on his own lap.

Alf spoke up. 'Ah, that there's the runt, never been much of a mover. The grey one there has been mothering it a bit, those two stay pretty close.' Ben was scrutinising the little white kitten. 'It's healthy enough, just a little smaller than the others.'

Amanda stroked the little white head, and Ben put it on her lap with its sister. 'This one's a girl too.'

The grey one immediately nuzzled against her sister, giving it a little hello lick.

'Can I buy two?' Amanda asked. Ben looked shocked, and his face soon changed into a surprised smile. Mr Jenkins chuckled. 'Of course you can, love, but they are yours. Ben here does enough for us, so consider them a gift.'

Amanda blushed. *Why did people treat them like a*

dating couple whenever they were together? She glanced at Ben to gauge his response, but he was looking back at her with a neutral expression.

'They will be great buds, I bet. Shall we collect them tomorrow? I can come with you after work, we can call at the pet store in town tonight if you like, get their things ready?'

She looked at him, obviously surprised at the offer.

He shrugged, trying to play down his enthusiastic plan-making. 'It's nothing—I have a car and you don't know your way around.'

Amanda nodded. It made sense, so she chose not to dwell on having to spend more time with him.

She was already mentally planning where to put things in her flat for her new little playmates as they waved goodbye to the kittens and the Jenkinses.

* * *

After a short but oddly expensive trip to the pet store, which luckily opened late, they were soon pulling up outside A New Lease of Life. Ben jumped out and came to open her door before she got chance to even touch the door handle.

'Thanks,' she said. He reached out his hand and, taking it, she jumped down to the pavement. He walked with her to the boot and opened it up. He started to bring the bags and boxes out. Amanda grabbed two herself and headed for the flat door, Ben following close behind.

'These kittens are spoilt already, Amanda, you do

know that, right?' She laughed, and Ben's heart danced at the carefree sound. *She has a nice laugh*, he thought to himself, enjoying the sound.

* * *

After carrying the bags up the stairs, Amanda opened up the flat door and headed to the kitchen area to put them on the counter. She opened the fridge and was grateful that she had stocked up. She had to offer him something, show him she had some manners akin to his own after he had ferried her about. She missed having a car for the first time in her life, after years of taxis and commuting in London, she had never even thought about transport when moving here. Turning to offer Ben a drink, she saw that he was laid out on the living room rug, putting together the large scratching post play centre that he had recommended she buy to save her furniture from little curious claws.

'Er, you really don't have to do that,' she said, not wanting to make him feel obligated to help his neighbour any more than he had already.

He stopped what he was doing and set his grey eyes on hers, shrugging his shoulders. 'I don't mind,' he said coolly. 'Unless you want me to go?' He made a motion to stand.

'No!' she said a little too quickly. *What? Amanda, you hate the guy. Let him go.* She had to admit to herself though, they had actually got on tonight, and she wasn't really in a hurry to spend yet another evening alone. 'No,' she tried again, making her voice sound less interested. 'It's fine. I appreciate the help today, by the way. Can I offer you a drink? Tea, wine?'

Ben settled back onto the floor. 'Er, wine, please?'

Amanda nodded, a maelstrom of emotions whirling through her. She poured the wine and set a glass beside him, adding a small plate of cheese and crackers as an afterthought. She hadn't had the chance to eat at tea-time, and she assumed that Ben might not have had a chance either.

See, Benjamin, she said with her eyes as she laid the plate on the coffee table, *us city girls have manners too.*

She sipped at her wine as she watched him work, his hair tousled, tongue peeking out from between his lips in concentration. The tableau of domesticity made her stomach lurch. She had been independent for so long that the thought of a man in her flat fixing together furniture was alien to her. When she had dated Marcus, he hadn't even so much as thought of picking up a screwdriver to do anything in her flat. She had even paid a handy-man to put up her bedroom curtain pole. Watching Ben help her, unasked, without thought of even being asked, thawed her heart a little. She took her glass across and sat on the sofa. Ben noticed her movement and smiled at her, taking the wine glass from the table.

'Thanks, you didn't have to bring me that.'

Amanda placed a piece of cheese on a cracker and took a bite, motioning for Ben to do the same. He nibbled on his as he worked, fixing parts together and twisting them tight together expertly with an Allen key. Before too long, the cheese, wine and play centre were all finished. Ben put it down where she asked him to, and they got to work setting everything else out. Seeing that everything was done, the two of them stood looking around the room awkwardly.

She was just thinking of something to say when Ben spoke.

'So, see you tomorrow? Pick the kittens up?'

Amanda shook her head. 'No, it's fine, really—I will get a taxi.'

Ben shook his head. 'It's no trouble, honestly. Dotty would kill me if I let you do that.'

Amanda nodded once. *Just accept, be nice.* 'OK, thank you,' she said slowly.

Ben nodded, walking to the door. 'Tomorrow then,' he said, towering over her.

She suddenly felt a frisson of tension as they stood near to each other, the door to her flat ajar. He reached out a hand and Amanda's heart leaped, till she realised he was holding it out for a handshake. She shook his hand, ignoring the zap she felt when their fingers connected.

Ben left, and she flounced down onto the sofa, fresh bottle in hand. Pulling the blanket around her from the sofa back, she noticed one side bore the scent of his aftershave. Nice, woody but gentle, it suited him. She

inhaled the smell and wrapped the blanket around her.
How could a man be such an arrogant arse and be so
nice to others around him? His behaviour at the Jenkinses' had shown her another side of him tonight, and
she couldn't quite work him out, which unnerved her.
Amanda was good at sussing people out normally, and
she wondered when that skill had left her. Perhaps it
was just around attractive men. She hated to admit it,
but as mean as he was, Ben Evans was a good-looking
man, and Marcus was no gargoyle, despite his other
less attractive attributes. She poured herself some wine
and flicked on the DVD-player. Mr Darcy popped onto
the screen again, sour-faced at the ball. She snorted
to herself as she threw back the contents of her glass.
*Maybe this was her type: arrogant, attractive, infu-
riating men.* The thought sufficiently depressed her
enough to refill her glass.

* * *

She was swimming again, thrashing through the water,
Marcus hot on her heels. Kicking her way through the
dark blue depths, towards the light, she once again felt
the fingers encase her ankle, pulling her down. Opening her mouth to scream, the water filled her lungs,
her chest heavy, sloshing. She whirled around, her own
hands reaching for her leg, seeking release before the
world turned black…she could see the light, just above…

Opening one eye, she was aware that the light was
brighter. Focusing with both eyes, she realised she was

home. Something tickled her nose as she stretched. The blanket, still smelling of her visitor, was wrapped around her tight.

Ten

Something felt different as Ben walked across the drive from his house to the practice. He couldn't quite put his finger on it, but something had changed. It wasn't till he looked at Dotty, who was making brews in the kitchen, that he realised. Dotty was smirking at him as she handed him a strong tea in his favourite mug. Ben frowned as he took it from her. 'What's with the grin, Dotty?'

Dotty laughed. 'Good night, was it?'

Ben flushed as he realised that he was busted. He felt guilty, even though nothing had happened last night. They had got on though, which had surprised him. Although he still wasn't holding any truck to her fancy ideas.

Dotty's swift poke into his ribs with her index finger

brought him back to the present, almost showering hot tea down them both in the process.

'What?' he protested, an awkward laugh following. 'I took Amanda to the Jenkinses' farm yesterday, that's all. She wanted a cat, so she asked me. Because *you* told her to, remember?'

Dotty grinned. 'And, how did it go? Did you ask her out?'

Ben shook his head violently. 'No! Why would I do that? I helped her put the equipment together, had a glass of wine and left.' He saw Dotty's excited expression. 'Dotty, it was a drink. Nothing more. We don't get on. She is not like us.'

Dotty shook her head and opened her mouth to speak. Ben put a finger up in protest.

'Dotty, I am not interested in chasing some Londoner solicitor who wants to modernise Westfield with her fancy boutique, OK?'

'Do you even know what her shop will do?' Dotty asked, hands on her hips now.

'Yes, of course I do, fancy boutique stuff that will drive the tourists away, fancy gadgets and the like, over-priced coffees and fancy cakes, stuff that is ten a penny in the city. She will soon get bored with our slow pace, and then she will pack up and leave, and we will be left to pick up the pieces. Usual story.'

Dotty shrugged then, huffing loudly, left the kitchen with her own drink and walked through to reception.

'You are a fool, Ben Evans,' she shot over her shoulder as she stomped off. 'Don't judge a girl by her past.'

Her determined stomp made Ben wonder what he had said to get her annoyed. He drank his tea and went to set up for the clinic. *It was just a drink,* he convinced himself. *Once the kittens are home with her, then we won't have a reason to spend time together any more.* The thought of their tentative friendship being cut short filled him with a little unease deep down, but it had to happen. It's not like he needed to get to know her, right? Maybe he was judging her, but rather that than waste time trying to get on with someone who would leave when winter set in.

He started to set up his area, resolving to keep his mind on the job. And away from the thought of how Amanda felt as their hands had touched. *Stop it, Ben*, he chided himself. *A girl like that will never be content with this life, with you. This is just a stopgap for her. She will move on, and you will be left. Again. And this time, she will take more than your best friend.*

* * *

In reception, Dotty cast furtive glances at Ben's door as she picked up the phone. Somewhere else in the village, the phone was ringing. As it was picked up, Dotty whispered into the receiver, cupped between her hands. 'It's me. We have a problem. It's not working like we hoped.' Dotty nodded vigorously as she listened to the voice on the line. 'I agree, we need to move things on. Can you do it today?'

The voice on the line agreed. Dotty said her goodbyes and, placing the phone back into the cradle, took a quick glance at the door and grabbed her mobile from her bag. Tapping out a group text, she sent it with a flourish and stashed the mobile back into her bag just as the first client walked in. The text had read: STAGE 2: BAKER STREET IS A GO. EAGLE IS FLYING TODAY.

Greeting the first customer, Mrs Eggleston and her dog Flossie, who was suffering from acral lick dermatitis as a result of Mr Eggleston forming a cover band who practised in their garage three evenings a week, no one would suspect a thing as Dotty, mild-mannered receptionist, went about her double life.

* * *

Placing the Wild & Wolf telephone receiver back into its cradle, Agatha Mayweather looked at the two dogs at her feet. Her latest projects were proving more troublesome than organising the summer fair, and that was a feat in itself even with her years of experience. Buster turned his head in question at his master. 'Well now, Buster, it seems we have a little visit in order. Good job your check-up is due, isn't it?' Rising from her chair, Buster and Maisie jumped to their feet, ready for the off. 'Taylor?' she called. No answer. Frowning, she headed past the large hall, through the kitchen and out the back door, hounds following at either side. 'Taylor?' Agatha could hear music coming from the garage. Tutting at Taylor's choice of soft rock, she walked to the garage, the noise of the radio and tinkering of tools getting louder as she approached. Taylor was half hidden under one of the cars, Mr Mayweather's Silver Shadow, which mostly stood resting in the garage, other than special occasions. His legs protruded out from underneath, his left foot tapping to the music of the drums.

'Taylor?' she said again. A thunk was her answer, as Taylor headbutted the chassis of the car. A muffled expletive could be heard coming from the car as he shuffled out. 'Mrs Mayweather?'

Agatha was slightly taken aback at the sight of her lifelong friend. Dressed in casual jeans and a mucky white T-shirt, Agatha could see his muscles underneath the thin cotton material. She looked away quickly, pretending to focus on the car instead. *For a man of his age, he was certainly trim*, she thought to herself, before she brushed the thought away sternly. 'Sorry, Taylor, I didn't mean to interrupt you. I was just wondering if you could take the children and me into town, we have an appointment at the vet's.'

Taylor wiped his cheek with the back of his hand, leaving a smear of oil across his face. Agatha resisted the urge to laugh, and pursed her lips together to prevent a giggle escaping. Taylor looked at her, an amused look on his face, as he produced a rag from his back pocket and proceeded to wipe his hands on it.

'More good deeds, eh, Mrs Mayweather?'

Agatha almost nodded till she realised he was mocking her. 'No, Taylor, of course not, just a check-up. And please, for the love of God, call me Agatha.'

Taylor chuckled, pushing the rag back into his pocket. 'Give me half an hour, Mrs Mayweather, I'll get cleaned up.'

Agatha nodded primly, turned on her heel and headed back to the house. She could hear Taylor's amused snickers all the way to the back door.

Damn that man, she thought, smiling despite herself.

* * *

Taylor watched her hostile retreating form. *Damn that woman*, he thought, feeling the telltale spread of warmth in his heart.

Eleven

Amanda was just setting the new coffee machine up when the tring of the bell rang out in the front of the shop. *Brilliant, customers!* She wiped her hands on a tea towel, tucked an errant strand of hair behind her ear and went to greet them. Dotty, Marlene, Hetty and Grace stood in the doorway, laden down with shopping bags. Amanda smiled nervously as she watched them surveying the shop. She had tidied up that morning, and now she just had some fabric laid out. To be honest, she was hoping that they had some ideas on what she could make with it. After all, they were using the craft club as a cover, but they still needed stock to sell at the fair. Grace immediately rushed forward, embracing her in a large hug. Amanda caught a whiff of lavender. 'Oh,' she said, her head smushed in silver hair. 'You smell lovely!'

Grace chuckled as the ladies set to work, emptying

their bags onto the large wooden table. 'It's lavender, dear. We collected a lot from the village, as we thought that we would make lavender bags to sell at the summer fair. They are always popular with the tourists.'

Amanda grinned, picking up the fabric bundle. 'I have just the fabric to use too.'

Hetty reached into her large fabric bag and pulled out notepads, pens and a map of Westfield.

'Got somewhere in the back we could pin this, dear? We need to start co-ordinating our efforts for the community centre.'

Amanda nodded, pinning the map to one of the walls in the expansive back room. Hetty pulled out some push pins and started to pin various areas with different coloured pins. The women all nodded along as she placed pin after pin, the odd grunt of approval being heard in the quiet of the room.

'So here we have it,' Hetty said proudly. 'These are the sectors we have petitioned, and everyone is signed up. We can collect more at the summer fair, but we need an event to raise the roof funds, so the council have a chance of fighting the closure.'

Amanda watched in wonder as the women scribbled away in their notepads. She had seen rooms full of the greatest legal minds in England work less effectively and efficiently than these women. Then it hit her! She was a solicitor, she lobbied in courts, fought and won cases, took on large corporations in her sleep. She could help! Her brain started to work faster, at the possibility of really making a positive difference to Westfield. That would show people she was here to stay. Especially Benjamin 'I don't like change' Evans. The thought of wiping that 'holier than thou' look off his face would be worth the effort alone.

Amanda piped up, and the women all stopped dead, looking at her in surprise from their poised forms.

'We should have an event!' she said excitedly. She grabbed a large piece of paper and, after spreading it across the table, she grabbed a pen and started writing.

'A huge event, something quintessentially Yorkshire, something different, to bring the crowds in.'

The ladies all shuffled around the paper.

'Like what though? We already have the summer fair, but that won't raise enough.'

Amanda frowned. She tried to remember all the boring charity events her parents had dragged each other, and her, to over the years. Vegas-themed casino night, rainforest-themed conservation events, balls, operas…

'A play!'

The women all looked at each other, their expressions unreadable. Amanda was on a roll, her hands flying over the paper as she wrote.

'An open-air play. We are in the heart of Yorkshire, right? We could host an Austen-themed play! People can dress up, we can have serving staff, music—you said yourself that Westfield has a historical society! We could get them involved, get the local and national press to come, charge money for tickets, all themed on Austen.'

Hetty jumped into life. 'The society are always putting them on, but not on this scale. People would pay from far and wide to come to that, I am sure!'

Grace, sat knitting with a notepad poised on one knee, stopped what she was doing. 'That, my dear, is a good idea.'

Amanda grinned as the women all talked excitedly around her. *Wait till Ben gets a load of this.*

The day whizzed by, and Amanda, for the first time since her arrival, felt like she was running a real business. The ladies were a joy to be with, they drank plenty of coffee and tea—Hetty seemed to be addicted to the stuff—which they gladly paid for, and the little hive of activity they created seemed to break the ice with the locals too. Amanda even made a few sales. By the end of the day, Amanda's feet hurt, and her till actually had some decent takings in it. The ladies all left at teatime with murmurs about her having a good evening, and whispers in Dotty's direction. Dotty herself gave her a motherly cuddle before she left, and even made a show of fluffing Amanda's hair, telling her she should curl her long hair once in a while.

When the last person had left and Amanda had cleaned up, she actually felt very alone, and was grateful for the evening plans she had with Ben. She couldn't wait to pick up the kittens, and was looking forward to having some company to share her new home with. Thoughts of Ben from the night before came into her mind, and she blushed at them. She went to double-check the coffee pot and heard the front doorbell go. *A late customer?* Amanda walked back through to the front of the shop and caught her breath as she saw Ben leaning over the table, looking at the day's work. After the morning of furtive planning, the afternoon had been taken up with making stock, her for her shop, and the ladies for the summer fair. She smiled as he sniffed one of the lavender bags, and found herself staring at his bottom in his black chinos. He looked like he had just got ready, all neat and tidy, and the little curls at the nape of his neck still looked damp from his shower. Amanda felt the sudden need to wrap them around her fingers.

'Hi,' Ben said, turning to her suddenly. She jumped and gave out a little surprised noise. Ben laughed. 'Sorry, I didn't mean to frighten you.' His apologetic grin made her pulse rise, his cheeks dimpling with the movement. She tried to speak but her voice had given out. Clearing her throat, embarrassed, she tried again.

'What, no, you didn't—I was just locking up. Are you ready already?'

Ben frowned, looking at his watch. 'We did say six, right?'

Amanda glanced at the art deco clock on the wall. It was ten past. *How was it this time already?* She glanced down in dismay at herself—loose bits of cotton were stuck to her jeans, and her pink top had little beads of lavender buds stuck to them. She already knew she had little make-up on. 'Sorry, Ben, I must have lost track of time. Not like me! Shall I change?'

Ben shook his head. 'No need, you look gorgeous.' He looked panicked for a second, and the emotion soon washed from his face into a lopsided grin. 'Er, I mean, the Jenkinses won't expect you to dress up, and you look...er...OK.'

Amanda didn't even hear him. She was still stuck on his first statement. *He thinks I'm gorgeous,* she thought to herself. *Not bad for a city girl come country lass, after all.* She smiled at him, grabbing her purse and keys from the side. 'Thanks, Ben. You look nice too.'

Ben blushed, and the two of them stood nervously. *Man, this was like high school territory all over again.*

Ben willed his face to stop betraying his reaction to her words.

'Shall we go?' he asked. Amanda nodded, willing the awkward moment to pass.

* * *

An hour later, Ben and Amanda were lying on the rug in Amanda's sitting room, watching two grey and white bundles of fluff navigate around their new home. The bigger grey one was trying to bat the end table at that moment, whilst the white one was trying to bury her way under the settee. Amanda giggled. 'They are like little drunk people, tiptoeing around!'

Ben chuckled, watching her face light up. It was nice to see her smile. Maybe she would stick around for a while after all. He hadn't expected her to take a pet in, never mind two, and he knew enough about people to see that she wasn't the type to make a commitment to them and then leave. What *did* she leave though? She changed the subject whenever anyone mentioned London, and all he knew was that she had worked in law. No mention of her family, friends…or anyone significant, just the odd feeling he had sometimes that there *might* have been someone.

When he wasn't with her, he found himself wracking his brain with possibilities, worries, niggles, and he found it more and more difficult to rein these in as the days went on. Amanda must have sensed his thoughts, because she looked over at him in question. 'Something on your mind?'

He didn't return her smile, and looked really uncomfortable as he spoke. Amanda held her breath as she waited for him to speak.

'I just wondered, are you happy here?'

Amanda puffed out in surprise. 'Happy? Yes, I am. Why?'

Ben's frown diminished as he smiled, his dimples peeking at her. 'I just never hear you talk of home, of London, and I wondered why.' He ran his fingers through his hair. 'I am not prying, I'm…just interested.'

Amanda sat up then, pushing her back into the settee. 'I left London quickly. I kind of had to. I…was… unhappy. I left my job, and my career.'

Ben moved to sit beside her, the kittens dashing around the rug in front of them.

'That must have been awful. Did you not have any family to support you? Your parents?' He pointed to the photo frames on her mantelpiece.

Amanda shook her head. 'No, it's just me. My parents work in law, and they love it. They don't understand people who don't follow their lifestyle. There was someone, but…he wasn't who I thought he was.' Ben nodded. He knew there must have been someone, she was beautiful and independent. Of course there was a man. He found himself wanting to punch the man for hurting his Amanda. *Not your Amanda, Ben, remember. You are not what she is looking for, and you can't take the risk anyway. You need to stay away, Ben, but you are failing.* 'Do you keep in touch with anyone?'

Amanda winced. 'To be honest, I turned off my mobile on the way out of London and haven't had the guts to turn it back on since.'

Ben nodded. *Was she hiding? What could be so bad?* He wanted to question her, find out what she was thinking of, and who, but he thought better of it. After all, he had plenty that he didn't want to discuss either, so who was he to talk? As he looked at her, playing with the kittens, he felt grateful that she had even answered his questions. She wasn't what he expected at all from a city girl. God knows his wife had been a force larger than life, but Amanda was different—softer, quieter. The more he saw her, the more difficult it was to imagine village life without her in it, and this notion both thrilled and terrified him in equal measure.

* * *

Amanda stroked her new little flatmates and tried not to blush as she felt Ben watching her. He had watched her a lot today, but she couldn't fathom out whether this was a brilliant development, or a signal of impending doom. From his looks and now his questions, he was obviously trying to fathom her out, but for what purpose Amanda could only guess. She had pretty much given up denying to herself that she was attracted to him, the telltale skips of her heart whenever he was near had put paid to that, but she didn't know her next move. Was there a next move? The kitten appeal for help had been genuine, she really did want to get a cat, but she couldn't fully deny that his help was strictly needed. She was a resourceful woman after all, any idiot could hunt down a pet. She just couldn't resist the chance to get to know him better, to fathom him out, but that had backfired. Being as picky as she was with the opposite sex, and as driven as she was, partners and love interests had been few and far between, and she hadn't really been that bothered before. Before Ben at least. The plan had been to suss out just how much of an idiot he was, and put paid to the girlish daydreaming. *Nice plan, Amanda, now you really are in trouble.*

Twelve

Agatha stirred from her slumber as a clatter came from the kitchen downstairs. She jumped up, pulled off her night eye mask and ran to the doorway in bare feet. The dulcet tones of Taylor rang up the stairs as he scolded whichever dog had been up to no good, and Agatha relaxed and tittered at the expletives coming from her companion's mouth. She walked over to the nightstand, quickly ran a comb through her hair, pinched her cheeks and then settled back under the covers, just as Taylor came in, tray in hand.

'Mrs Mayweather?'

Agatha opened her eyes and smiled at Taylor, before taking the cup and saucer he had placed on the tray. Alongside that was a plate bearing marmalade and toast, and a small vase holding a single red rose and a spray of baby's breath.

'Ooh,' Agatha exclaimed, dipping her head to smell the bloom.

'The garden is full of them, a good crop this year.' Taylor smiled. 'I thought you might like a little colour this morning.'

Agatha smiled back at him. 'Lovely, thank you. I shall have to visit the gardens this afternoon, speak to Archibald.'

Taylor snuffed. 'Just don't call him Archibald, eh? You know he hates it.'

Agatha lifted her chin in defiance. 'Traditions are nothing in society these days, but not here. I intend to keep up the pretence for a little while longer, thank you.'

Taylor rolled his eyes good-naturedly. 'No problem, Mrs Mayweather,' he said, with great emphasis on her full name. Agatha tutted and huffed in response, making Taylor's grin all the broader. He crossed the room, tray in hand, and placed the vase on her dressing table. 'On another note, your recent foray into espionage seems to be paying off. Dotty says that Amanda has a cracking idea to save the community centre, and I think you will like it.'

She narrowed her eyes at him. 'What "espionage" is this you speak of? I merely helped a newcomer to earn a bit of cash and got us somewhere safe to meet, away from Mr Beecham.'

Taylor nodded, tapping the side of his nose with his

free hand. 'Fair enough, nudge nudge, wink wink, and all that. Your secret is safe, Bond.'

Agatha squeezed the duvet between her fingers, stifling the urge to throw something at his retreating form. *That man is so infuriating!* She finished her brew and went to sit at her dressing table. The smell from the flowers surrounded her and she reached out tentatively to stroke a blood red petal. Her eyes glanced across to the photo beside it, displaying her husband's smiling face. Her smile dimming slightly, she started to get ready.

The summer fair was a matter of a few weeks away, and there was still much to be done to get the village, and her own house and grounds, ready for the onslaught of visitors to their beautiful haven. And, if she had her way, there might even be a wedding to add to their celebrations before too long. That really would be a jewel in her organisational crown, she thought, as she brushed her hair for the second time that morning.

It wasn't till that afternoon, when she was speaking to suppliers in her office, twiddling a loose strand of hair, she registered that for the first time since her husband died, she had cared what a man thought of her appearance first thing in the morning. The reasons eluded her still, but gave her food for thought. Food for thought, and an extra sherry that teatime.

* * *

Meanwhile, back on Baker Street, Amanda was standing up on a stool in the beginnings of a gown, whilst the ladies of the elite pranced around her, showing her fabric swatches, moving her body parts this way and that, tape measures a flash around here, around there, as they animatedly chattered, took notes and even made chalk lines on her clothing. For her part, she was so bemused that she simply let them do their will and, before too long, she was actually enjoying herself immensely.

That morning, the ladies had been all of a flutter about the Austen event, and apparently it had even got the Mayweather seal of approval, so it was all systems go, and the print shop in the village was hurriedly making flyers and tickets for the event. Everyone in the village was excited and the shops in town had been deluged with people buying supplies to make their own costumes. The women had instantly put themselves forward as Amanda's chief costume makers, and would brook no refusal.

Amanda was horrified at first, never even connecting that the event may require a costume for her, but secretly she was ridiculously excited about dressing up and having an Austen adventure. *Keira Knightley—eat your heart out, girlie, Amanda Perry is hot on your tail.* As she watched Grace and Dotty argue about whether the sleeves should be taffeta or ruched silk, she wondered momentarily what she would have been doing at this time of day six months ago. Nose deep in a file probably, mainlining expensive to-go coffees and barking instructions at her secretary. In this moment, she felt as far away from that woman as she ever did, and the thought warmed her. The shop bell trilled and Ben walked in. She flushed as their eyes met, and Ben's gaze wandered over her body momentarily, on show like a shop mannequin.

'Oh, Ben! You can't be in here! We are busy!' Marlene scolded.

Ben laughed. 'It's fine, I won't be a minute. I just wanted to say hello, see how the kittens' first night was. Agatha has roped me into this event, and said I should come and help organise it.'

Hetty giggled and Amanda thought she heard her say something like 'Nice one, Ags' under her breath. She hoped that Ben didn't hear it too. One look across at him however, and she knew that he had. He rolled his eyes dramatically and smirked at her, and she giggled out loud before she could stop herself. Grace glanced up from her skirts and winked at her. *Were this lot trying to push them together?* Amanda marvelled once again at the relentless beat of the jungle drums in this small town. When she had lived in London, even seeing a neighbour once a month in the stairway was considered a social occasion.

Dotty looked at Ben then, and Amanda could practically see the cogs turning.

'Ben, you don't have a date for the play. Why don't you take Amanda?'

Amanda wanted the earth to split open and suck her

under. She felt her face explode with embarrassment, and suddenly felt a bit faint perched on the stool.

'I was just thinking that myself!' Hetty exclaimed, nodding vigorously.

Ben smirked at Hetty. 'Just occurred to you that, did it?'

Her face dropped, a guilty look passing across her face. *Busted.* Marlene swatted at him then, catching his hand with an open palm.

'Don't tease, Ben, it doesn't become you. Now, are you going to ask her or not?'

Amanda's stomach flipped. *Awkward! A pity date from a man who didn't like her being in the village was not the most romantic event ever, was it?*

'Er, no, I am fine going alone,' she said.

Ben raised his eyebrow. 'You do realise we won't get any peace if we don't. I would be happy to take you, if you want,' he said, rather flatly.

Amanda was trapped now. All eyes on her, she swallowed hard.

'Erm, I suppose we could. For a quiet life, I mean.' She shrugged like a teenager. *No big deal,* she thought. *They could part ways once the event got started.*

Ben smiled a little. 'Good, settled then, ladies, OK?' The ladies all nodded, murmuring their approval collectively. He looked at Amanda then, and she looked back at him nervously. His expression wasn't readable, and she couldn't tell if he was mad or just put out. 'How are they settling in?' he asked her, obviously trying to change the subject.

'The kittens were fine, Ben, they only kept me up a couple of hours in the night. They are settling in lovely, thank you.'

Ben nodded. 'Good, hope you get more sleep tonight. I shall see you soon, OK?'

Amanda nodded. Ben turned back from the door, and looked at her again.

'You look nice by the way,' he said, and then he was gone. Amanda stood, mouth gaping like a floundering fish as the ladies all looked at each other, and set to work.

* * *

Ben's morning went fast. So fast, that he couldn't even remember how many patients he had seen, how many people he had spoken to, or whether he had even eaten anything. All he saw and thought about was Amanda in that dress. She was a vision, pins sticking out everywhere as the women bustled around her like Cinderella's cartoon mice. Her hair was tousled in a loose bun, something she seemed to do a lot, and he found himself thinking about taking the clip out, brushing the hair back from her shoulders, touching the once alabaster skin of her collarbone. She had changed physically since being in the village, her hair was lightening from the sunlight, her skin getting more tan from the fresh air and sunshine, her whole body seemingly uncoiling itself a bit more daily. He found her more attractive every time they saw each other, and today, he felt like she saw him too. He knew that the women of the village had made it their mission for her to be a pet project in the 'Find Ben a Wife' campaign that was no doubt spearheaded by the infamous Agatha Mayweather. Not that he was offended, although it was embarrassing at times. He knew Dotty was in it too, but instead of feeling angry, hemmed in, he was actually very touched by the women's attentions to his love life. It did need a kick-start, that must be said, but the kick had to come from him, and they had picked the wrong girl.

As though conjured from his mind, Dotty walked into the consulting room, a tin foil square package and a bottle of water in hand.

'Ben, we have a break in patients now, so I have made an appointment with Mr Denton. Here, take some lunch with you.'

Ben looked at Dotty, frowning as he took the sandwich and bottle from her.

'Denton, the tailor?'

Dotty nodded, a wry smile dancing around her lips, never quite settling.

'Yes, that Denton.' She shrugged off Ben's questioning look. 'You need a costume remember, for the open-air event?'

Ben grinned, walked towards her and grabbed her in his arms, swinging her around.

'What would I do without you, eh?' he said, teasingly.

'Oh gerroff!' Dotty said, laughing. He put her down and she stroked his cheek tenderly. 'Listen, Ben, I made a promise to your dear departed mother and father that I would look out for you, and that's just what I am doing. So do as you are told.'

He nodded, a lump in his throat forming at the thought of his parents. 'And the rest of your cronies? What are they up to?'

Dotty blushed before what he said sank in, and he earned a quick cuff round the ear for his trouble, or as close as she could with him towering over her.

'Ben Evans, you are not too big to go over my knee! Those ladies are not doing anything, I can assure you.'

Ben nodded, dropping a kiss on his friend's cheek.

'OK, I'll believe you, thousands wouldn't. Well, I am off to get my suit then.'

Dotty broke into a gleeful smile. 'Have fun, Ben, and pick well.' Ben looked at her questioningly. She looked back at him, eyes glistening with mischief. 'I have heard, from a little birdie, that your date looks very nice indeed. Have to make a good impression, don't we?'

Ben groaned and walked out of the door. Dotty watched him cross the driveway, get into his jeep and drive away. When he disappeared out of sight, she picked up the phone and dialled.

It's me,' she whispered breathily. 'He has gone now. I briefed Denton on her outfit and he is going to work his magic.' The voice at the other end of the line said something back. Dotty frowned. 'Can we not just fight it? We will raise the money for the roof, surely that's enough to get rid of him?'

The voice on the end got louder and Dotty grimaced. 'OK, OK, I know, just a thought. Let's just cross our fingers then and hope for the best.'

After placing the receiver back in the cradle, she tapped out a text and sent it to a group stored in her phone. She then brushed herself down and made a coffee. Spy work done, the filing was next. After a nice cuppa and a garibaldi.

Thirteen

Marcus was hiding. Not even metaphorically either, but literally hiding. He was crouched under his desk, one bum cheek being poked with the plastic of the swivel chair leg, the other cheek rammed up against the hard mahogany of the desk. His phone kept ringing on his desk above, as it had done incessantly since he had walked through the door at eight that morning.

Angela had been marauding outside, pacing the corridors like a lion stalking its prey. In this instance, that prey was him, and he felt every inch the scared little antelope. The door to his office suddenly opened, and Marcus prayed it wouldn't be one of the partners in the firm. He was pretty sure that they were on to him, and he worried for his future. Having newly been made partner, he was still earning his stripes and he was feeling the pressure more than ever, especially since he no longer had Amanda to back him up. He saw a pair of red patent high heels stood in front of his desk, and he wrapped his hand over his mouth to stop the squeak that threatened to jump out from his lips. 'Humph,' he heard a female voice grumble, and then he saw the heels retreat. His office door closed and he breathed out a sigh of relief. The phone started to ring again, and Marcus shuddered at the sound. *Keep it together, man, you can do this.* He uncurled himself from under the desk, his cheek completely numb now, pins and needles reverberating around his posterior as he bottom shuffled out from under his desk. Picking up the phone, he wiped at the sheen of sweat on his face. Today, he had to get himself together.

'Hello?' he said weakly into the receiver.

Celine's clipped tones came back over the line, making his testicles shrink into his body at warp speed.

'Marcus, is that you?'

Marcus shuddered. 'Mrs Perry, hello! Lovely to hear from you.'

Celine ignored his greeting. 'Marcus, what the hell is going on there? Amanda hasn't returned my calls or emails, and her phone is switched off. She should be back from vacation now, and today I went round to her flat, and someone answered the door and informed me that she has sold it! What on earth is going on? You are supposed to be her friend, why didn't you call me? Her father is scouring half of London looking for her!'

Marcus winced as Celine prattled on and on in her plummy tones. 'She has the partnership to think of. I swear, I don't know where that girl's head is at sometimes! Marcus, are you there? Marcus?'

Marcus sighed. 'Mrs Perry, I am sorry to tell you, Amanda doesn't work here any more. I don't know where she is, I have been trying to find her myself. The estate agent won't tell me anything, and she hasn't been in touch. Elaine has been trying her too, but we haven't come up with anything yet.'

Celine was quiet at the other end.

'Celine?' he ventured. 'Are you there? Hello?' Marcus could hear her speaking quietly and hurriedly to someone in her room, her hand over the receiver. He was about to hang up when her booming voice jangled in his ear.

'Marcus, I have cleared my schedule. I am sending a car for you. I shall see you at my house in an hour.'

'Er…but I have a—'

She cut him short. 'Marcus Beresford, my daughter is missing. Whatever you have on today, bloody well cancel it and get your miserable arse in that car!'

Marcus found himself nodding to the hang up tone. Wiping his brow, he sniffed at his armpit. He needed a fresh shirt and sharpish.

* * *

The next few days in the shop passed by in a flourish, with Amanda being hectic, serving customers, chatting to the ladies and using every other spare minute making up orders and stock for her stall at the summer fair. A couple of nights ago, in a flash of late-night inspiration, she had been in the shop in her pyjamas in the wee small hours, working on a new idea. One that was sure to appeal to the villagers and tourists alike, and help her use up her fabric and fur scraps to boot.

She had finished up last night, and this morning she danced down to the shop, coffee in hand, to wrap them up. Today heralded the day of the Austen Open Air Event at the Mayweather estate, and the sunshine seemed to have burst through her window as she had stirred that morning. She couldn't believe how the village had pulled together to do so much in such a short space of time. The sense of community here was amazing, and Amanda found a reason every day to be grateful for her new life.

Selecting some blue tissue paper and a fetching cream ribbon, Amanda wrapped up the gift neatly, placing it in a little gift bag for later. She reached for her smartphone to take a picture of her handiwork before she realised, and chastised herself for not having the guts to turn her old handset on. She resolved to buy a new SIM card that weekend, then she could start to upload her work onto social media, show off her new business. She had closed down all her social media accounts before she left, so people wouldn't be trying to contact her. She wasn't ready to face people yet, so it was better to stay off the grid. She mentally shook off the pit in her stomach, trying to ignore the gnaw of dread that she got whenever she thought of her old life, and tried to catch her breath. For a woman in control of her own life, she sure was acting pathetic. She couldn't live like this much longer, she had to either bin the phone, or deal with the messages that she knew would be there.

Either way, she had to move on.

Looking around the shop, she marvelled at the difference a few weeks had made. The ladies had left their own little marks on New Lease of Life, and it was comforting for Amanda to see them. Little things like Marlene's teacup, Grace's knitting needles sat in a wicker basket of wool, even Agatha's influence could be seen in the window display they had created together. Amanda had suspicions that she and Ben's…whatever it was, was subject to the women's meddling, but, as time went on, Amanda felt less overrun and cajoled than she did. She counted the women as friends now, which was pretty much a first for her. It was a first, and it felt really nice.

* * *

Ben adjusted his cravat and looked nervously into his bedroom mirror. Donning his top hat, he realised he looked ridiculous, but he wasn't bothered about the costume. He was bothered about what Amanda would make of it. He had never felt that way around Tanya. He had learned to pretty much ignore her comments as nothing he said or did was ever well received by her—it was seen as something that could be altered, improved upon, or stamped out. He had allowed her to do this too, till, on the day she left, he no longer recognised the man in the mirror before him, and didn't like him very much either. Today was different though; Amanda was different. He found that he did care what she thought of him, especially as they differed on so many things. Maybe she would stay in the village, and maybe he had misjudged her. Dotty spoke nothing but praise for her and her efforts in not only coming up with the play idea, but helping to organise it too. Ben was finding it harder day to day to deny the small feelings of hope he harboured, and today would be the test. It would be them together, alone but in the backdrop of a social event. They hadn't discussed the shop, so there had been no arguments, although they definitely challenged each other sometimes. Her idea for the event was a stroke of genius and he had to admit that perhaps he had misjudged her a little.

Ben felt the frisson of excitement at the prospect and hoped that this evening's work would be the turning point. If something happened tonight, something that set off an alarm bell in his head, then Ben would walk away. He needed to, to protect his heart, because he just knew, if she left now, she would take the broken shards of his growing regard with her, and he couldn't let himself get hurt like that.

Adjusting his cravat again, feeling it choke him, he looked at himself again in the mirror. After picking up his keys, wallet, and small package, he left, heading for a New Lease of Life. The irony was not lost on him as he drove.

* * *

Pulling up to the Baker Street shop minutes later, Ben took a deep breath, grabbed his hat and pressed the intercom button. He was buzzed straight up and, putting his hat on, he ran up the steps two at a time, pleading with his heart to stop beating out of his chest. The interior door was open and he knocked lightly before walking in. The front room was empty, apart from the two kittens, snuggled up together asleep in their basket next to the hearth. He smiled at the domestic scene, and then Amanda walked out of the bedroom. His breath caught as their eyes locked. She was wearing a cream gown, lace trimmed delicately down the neckline, and sheer chiffon sleeves covering her arms. Her hair was up and curled, and tiny creamy pearls dotted around her hair. She was beautiful.

'Hi,' she said, shoulders hunching with nerves. A shy smile glanced across her lips, and she blushed under his gaze. *Say something, Ben, stop staring!* He took a step towards her, half expecting her to drop back, but she took a tentative step to meet him.

'Hi,' he said, voice cracking. 'Hi,' he tried again. 'You look stunning. I brought you something.'

Amanda's face lit up under his praise, her smile broadening, and the room seemed to explode with light. Ben took out the little box from his jacket pocket. 'It's just something little,' he said.

'Which of the ladies did this then?' she asked teasingly, smirking at him sarcastically.

He didn't return her expression, instead looking very much out of his depth.

'Er, actually, it's from me. To say thanks for helping the girls try to save the community centre.'

Amanda took the box from him and pulled at the ribbon with slender fingers. Inside, nestled in the tissue paper lining the box, was a cameo on a necklace. Amanda gasped. 'It's lovely, Ben! You shouldn't have.'

Ben shook his head. 'Of course I should. It will look lovely with your outfit. I got it from the antique shop in town. I just passed by the window one day, saw it and thought of you. It's a thank you, for all the work you have been putting in lately for the village, that's all.'

Their eyes met again, and Ben had to remind himself to breathe. *Was she feeling this too? Am I just being a creep, or does she feel this?*

Amanda touched his arm. 'Thank you. Will you put it on for me please?'

Ben nodded, not trusting himself to speak in case he sounded like an adolescent boy breaking in his new voice. He moved to the back of her and clicked the clasp shut, his lips tingling with the urge to lay them on the soft nape of her neck. Amanda fingered the necklace, gazing at it against her dress. Ben moved to the front of

her, he needed to get her out of this room before he did
something and he couldn't run the risk of spoiling the
evening, or cutting it short.

'Shall we go?' he said, motioning to the door. Amanda
nodded and moved to the counter, picking up a sky-blue
gift bag. 'I got something for you too, to thank you for
your help since I have been here, but it seems a little
silly now.'

She moved to put the bag back on the counter, but he
made a grab for it.

'Don't be daft, let me see.' He unwrapped the tissue
paper and touched something furry. 'Not a kitten, is it?'
he said, laughing. Amanda looked nervous, making a
grab for it again. He dodged her easily and ran to the
door. 'Nope, it's mine!'

He pulled the fluffy thing out. It was a cockerel, hand
stitched, bright fabric colours mixing perfectly together.
On one wing, the name 'DARCY' was embroidered in
blue. Ben loved it. Loved that she had made him something, put thought into it, not just buying him hip—and
scratchy—imported underpants from Milan like Tanya
had.

'It's my Darcy!' he said, turning it this way and that,
looking at it intently.

Amanda blushed, turning away. 'It's rubbish, isn't it?
You don't have to take it, it was just a silly gift, nothing like yours.' She touched the necklace as she spoke,

and Ben was insanely pleased that she now wore something of his.

He looked her in the eye as he put the little gift in his jacket pocket. 'Amanda, I love it. Honestly. It's brilliant, you should make more, I bet they would sell.'

Amanda grinned, grabbed for his arm and headed down the stairs. 'I have something to show you.'

Downstairs in the shop, laid out on the large centre table, was an array of soft toys, all with little tags saying 'New Lease of Life' on them. Looking closer, Ben recognised Darcy and his other chickens, and turned to beam at Amanda.

'Are these all animals from Westfield?'

Amanda smiled, picking two up. 'Yep, look, Gwendolen and Ophelia, and Pinky and Perky over here, too, and Agatha's dogs.' She showed him the little cow and calf, both with little name tags on and the shop logo.

'Pinky and Perky?' he asked, frowning.

'The kittens,' she laughed. 'Seemed to fit them.'

Ben nodded. 'These are amazing, Amanda, really. You could really have something here.'

'Not too city slicker? I would hate to ruin Westfield, after all,' she said teasingly.

Ben looked suitably sheepish. 'No, these are very Westfield.'

Amanda put them back, her dress swishing as she moved around the table. 'I am hoping to debut them at the summer fair next week. I just want to ask the owners if they mind first. I think it could be a little theme for the shop, you know? I can sell them online too.'

Ben was in awe. 'You have been busy, haven't you, while I have been slacking off birthing lambs?' He chuckled. 'We can put an ad in the vet's too, ask people to volunteer their pets' likenesses to be made too. I bet people would love it. Plenty of people around here love animals.'

Amanda was touched by Ben completely being onboard and helping her ideas along.

'Thanks, Ben, that would be great. Shall we go?' She held out her hand for him to take, and he was suddenly jealous of the long glove on her hand, as his hand closed around it.

* * *

The early night air was perfect, warm without the clammy threat of oncoming rain. The sky was clear, and the sun was only just shuffling into setting, making the horizon a beautiful backdrop to the ladies and gents in the play. People sat dotted around the hillside, lying out on picnic blankets, sat in garden chairs festooned with ribbon and cotton covers for the occasion. Gentle chatter and occasional tinkles of laughter could be heard at times, but the play was going well and, on the whole, uninterrupted, although Maisie did at one point take a fancy to the fellow playing Wickham, aiming for a leg hump at an inopportune moment, much to Agatha's disgust and embarrassment. Ben and Amanda had watched as Taylor strode up, laughing as he led Maisie away, tail between her legs. He deposited the feckless hound in front of her brother and Agatha, and Amanda noticed that Agatha coloured as Taylor whispered something into her ear.

Sitting on a picnic blanket mountain with Ben, she started to wonder. Maybe the women of Westfield were not as clued up as they thought they were. *Should I?* she wondered, a thought whizzing around her brain. Turning to Ben, who was watching the play with a relaxed look on his face, she hesitantly spoke up.

'What's the deal with Agatha and Taylor?'

He looked at her, an inquisitive look on his face. 'Why?' he drawled out, making it sound funny, like a four-year-old asking the eternal question of its creator.

'I just wondered, that's all,' she said, poking him in the ribs. She loved how relaxed they were with each other today, finding little excuses to touch each other. Well, she was, she wasn't sure about where Ben stood. Far different from their first few meetings, when she could have cheerfully throttled him. 'I just wonder why they are both on their own.'

Ben poured her another drink of the chilled white wine he had bought from the passing waiter, one of many milling around the grounds, selling food and drink to the many ticket holders at the event. 'Taylor was going to leave Westfield when he left school. He planned to work in the city, I forget which profession, but his mother got sick, and he stayed on to help his father, who worked for the Mayweathers, and then he just never left.'

Amanda nodded. 'That's sad, but he seems happy.'

Ben shrugged. 'He is, I think. Agatha married Mr Mayweather Junior, promoted Taylor up from butler, and they have been friends since school, so they rub along nicely together. In fact, I think Taylor can deal with Agatha better than even Mr Mayweather could before he got sick.'

Amanda giggled at this, as she looked over at Taylor being scolded by Agatha for something or other, his gait indicating he was paying little or no attention either way.

'And what about them together? Do you think they like each other?'

Ben chucked her a sly grin. 'Why, Amanda, are you going for the crown of village meddler this year?' he said, pretending to don a hat on her head.

'No!' she said, indignant. 'But…perhaps if we just suggested it, a little?'

Ben chuckled, a deep throaty noise that sent a little quiver down Amanda's spine. *If she could bottle that noise…*

'I think, to be honest, Taylor does have a soft spot for her, and she him, but I'm not sure about anything more. I mean, what if we do "meddle" and mess things up? After all these years, they are definitely in the friend zone now.'

Amanda formed a thought and it jumped out of her

mouth before she could even attempt a grab for it. 'Is that where we are?'

Ben looked at her, his expression unreadable. Amanda quickly turned her head and looked out over the Mayweather estate at the people watching the play, not daring to look at him, move, breathe. She heard him then, softly. Felt him at her ear.

'Do you want to be friends?' he asked, something making his voice sound urgent, breathy. She started to nod her head, and turned to face him, only to look straight into his beautiful grey eyes. The colour of her kittens' fur, but this grey felt like looking into a black hole, something that could pick you up and suck you into its vortex, swishing you around till you were a quivery, jelly-like blob of warm feelings and mush. She continued to stare into them, transfixed. Ben spoke again, and she felt his breath on her cheek. 'Amanda, do you want to be friends?'

Amanda didn't answer. She couldn't put the words together. Instead, she closed her eyes, and slowly, barely, brushed her lips against his. Pulling back, she opened her eyes slowly. Ben's face told her everything she needed to know. He reached for her then, putting his slightly calloused hands on either side of her face, meeting her lips with his. They kissed slowly, tenderly, and Amanda was just curling her fingers into his hair, deepening the kiss when a round of applause rang out across the hillside. Embarrassed, the two pulled apart, but the applause had been for the end of the play.

Their moment of passion had passed by seemingly undetected. Amanda stood up and smoothed her clothes down, flushed. Ben jumped up too and they both started to speak at once.

'I...'

'Amanda, I'm sorry, that shouldn't have happened.'

Amanda felt as though she had been slapped, even though she was trying to say the same thing.

'I know, I'm sorry, Ben, but I can't.'

His confused flushed expression mirrored her own and they both looked away, packing up their things in silence, still absorbed in each other, and thoughts of what had just happened. So absorbed that they hadn't seen the flash of Marlene's camera as they kissed, or seen Agatha's most unbecoming-of-a-lady fist pump as she jumped into the air. Taylor laughed and tittered for the rest of the evening, and only got jabbed in the ribs by Agatha three times. Progress all round.

Fourteen

London

Marcus couldn't deny it any longer: he was in big trouble. The Kamimura account was complicated, too complicated, and the partners were starting to cotton on to his inability to cope, he was sure of it. Add to that the Perrys breathing down his neck every day, asking questions he didn't want to answer, and quizzing him on aspects of Amanda's life that he had no idea about, he was beyond stressed. He jammed his finger into his collar, pulling at the pale blue silk tie he had on, which currently felt like a garrotte. He had been in since seven, which was a first for him, and had done nothing but stare at the account file for two hours. His office walls were closing in on him, and every time he turned his back on one, he felt sure it tiptoed up behind him, ever closer, playing their own Mr Wolf mind games with his head. He could feel the sweat pooling in the small of his back, soaking his shirt through. Trickles of moisture dripped down his spine like icy fingers, the air conditioning in his large new office doing nothing but circulate the stale smell he expelled. He would give his Mercedes for an open window right now, but he half feared that he would use it as a jumping platform to the freedom of death instead of enjoying some fresh air.

He half wished he smoked, for the excuse to have a fag break and a heavy dose of stress relief. Looking at the clock, he realised that the secretaries would all be in the coffee room about now, getting the orders of breakfast and caffeine ready for their respective bosses. He decided to chance bumping into Angela and made a dash for it, power-walking past the water cooler. Elaine, Angela and the other secretaries all stood around the kitchen area, clinking cups and teaspoons, putting bread in to toast and chatting. As soon as he rounded the corner, they all stopped and glared at him. He swallowed hard and smiled at Elaine, his target on this suicide mission. Ignoring the tuts and stares of the other women, he went to stand next to her. Angela started to move towards him, breasts jutting out of her tight black dress, red lips grinning at him, but she frowned and held back when she saw where he was going.

'Er…Elaine, I…er…just wondered, have you heard anything from Amanda?' He said it cautiously, spat the words out nervously as though he had asked her age, or menstrual cycle. He knew she had been looking for her boss, but previously the bravest he had gotten in way of contacting her was emailing her through the office network.

Elaine rounded on him instantly though, and he reared back at her venom. Her voice shaking with barely controlled anger, she spoke in a low growl.

'No, I bloody well haven't, and whose fault is that!?' Marcus went to speak, but she cut him off with a finger in his face. 'No! You may be a partner here now, *Mr* Beresford—' said mockingly, as though she really wanted to call him something far less polite '—but we all know what you did, and no one has managed to track her down. Her parents are worried sick! If you can't do your blinking job, then flippin' well work it out and leave Amanda out of it!' She nodded goodbye to the girls, ignoring Angela completely, and turned on her heel, coffee cups in hand.

Marcus sheepishly smiled at the other girls, but all he got back was disgusted stares and the back of their heads as they all followed suit. Within seconds, the kitchen was empty, bar him and Angela. She took this opportunity to sidle up to him, her index talon running down the front of his buttons whilst her other arm snaked around his back, pulling him into her breasts. If she noticed the sweat patch, she never missed a beat, to her credit.

'What do you want to speak to her for anyway, Markie?' she simpered, calling him that stupid pet name he deplored again. 'You know she won't have you back, not after she found out about us, so why bother?'

Marcus shuddered inwardly at the 'us' word. *Was this his life now? Stuck with this trampy social climber, destined to be Angela and Markie?* He wished to God that he had thought with his head more those months ago, instead of a more feckless and reckless part of his anatomy. The look on Amanda's face when she had walked into his office to find him in flagrante with Angela was not one of his finer moments, that was for sure. He never even got the chance to explain. Two days after that, she had been fired after the colossal cock-up with the Kamimura account and he was made partner, a role that Marcus had no doubt was earmarked for his ex-girlfriend. And now he was stuck with this bimbo, clueless about a job he was supposed to be master of, and the Kamimura contract was due to be completed. Signed, sealed, delivered, with a great deal of back-slapping credit and company bonus to be had for his trouble. Except he couldn't do it, he never had been able to, and the clock was ticking. As Angela nibbled on his ear lobes, whispering their—her—plans for dinner that evening, Marcus's cogs were turning. He needed a plan, and fast.

* * *

Amanda stood in front of the ladies as they sat chatting and crafting away at A New Lease of Life. 'Ladies, I have a plan.'

The ladies all turned round, needles poised, to look at her. Grace piped up first. 'A plan, dear? Do tell. Is it for Ben?'

Amanda rolled her eyes. 'No, Grace, it's not for Ben. I do think of other things from time to time you know.' The ladies tittered at this, and Amanda realised what she had alluded to and blushed. 'No, this plan is for Agatha. Now we have raised the money for the roof, we can afford a couple of days off from the community centre project.'

The ladies all listened intently, intrigued now. She was heartened by this. *So far, so good.* 'The plan involves her and Taylor, actually.'

Marlene shook her head, raising a hand in objection. 'You are kidding, aren't you? We can't interfere with Agatha, she would bloomin' murder the lot of us, and have a smile on her face while she did it!'

Dotty laughed, tapping Marlene on the arm. 'Can you remember when Tanya tried to plan a fashion event in the village? I thought Agatha was going to have a stroke! Sh— Oh, sorry, Amanda.' Dotty coloured as she realised her faux pas.

Amanda laughed. 'Dotty, I won't turn to stone. Ben and I are just friends, and we are barely even that really.' She thought of the confusing kiss at the play, and the awkward ride home in silence afterwards. 'I would actually like to hear about Tanya. Ben doesn't talk about her.'

The ladies all looked a bit nervous, as though someone had finally pointed out the elephant in the corner of the room.

Hetty, no nonsense as ever, piped up. 'She wasn't cut from the same cloth as him, love, it would never have worked. That girl was a city lass, through and through, and our Ben, well, he is our Benjamin, he belongs here.'

Marlene chortled. 'You never liked her, Hetty, none of us did really. We only put up with her for Ben.'

Amanda nodded, wondering how much Ben thought about her, and whether he compared the two. She considered herself to be a village girl these days, London seemed a lifetime ago, but what if Ben wanted a city girl? That was obviously what he went for at one time in his life, for him to marry Tanya. He would be going after the girl she was, and not the woman she was becoming, and that couldn't end well. She shook off the thought. Ben didn't know what he wanted anyway. The kiss had felt like an urgent need he had, rather than a thought out plan. He said it himself, the kiss was a mistake. She had agreed with him, so no harm done, right? Being around these women day in day out had mellowed him a bit, but after that, she was in no doubt that he was all man. If he wanted to be with her, wouldn't he have made the move after the kiss, said or done something, instead of giving her the vague speech he had? *What are you thinking, Amanda? You moved here for a new start, men- and stress-free, and now you are pining for a*

man who declares you the village Antichrist one minute
and grabs you for toe-curling kisses the next. Go figure!

'Anyway, I think that our dear Agatha and Taylor
could do with a helping hand, to nudge them together.
It's worth a try, don't you agree? I was thinking that we,
the villagers, could rustle up a little thank you gift, to
thank them for all the hard work they do. I was thinking a meal out, there is a posh place near Harrogate we
could book them into, then they are away from the village. Worst-case scenario, they have a nice meal out, a
change of scene. I need your help though, it has to come
from you ladies—she would suss me out a mile away.'

She watched nervously as the ladies muttered amongst
themselves, the occasional 'she'll bloody swing for us'
and 'man up, Marlene' coming from the gaggle. One by
one the ladies all turned to look at her. Amanda knotted her fingers together, praying that she was doing the
right thing. When she had first told Ben her plan at the
play, he had eventually—after much laughter—agreed
to help, providing she could, in his words, 'get the silver brigade on board without killing each other'. She
remembered how he had hugged her after, calling her
a daft thing. She grinned to herself like an idiot, belatedly remembering that this had happened before the kiss
ruined the night. She pushed the thought away and con-
centrated on setting her face straight when Dotty spoke.

'OK, first we have some stipulations.' Trying to keep
her face neutral, Amanda nodded. 'Firstly, we can't tell

anyone what we are planning, on pain of death. Secondly, you and Ben have to do the same, go for a meal somewhere, before the summer fair, our pick. And thirdly,' she said, smiling to herself, 'if this works, Agatha can never get wind that it was down to us, because we will never hear the end of it when Taylor annoys her.'

Amanda clapped her hands together in glee. 'So you are in?'

Grace nodded. 'And you, are you in?'

Amanda remembered the second request from the ladies. A meal out with Ben. *Hmm.* She shrugged in what she hoped was a nonchalant manner. He wouldn't agree to that, so she would be off the hook. 'I can take one for the team, if it means we are on. Sure,' she said, shrugging.

The ladies all smiled at her.

'That settles it then, we shall make the arrangements, we have money in our kitty for the meal, we can use that,' Grace, the unofficial treasurer of the group said, flipping through a notebook she produced from her bag.

'I will pay for our meal then, 50/50?'

Grace nodded, obviously calculating something in her brain as she scribbled with a pencil she usually kept behind her ear. Amanda went off to make the coffee, excited at the prospect of playing matchmaker. Behind her, the ladies all did a little victory dance, before returning to their work.

Fifteen

Two days later, the ladies brought more than scones with them to the shop. They had a menu for a nice gastropub on the outskirts of the village, and details of that night's booking. Dotty was practically jumping up and down in excitement as she told Amanda about the little rustic setting of the converted farmhouse which was to be the scene of her and Ben's meal that evening. Amanda laughed at her exuberance.

'OK, OK, Dotty. It sounds perfect, but it won't happen. Things between Ben and I are awkward, to say the least.' She took the menu from her and marvelled at the choice of food. It sounded lovely, and she was a little sad that she wouldn't get to go, or to give her new dress, bought from a little vintage shop in the village, a good night out.

Dotty touched her arm. 'I will tell Ben this afternoon,

and get him to pick you up at seven. It will happen, trust me. I wish you would get a mobile though, dear. Who doesn't have one in this day and age?'

Amanda's face fell as she thought of her forgotten smartphone languishing in the drawer upstairs. 'I know, I know, I will get a new SIM card today from the village, OK?'

Dotty nodded. 'Perfect. Then you can ring Ben on it, can't you?'

Amanda groaned. 'Yes, Dotty, I get the gist.' She laughed out loud. Of course, she was right, it was ridiculous not to have a mobile. She used the internet for her business research, of course, but steered clear of any social media, and she would like to advertise herself on there, and maybe even get a new email address. It was time to come back into the world, she thought to herself. She resolved to make a start that day, beginning with a new number.

* * *

Ben was in the practice later on when his mobile buzzed on his desk. He was busy checking X-rays, writing lambing reports on his patients, coffee steaming on his desk, soft rock pumping through his computer speakers in the background. Dotty was at her group, so he knew she was not there to complain about his taste in music, or his occasional air guitar through the surgery.

He read the text on his screen and smiled to himself. It read, 'I am back in the land of the texting. Amanda.'

He frowned as he thought of the sender. The kiss had been reckless, a mistake. An amazing, mind-blowing mistake granted, but Amanda wasn't right for him, he knew it, deep down. They drove each other crazy! He kept seeing glimpses of the city girl in her, her melancholy attitude when her old life was mentioned. There was more to the story, he knew it, but he didn't want to push her. He typed back, 'Wow, and they say us village dwellers are behind the times. Ben.' He tapped 'send' and sighed. The more he got to know her, the more he got the impression he had misjudged her, but he just couldn't take the risk. He would have to keep his distance from her for a while, cool things down. He really liked her, and being around her was becoming harder and harder to do. He just couldn't take the chance of getting hurt again, and now, after his kiss, he ran the risk of losing her friendship too. Losing his parents, wife and best friend all in the space of a few short years had taken its toll, and he didn't relish trying to stick himself back together after yet another person leaving him.

He ruffled his hair with one hand when his phone beeped again. Picking it up, he tried not to grin as he read 'The ladies are in on the plan, but played us at our own game. Dotty will fill you in. Sorry! A.' Ben wondered what she meant by that, but guessed it was to do with their meddling. Whatever it was, Ben didn't have to be a genius to work out that keeping his distance from Amanda was going to be a lot harder than he thought, in more ways than one.

* * *

Amanda grinned to herself as she got a ping back. She was sat at home, drinking a well-deserved cup of tea as she relaxed on her lunch break, Pinky on her lap, Perky wrapped around her bare feet on the settee. She had managed to change her SIM card and block any messages coming through to her phone, and she felt so much better now for having exorcised that demon. She pulled up the text screen and frowned as she read Ben's short reply of 'OK. B.' Bit short, no kiss? What did this mean? Amanda dissected the whole text conversation like a teenager, reading affection or rebuttal into every semicolon and emoticon sent over the airwaves. *He's probably just busy*, she told herself. *It has been weird since the kiss though, you know that*, her inner voice replied. Groaning loudly, causing Pinky to backflip in surprise off the settee, she slammed her phone down on the side table. *Men-free, my ass*, she scolded herself. *Sat here like a sulky teen, I mean really. You don't even want a relationship. Especially not with a man who thinks Starbucks is the epitome of evil.*

She scanned her attire then; fluffy socks made to look like sheep—Marlene's creation, and a best-seller—ripped jeans, a plain top and a crazy cat lady hairdo. She was about as far from her old high-powered self as could be. What occurred to her then, what unsettled her thoughts, was the notion that the old her had been the mask the whole time, and her true self was the unkempt romantic sap she currently was. Pinky jumped back onto her lap and resumed her position, purring loudly. As Amanda stroked the ball of fluff, she made a deal with herself. If the meal happened, that would be the last time she would spend any time with Ben. Give it up as a bad job and embrace spinsterhood wholeheartedly. Perky lifted her head up at that moment, giving a lazy little wink as she adjusted position on her owner's feet. Amanda took that to mean *Whatever, Mum, we'll see*, and she spoke aloud. 'I mean it Pinky, D-Day is upon us.' Both cats slept on, clearly not giving a toss at her predicament. Amanda tutted. *Bloody furry traitors, they love Ben, what do they know.* She had made up her mind, one more night, that was it. The women would just have to move on. Amanda just hoped that she could stick to her guns, hold fast in her resolve against those gorgeous grey eyes.

Reaching for a paperback, she settled in to enjoy her break. She would leave the spy game to the women of Westfield for the day, let them deal with the cloak and dagger, and try not to tie herself in knots for once. Pulling the settee blanket around her shoulders against the unseasonal chill she felt, she suddenly had a flash of herself: many years from now, sat in a chair reading, her fur babies sleeping on her as they did now. Was this what the future held? Comfort, contentment, with a side order of crippling loneliness? She thought of Agatha then, rattling around her huge house with her 'children' for company, and she realised: one last chance at happiness might not be as bad as it sounded. Worth the shot, at the very least. What-ifs were soothing bedtime stories for no one, and Amanda would rather cope with the nightmares of memory, than the alternative.

Sixteen

In the vet's practice that afternoon, Dotty Arbuckle felt ready to pop. Ben Evans was the most exasperating man she had ever met, and she told him so.

'You, Ben Evans, are the most exasperating man I have ever met! Just take the girl out for a meal!'

Ben slapped the side of his face with an open palm, his frustration evident. 'Why? So you ladies can feast on the intrigue of it all? No!'

Dotty folded her arms across her ample breasts and shook with anger. 'Benjamin, don't be rude! We just have your best interests at heart! She is a lovely girl, and, Lord knows, you need some happiness in your life, so take her out! It's all arranged, she agreed to it, she wants to go!'

Ben huffed loudly. 'What choice did you give her! You railroaded her into it, and she probably doesn't want to appear nasty, don't you get it? She wants to help Agatha, she is new here, she obviously wants to fit in, but she is not one of us!'

Dotty pounced on his last statement. 'Exactly, Benjamin, she wants to fit in, which would imply that she wants to ruddy well stay here! Don't you get it, Ben? She likes you!'

He sighed, leaning against the counter, his body suddenly sagging before her. Dotty frowned. The poor boy looked exhausted suddenly, and she wondered whether her tough love had gone a tad too far.

'Dotty, I love you, but you just don't get it. I…I just can't go there again. I am not strong enough. I know you all hated Tanya, and God knows she was the wrong woman, but she was there for me, and she still left. Besides, Amanda and I are just friends.'

Dotty finally understood, and her heart went out to the man before her, the man she loved like her own child. She had watched him grow from a cute grey-eyed little boy to a man, a strong, clever man who hid his heart for fear of it being crushed. The thing that was crushing him now, though, was fear. The fear of loss, of hoping for something, wanting someone, and taking that leap. She kept her arms crossed and tried her best not to run over to him and scoop him into her arms, but she eventually walked to him and placed her hand over his. Ben looked down at her wrinkled, soft hand over his own and smiled weakly at her.

'Ben,' she began softly. 'I know this is hard, duck, but I still remember your parents' hopes and dreams for you, and God bless them, you are a son to be proud of.'

He smiled at her, as he thought of the day he got the call telling him his parents had been taken from him. A silly crash, some idiot spinning around the country lanes, taking his parents off the road as they drove to the market in the next town, something they did every week. Dotty had been here to meet him when he came home, new wife in tow, and hadn't left since. 'You have to take a chance sometime, Ben,' she continued, hoping that he would listen to her. 'Amanda is not Tanya. She isn't going to leave, or break your heart. She is happy here, and we all love her. Your parents would never have left you by choice, my darling, and you need to make a life of your own now.'

She waved her hand around the surgery, and Ben looked at everything he had accomplished, taking over the surgery and house from his parents, making their legacy both work and thrive. He nodded slowly. Dotty patted his hand and he lifted it into his and kissed the back of it.

'As usual, Dotty, you have a point. I do need to do something, I know.' He thought then of the kiss, the kiss with so much energy and promise, and he cursed himself for not saying more to Amanda when he had the chance. Smoothing his tousled brown hair back from his face, he smiled. 'So, when is this dinner booked for then?'

Dotty grinned at him then, clapping her hands together as he rolled his eyes at her. 'OK, OK,' he laughed. 'Go on, tap the jungle drums.'

Dotty giggled and pulled out her phone, ignoring his dig as she typed.

* * *

Ben felt sick to his stomach as he pulled up to Baker Street that evening. It was ten to seven, and he was washed, brushed up and terrified. Hetty had 'come by' the practice earlier that evening, bearing a huge bouquet of flowers she 'just happened to pick' from her garden, all trimmed up with crepe paper and ribbon, and Dotty and Grace had even knocked at his door an hour earlier to bring him some wine and cheese, 'in case' Amanda fancied a nightcap after their meal. Ben had answered the door in surprise and Grace had instantly ushered him in, vetoing his outfit choice in seconds. Before he knew it, Dotty was cleaning the kitchen and Grace was thumbing through his wardrobe, selecting a dark blue shirt that showed off his tan, a pair of black slacks and a grey silk tie that matched his eyes. Her words, not his. Then they had smothered him with kisses and good luck wishes, and breezed out of the door, leaving Ben feeling like a tidying and organising whirlwind had just hit. Hurricane Grandma.

He slowly turned off the engine and reached for the flowers from the passenger seat. The Friday night was warm, even for late July, and he could hear the crickets and birds chatting away to each other as he opened the jeep door. Looking at Amanda's shop, he noticed that she now had planters on all her windowsills, bearing colourful flowers, and her shop window was full of the little animals she had been making. The vet's advert had obviously worked well, as Ben recognised the likeness of many of his clients in the faces of the soft toys.

He closed the jeep door, walked to the buzzer, taking a deep breath, and pressed the button. He had decided, after tonight, he would listen to his instincts and walk away. He owed it to himself, and the pushy women in the village, to close this down. He would keep his distance, be aloof and walk away. He felt better, having a deadline, but he didn't know which scared him the most, her letting him go or her trying to keep their friendship. He didn't get any more time to dwell on it as she buzzed him up.

He walked up to the flat door and knocked softly. Amanda had soft rock on in the flat, and he smiled to himself at her music choice. They had so many interests in common, it was strange. She opened the door to him and he blinked hard. She looked lovely. Her brown hair was curled slightly, hanging in loose ringlets around her face, and her dress was a fitted cream number that showed off her tanned body well. She had matching cream pumps on, with high heels. As he looked her up and down, he saw a bundle of fluff by her leg. He bent down in the doorway and stroked the kitten's cheek, before looking back up at her. She laughed as Perky, the white one, barrelled up from behind the settee and ploughed into him. He laughed too and, picking her up, walked into the flat. Amanda closed the door and grinned at him. 'They have made themselves at home. Hi.'

Ben smiled back at her. 'Hi, I brought you these.' He rearranged Perky into his arms as he handed her the large bunch of blooms.

'Ooh,' she exclaimed. 'Thanks, they are beautiful! The ladies did well.' He opened his mouth to apologise, but she winked at him to show she was teasing and went to put them in water, Pinky following close behind her. 'Sit down, I won't be a minute.'

He sat down on the couch, Perky immediately settling down on his lap. He noticed her laptop was on the coffee table in front of him, showing a Facebook page.

'You really are back in the land of the living,' he said as she came back over to him, placing the flowers on the hearth. Pinky took a swipe at one of the flowers, and got a faceful of pollen for her trouble. She sneezed loudly and scampered off.

Amanda rolled her eyes at the cat, and sat next to Ben. She took the laptop off the table and showed him the pictures. 'Yep, I set up a new profile for a business page. I have had orders already for the little animals. It's great!'

Ben smiled at her, looking through the pictures, all placed in arty poses with the shop in the background.

'These look great. I see the villagers have taken to your animals, too.'

Amanda nodded. 'I have had lots of people come to the shop with photos of their pets, it's amazing. Thanks for putting the advert in the vet's.'

'No problem,' he said softly.

Amanda smiled again and they fell into silence. He took this as a sign to move.

'Shall we set off? We have reservations, I believe.'

* * *

A short time later, on the outskirts of the village, they pulled up outside a bright white public house. It was set into the hills, surrounded by green fields, with a small shale car park at the side, and a wooden decking area for outside eating. Ben and Amanda headed for inside, but seeing that it looked really busy, they decided to eat outside, as it was still light. Ben went in to get some drinks and a menu. Amanda sat down at one of the tables in the corner. It was lovely. The outside area was surrounded by flower-covered trellis, and large heaters were placed near the tables for comfort. It was lovely and warm, and she was grateful that there was no breeze coming at them from the outdoors. A circle of tea lights flickered in a glass bowl in the centre of the table. The whole thing was very summery and romantic, and Amanda knew now why the girls had chosen it for their date. She half expected them to jump out from the hedges and start playing violin, and was suddenly grateful that the pub was on the outskirts of the village. Ben came out from the front door with a menu under one arm, a glass of rosé wine and a pint of lager. Passing the wine and the menu to her, he took a seat on the four-seated table. Instead of choosing to sit next to her, he sat across from her, she noted, and she tried not to feel disappointed. She said thanks and they both took a large gulp of their drinks. Noticing what the other had done, they both laughed, and it seemed to break the tension a little.

'Bit nerve-wracking, isn't it, being set up for a date,' Ben said, a statement more than a question.

Amanda nodded. 'Yes, it is, I am sorry.'

Ben frowned. 'Why, er… Why? Are you sorry, I mean.' He looked upset, wary even.

Amanda looked at him. Now or never. 'I know you are doing this for me, because of the deal with the ladies, and I am sorry you got dragged into all this.'

Ben's brows knitted together, and he said nothing. He took another swig at his pint and then, running his fingers through his hair, he moved into the chair next to her. She gasped a little at his sudden movement. *What was going on?* He looked at her, square in the eyes. 'Amanda, I will admit, I was a bit unsure about coming tonight, but it's not your fault. You haven't done anything wrong. It's just…me.'

Amanda nodded, choosing to suddenly study the rivulets of water running down her wine glass instead of looking at him. *See, he is just not that into you, woman.*

And now you are stuck with him all night, and he has to drive you home! Fab. Ground, swallow me now, please.

'Amanda?' he said softly, putting his fingers under her chin and turning her head to face him. 'Have I upset you?'

Amanda shook her head and swallowed hard, still not looking at him. She didn't trust herself not to cry, and she knew that if she took one look into those deep grey eyes, she would end up bawling like a baby.

'Amanda,' he said again. 'Look at me.'

She flicked her eyes to his then, and his expression confused her. He looked worried, his eyes full of concern.

'Ben, there is nothing to worry about. We are just friends.' *There, you said it*, she thought to herself. *Let the chips fall where they may.*

Ben's expression changed to shock, before his wall came up again, locking his expression away as usual. 'That's good, er...yes...good.'

Amanda nodded.

'We can just be friends, then, that's fine. The ladies will get bored eventually.'

Her heart thudded to the decking at his words, floundering like a fish before finally flatlining. But Ben didn't move his hand from her chin, and she couldn't bring herself to move away. He looked at her again, a frown on his face.

Amanda put her hand over Ben's hesitantly, and gently

moved his hand away from her face. Ben put his hands on his lap, and looked at the candles on the table.

'I haven't dated in a long time, not that the women in the village haven't tried. Dotty even tried to get me into online dating once.'

Amanda nearly laughed at this, picturing Dotty on the net, scanning for eligible women for their Benjamin to date.

'I can just imagine that,' she said, looking at him fondly. Ben laughed with her. 'It was pretty bad, there was even talk of a speed-dating night at the Four Feathers,' he chuckled. 'When my wife left, I was hurt. They are just trying to help. I think they had their heart set on us getting on better than we did.'

'What, because I am a fat cat, determined to tarmac the village into a shopping complex?' she laughed, trying to break the tension. He was trying to explain why he didn't want her, but Amanda couldn't bear to hear it.

Ben hung his head, obviously embarrassed.

Amanda stopped laughing then, waiting for him to open up.

'I got hurt too, in London. It's always been pretty much me though, my parents never really bothered, they were too busy with modelling me into the perfect daughter to bother with my personal life, so I just got on with it. I can't imagine how you felt, losing your parents. I have heard a lot of nice things about them.'

Ben smiled. 'They were very much in love, I never

even remember one fight or disagreement growing up. I always wanted what they had, one day.'

Amanda sighed. 'So, why are you telling me all this?'

Ben locked eyes with her again. 'I just wanted to make sure you didn't think bad of me. I would like us to be able to get along when we bump into each other.'

Amanda nodded, swallowing down the slab of hurt that choked her windpipe. 'Don't worry Ben, let's just have a nice meal and forget about everything, OK?'

Ben nodded slowly, and they both turned their attention to their menus, surrounded by the twinkling candlelight.

* * *

Jasper the Westie was thoroughly miserable. He stood on the vet's table, ears down, shoulders hunched as Mrs Warburton prattled on to Ben about her prized pooch. He had been off his food for a couple of days now, and had generally been moody. He had even stopped pooping, so she was beside herself with worry. Ben felt along Jasper's ribs, his stomach and could feel no blockages, and his weight loss was not significant enough for concern. He was slightly perplexed, and was just trying to think of his next course of action when he lifted his tail and found the culprit. Turning to Mrs Warburton, he resisted the urge to laugh.

'Mrs Warburton, do you floss?'

The woman looked at him, nonplussed. 'Of course I do, Mr Evans, every day.' She flashed her teeth at him, tapping one of her top teeth with a finger. 'These are all me own, y'know.'

Ben nodded. 'I think I know what's wrong with little Jasper here. You see, dogs like to floss too.'

Mrs Warburton looked confused until Ben pulled up Jasper's tail and showed her the white threads protruding from her companion's bottom. 'Oh,' she said. 'Oh Jasper, you silly boy!'

'When you throw away your floss, make sure he can't get to it. They love the smell of it. It happens quite a lot. He will need an X-ray to see if there are any complications, but, other than that, he is probably just feeling a bit full and scared to poo. He should pass it in a couple of days. Let's see what the X-ray shows. We might have to keep him in for observation.'

Mrs Warburton nodded, sniffling into a hanky. 'Okay, Mr Evans. Oh, Jasper, you naughty boy!'

Ben gave her a hug. 'Don't worry, Mrs Warburton, we shall soon get him right as rain.'

She nodded, still sniffling, as he shepherded her out. He promised to call her as soon as he had news.

Ben washed his hands and checked his phone. *Nothing*, he acknowledged glumly. *Why would she get in touch, Ben? You both agreed it was going nowhere, you wanted to back off, and you did, and she isn't bothered. There's your answer.* He put his phone in the desk drawer and called for the next patient. Thank God the surgery was busy today.

* * *

A few hours later, Jasper was tucking into a bowl of dog food when Mrs Warburton came to pick him up. The floss was not stuck to anything, and he had eventually passed it with a bit of help. He was now trying his best to take the enamel off the food bowl, obviously no worse for wear from his ordeal.

Dotty waved them both off, and looked at Ben, sat in his office staring into space.

'I am off now, duck, any plans for tonight?'

Ben looked across at her. 'Nope, no plans, Dotty. See you tomorrow.'

Dotty nodded glumly, planting a kiss on his forehead as she went to leave.

'Just as stubborn as your father,' she said over her shoulder when she left.

Ben put his head in his hands. *Can't argue with you there*, he thought to himself.

Seventeen

Vince Stokes was angry. Very angry indeed. So much so, in fact, that the vein in his forehead was tapping out its own heartbeat, pulsing against his brain as he barked down the phone at his secretary, Rosie.

'In a meeting? What bloody meeting? Tell his secretary tart that I want him in my office, now!'

Rosie replied meekly, wincing as Vince slammed down his phone in her ear. Sighing, she pushed away from her desk and walked briskly to Marcus's new office. Angela was sitting at her desk, just outside, filing her nails. The sound of the sandpaper against her long plastic nails set Rosie's teeth on edge, and she headed for his door.

Angela stood up and ran towards her. 'Er, excuse me, where do you think you are going?'

Rosie gave her a sideways glare. 'To see Marcus, because *my* boss wants to see him, and neither of you are answering the phones. What's the matter? Too busy?' she said, nodding at her hands.

Angela scowled. 'Marcus told me not to answer internal calls, FYI, because he is busy. *Capisce*?'

Rosie continued on, placing her hand firmly on Marcus's door handle. 'No, not "*capisce*". Mr Stokes wants to speak to him, now.'

Angela made a move to pull her hand off the door handle, and Rosie pressed it down. They both ended up in a pile of heels and hair in the doorway to Marcus's office, and they both balked at the sight before them. Marcus was asleep, head back on his swivel chair, snoring loudly. Energy drink cans littered the desk, along with balls of paper covered with scribbles, and a half-empty box of antacids. He jumped at the noise, falling backwards off his chair.

After bounding back up, he straightened his clothes quickly, looking with terror towards the door. Seeing the two secretaries extricate themselves, he sagged with relief, till he looked again at Rosie.

'Hi, girls,' he said brazenly. 'Don't fight over me, there is enough for everyone!'

Angela scowled and Rosie tried to hold down her breakfast. Walking to his desk, she began putting the rubbish into his wastepaper bin. 'Mr Stokes senior is looking for you, Mr Beresford—' she said his name like you would say, 'I have poo on my new heels' '—and he is not going to be ignored. He wants you in his office, now.'

Marcus's bleary eyes focused on her words and his face paled even further. He now resembled the colour of cold custard. 'I will be right there,' he muttered, dragging his fingers through his greasy, dishevelled hair.

Rosie nodded. 'If I were you, Mr Beresford—' again, she emphasised greatly the fact that she wanted to call him something far worse '—I would make this right. You still have time to do that, but you will have to act fast.'

Marcus looked at Rosie, who stared at him right back. He withered under her gaze, knowing full well she had the measure of him as a man, a partner and a human being.

She flicked her eyes across to Angela. 'When you have got rid of this tramp, and spoken to my boss, go and see Elaine. She might just be able to help you, if you help yourself.'

Angela huffed, a strangled semi-scream coming from her throat as she stewed on what Rosie had said, and she started to move towards her, claws out.

Rosie merely raised one hand on her way out of the office. 'Try it, Angela, I will take you down. And I would love to see security drag your bony arse out of here. We all would.' She walked out of the office then, still immaculate and showing no outward signs of being perturbed at all. The woman was as cool as a cucumber.

Angela was apoplectic and, slamming the door, she screamed loudly. 'Arrgghh! Marcus, are you going to let her speak to me like that?! I have never been so insulted in all my life, how dare she?' She was ranting now, to-ing and fro-ing across the carpet in front of his desk, bits of spittle flying out from her now smudged red lips. 'Does she not know who I am? I am soooo going to get her fired! You are going to sort this, aren't you, Markie?' she barked, stopping in front of his desk and turning to him.

Marcus sat at his desk, a pale ghost, with rabbit-in-the-headlight eyes. He opened his mouth to speak and, instead, a funny sound came out. A titter. Before Angela's eyes, Marcus crumbled into a crying, hysterically laughing mess. He was clutching at himself now, trying to catch his breath.

She looked at him, disgusted. 'Heard a funny joke, have we?' she sneered. 'You need to pull it together, Marcus, because you *are the joke.*' She hissed out the last words as she stared at him, arms folded.

He abruptly stopped laughing then, slamming his hand down on the desk with a resounding boom. Angela jumped.

'Get out, Angela, and don't come back. You are fired,' he said, voice quaking with rage.

Angela flinched as though he had shot her. 'Fired!? You can't fire me, I'm your—'

'You are nothing to me!' he shouted. 'You were a distraction, a bit of fluff, but I am beyond bored with you now, Angela. And you know what, you are mean. Mean, bitchy and cold. I was an idiot to even touch you.'

Angela's eyes glittered with anger, and her facial expression grew hard. 'You will regret this.'

Marcus chuckled as she stomped out the door. 'I already do, darling, now don't let the door hit you on your bony arse on the way out!'

Relieved, he ran his fingers through his hair, wincing at the greasy knotted mess. Reaching into his bottom drawer, he pulled out his spare change of clothes and his washbag. Heading for the company showers, he felt rather like a man taking his final preparations before being taken out. For a nice lethal injection. He didn't feel upset, or panicked, however, he felt relief. Great relief at making a stand for the right thing for once. And one thing was for sure, if he was to survive this at all, he needed Amanda. He needed to find her, and bring her home. What Marcus never considered was whether Amanda would want to.

Eighteen

Before Amanda had time to blink, the humid July turned into a very hot and summery August, and she awoke on the day before the summer county fair bursting with the joy of starting the next day in her new life. Friday morning brought with it the ladies group's coffee and cake morning, a new initiative that was working brilliantly, and brought even more crafty villagers out of their homes and into the shop, latest projects with them. Amanda had began to stock little extras in her shop, such as novelty buttons, zips, threads and cottons, and had increased her profit by half. Life was pretty amazing, and she had long since stopped fretting over her bank account, which had now stabilised somewhat and was starting to look much healthier after the recent catastrophic haemorrhage.

Amanda laughed at her companions as she padded

down to the shop, the kittens barrelling down the stairs behind her. They had taken to sleeping in the basket in the back, unperturbed and uninterested in the people coming in and out of the shop. She loved their company, and their little personalities were so different. Perky was far from her namesake, in fact she was the grumpiest cat ever when she wanted to be, and Pinky was an uncontrollable ball of grey fluff, always the first one into the path of trouble, while Perky looked on, judging and tutting from a distance. In fact, the only person, other than her, that they seemed to calm down for and adore was Ben. She supposed it was his way with animals, but she had a feeling it was more down to the animals having an innate sense of sussing out how people really were on the inside. She had to admit, as dreamy village vets went, though her experience was limited in this field, she believed Ben had to be in the top five, at least.

She was just chastising herself for thinking of him as she felt a drip on her nose. Bemused, she looked up to see a heart-stopping bulge in her ceiling. As she kept watching, the bulge suddenly bowed and burst, smacking Amanda in the face with a wall of water, and chunks of plasterboard and wood, one of which promptly conked her on the head, knocking her out. And that's how the ladies found her, ten minutes later, water gushing into the stockroom, both cats patrolling round her like sentries.

* * *

Amanda opened her eyes gingerly and smiled as she looked into the loveliest sight she had ever seen. Two swirls of grey and black, dotted with stars that twinkled and danced as she gazed at them. 'Wow,' she said, voice thick, dry as dust. 'So pretty.'

The swirls disappeared, leaving a plain cream backdrop. She heard a rumble then, two rumbles in fact, far away. She closed her eyes quickly as the noise increased. One of the rumbles was deep, angry, whilst the other was softer, trying to quieten the deeper one. She frowned, trying to decipher the sounds, and was suddenly glad her eyes were shut, as another bolt of pain shot across her forehead. 'Ouch,' she drawled.

The low rumble grew closer, and she felt someone's hand around hers. She gripped the warmth, squeezing it as hard as she could, which she suspected wasn't much at all, since she felt as if she had no bones. The grey swirls, which looked like galaxies now, swam back into view as she opened her eyes slowly.

'Amanda,' a voice said softly. The voice resembled the loud rumble she had heard earlier, but kinder now. 'You are in the hospital, you had a nasty knock.'

Amanda tried to nod, but a warm hand touched her cheek, stilling her. She smiled at the touch. A thought flashed through her mind. 'The cats?'

The face smiled down at her, galaxy swirls dancing brighter. 'They're fine. Dotty has taken them to mine, you are staying with me till the shop is fixed. Luckily, the stock is all OK, so you can still do the fair tomorrow, if you are up to it. Anyway, the girls are sorting everything out, Agatha is there, so it will all be organised like a military camp now.' A hand came across and brushed a loose strand of matted hair away from her face.

She smiled lazily, enjoying the view. 'I always knew I would drown eventually,' she said to no one in particular.

* * *

Ben frowned at her mutterings. *Drown?* He held her hand again. 'Amanda, you didn't drown, you are safe. They gave you something for the pain, I think you need to sleep it off.'

* * *

Amanda shook her head weakly, wincing at the pain it produced.

The hand around hers tightened. 'Sshh, shh,' the voice said. 'It's OK, just go to sleep.'

'I can't sleep,' Amanda replied, fighting the wall of what was trying to pull her under. 'He comes when I sleep, it all comes back.'

* * *

Ben's jaw tightened and flexed with anger. *If I ever meet this douchebag, I won't be responsible for my actions.* 'Amanda,' he tried again. 'Manda, you are safe now. I'm not going anywhere, it's Ben. You don't have to be scared.'

Amanda, fighting to keep her fluttering eyes open, seemed to relax at these words, and her eyes started to close. A small smile glanced across her face and she laughed numbly. 'Ben doesn't scare me, silly,' she said, each word spaced out as she fought to get them out before the drugs pulled her under. 'He's the one who saves me.'

* * *

And with that, she was out. Ben froze in shock, staring at her now peaceful expression. He looked down at their hands, still clasped together. Bending his head, he kissed her hand tenderly. *Save her? I can't even save myself.* He shuffled in his seat, making himself comfy by propping his head on his jacket, hand still in hers. He settled in for a nap, so he could be alert when she came round. As he fell asleep, he wondered how things would have been if they had met each other sooner, if their disastrous lives hadn't set them onto the path they were on. Would they have liked each other? Ben couldn't help thinking that things would have been so much easier if they had met each other first. When they were both brand new, not rebounding from pain and heartache. He smiled as she squeezed his hand, deep in sleep.

One thing was for sure, he was glad he was there today. When Dotty had rang him in a panic, he had pretty much flown to Baker Street, willing his jeep to be faster, quicker, beating the paramedics there, and his heart had been in his mouth the entire time. His heart hadn't hit a beat from the minutes between the call till he saw her, pale, unconscious, being stretchered into the ambulance. He hadn't felt like that since the day his parents died, and it had awakened a fear in him he didn't know still existed. He knew what it was, how he felt, he just couldn't work out what to do about it. Looking over at her again, her brown hair matted with dried blood, framing her pale, scratched and bloodied face, he registered how calm he felt now he was around her, close to her, and he decided to concentrate on that. One day at a time, till his fears subsided. The alternative was not something, especially after today, that Ben wanted to contemplate.

Nineteen

'Ben, I am fine!' Amanda huffed, as he wrapped her in yet another blanket. She was dressed in a loose cotton dress, slip-on shoes and a very fetching head bandage from the hospital. She had plasters and dressings on her head and arms, where she had been scratched and cut from the debris of the water leak. She was sitting behind her stall on a very large and comfortable garden chaise longue, feeling more like a bandaged mummy than Cleopatra with all the hospital's efforts, and blankets and cushions Ben had plonked her on. He shook his head at her, obviously irritated by her efforts to stop him helping her. He headed off to get them a drink from the nearby tea bar whilst she watched the rest of the stall-holders set up.

She thought of that morning, in the hospital. She had woken up in a side room with Ben sleeping in the chair next to her. His hand was wound tightly around hers, and he had splashes of blood on his clothes, and she wondered how he had got them. Why was he there? He slept fitfully, tossing his head occasionally, probably uncomfortable, and she realised from his five o'clock shadow that he had been there all night. He hadn't left her side since, although they had not spoken about anything, aside from her pain level and comfort. She was pretending to be annoyed at his attentions and mitherings, but, deep down, she was actually really enjoying being looked after by someone for a change, even though he was being a grumpy sod in the meantime. He was gruffer today, more protective, take charge than he usually was, and Amanda had to admit that she found him even more attractive as a result. *Great, club me now, caveman! Get a grip, Amanda.* She shrugged her own thoughts away as she battled against her old self, the tough independent woman she presented to the world. She had just had a concussion, after all—she was allowed a little romantic fantasy for her troubles. She blushed furiously at her own musings as Ben appeared in view, cup of tea and biscuits in hand. He sat next to her, perched in a plastic garden chair, and offered her the tea. She took it from him gratefully, and resisted the urge to smack him one when he eyed her like a baby drinking from an open cup for the first time.

'Ben,' she said, trying to keep the tension from her

voice. 'I have drunk tea before, I'm fine.' He looked away sheepishly then, nodding once. 'Are you not at the vet's today?'

Ben shrugged. 'No, I have taken a few days off, I have a locum friend—he has stepped in for me.'

Amanda's face dropped. 'Because of me?'

'I told you this morning, you are staying with me till the shop is fixed up, and you can't be left alone with a concussion anyway. It's all arranged, don't worry.'

Amanda kept her eyes trained on her tea. 'I could have stayed in a hotel, or with a friend. Agatha would have probably let me stay.'

Ben shook his head. 'No, she couldn't have done that.'

Amanda looked at him, puzzled. 'Why, cos she doesn't have the room?'

Ben's eyes darted around before he answered. 'Er, no, of course not, but...but the cats and the dogs together? Not a good combination. Besides, Dotty already packed you some things, they are already at mine, it's fine.'

Amanda nodded. 'OK, well...thanks.'

Ben positively sagged with relief. 'It's better for everyone, trust me.'

She wondered what he meant by that, and was about to ask, when the ladies arrived. Ben swiftly took his leave to go and check on the vet's stall as the women smothered her with kisses and interrogations of her night, before they started to set up the New Lease of Life stall.

* * *

As Ben looked back at Amanda, all swaddled up, laughing at something Hetty said, he felt a huge urge to protect her, and he resolved to hurry back, once the swarms had dissipated a little. He was glad that she hadn't pressed the issue of staying at his, or picked at how it had come about. The truth was, he wanted to look after her, and had knocked back the women's offers of putting her up. Since seeing her on that floor, vulnerable and hurt, something had shifted in him, and until he could figure it out himself, he couldn't put it into words. All he knew was that he wanted to be the one to look after her, keep her safe. That was all he could wrap his head around for now. She seemed to be mightily peed off at the prospect, but, so far, she was going along with it relatively quietly, although he suspected that this was due to her feeling too ill to put up much of a fight.

* * *

All too soon, the county fair was ready to open. The atmosphere in the grounds of the Mayweather estate was a positive frisson of excitement. A real feeling of community had descended, even more than Amanda usually saw exhibited due to the threat to the community centre, and she was loving every minute. The ladies had done a fantastic job with the stall; the stock looked amazing, everything was just so, all neatly labelled and priced, and all Amanda was allowed to do was make change for the sales, the float tin on her bundled lap. She felt ridiculous, but she didn't make too much of a fuss as she realised that, actually, she did feel pretty shocking. She was just grateful to be an observer of the day.

Agatha was not underestimated, she saw; the whole fair was amazing, ran like clockwork and looked effortlessly seamless. She saw a lot of people from the village that she knew now, from being out and about with Ben, at the surgery or from her shop. *Her shop!* She felt a huge pang of panic as she remembered about her shop, her livelihood, closed till the workmen of the village got today over with and returned to work. Every villager had a part in the fair today—Amanda even ventured that the church was on hiatus, as she could see the vicar, Mr Blendergast, judging the bonny baby competition, working his way through a huge plate of treats the mothers kept refilling, hoping to sway his sweet tooth towards their bundle of joy for the rosette. She tittered to herself at the sight, and immediately regretted it as a stab of pain zinged across her forehead. Ben was at her side in seconds, as if from nowhere, and he gently touched her face. He set two cups beside them. 'I knew it was too much, I said to the hospital you needed to be kept in another night, damn it!'

Amanda pushed him away feebly. 'Ben,' she said, stroking his arm as an afterthought, to relieve the hurt look her push away had provoked. 'Sorry, but I am fine. I am sat here like the Queen of Sheba, the girls are here, I am sat watching, not doing a thing!'

Ben's face smoothed out somewhat with relief. 'OK,'
he acquiesced.

Amanda glanced across at him, and he smiled bash-
fully back at her. She leaned forward a little, giving him
a little sign to kiss her, an impulse, but he looked away,
changing the subject. Amanda's face flushed, embarrassed by the apparent rebuttal. *Why the hell did you do
that, Amanda?* She frowned, her head suddenly feeling
very foggy indeed, and she knew it wasn't just down to
the concussion.

* * *

Ben watched her sip her tea, wishing that his was laced
with arsenic. *Bloody idiot*, he berated himself grimly.
She wanted you to kiss her, and you moved away. He
had wanted to kiss her, that's all he had thought about
since he saw her on that stretcher, but he was aware that
she was delicate, in pain, and he didn't want his passion to overtake him, and hurt her. So he had moved
away, trying to be the gent, and he knew from her face
that he had confused her. He wanted to slap himself.
Hard. One thing was for sure, for a man who lived with
loads of women looking after him, he sucked at figur-
ing them out sometimes. He finished his tea in a noisy
gulp, and turned to her quickly. Amanda was looking at
him as though he were mad. 'Ben, that tea is like lava!
Are you OK?'

He shook his head, ignoring the burning sensation on
his tongue. He took her barely touched cup from her,

set it on the grass and gently cupped her face. 'I have wanted to do this since last night,' he said, gently touching his lips to hers, trying to fight the urge to deepen it. Amanda made a little sound, and he froze, pulling away. 'Did I hurt you?'

* * *

Amanda's eyes were shut tight. The little moan that had just escaped her lips was a pleased sound, and she was mortified that he heard it. She opened her eyes and shook her head, smiling. 'No, Ben, you could never do that.'

Ben smiled, his white teeth flashing as they looked at each other.

The stall started to get busy then, and they reluctantly moved away from each other. *Almost worth a bump on the head*, Amanda thought to herself, as she dealt with a customer from her sick chair.

* * *

The fair was a resounding success, and the day soon wore on. Amanda was in her element—most of her stock was sold, and she had a whole notepad full of orders and contacts. The ladies had been amazing, wrapping up purchases, dealing with the throng of people, constantly keeping her wrapped up against the elements. She had also drunk enough tea to sink a battleship. She was just getting up to head to the Portaloos when Ben reappeared. He looked startled that she was trying to get up. He helped her move the blankets from her feet, he looked at her enquiringly.

'Do you want another drink? Because I can get you one, if you like?'

Amanda burst into laughter and then winced, twice, for her full bladder and pain in her head. 'No, no more tea I beg you,' she said, giggling. 'I...er, I need the toilet.'

'Oh,' Ben said, a small smile playing on his lips. 'I see. Let me help.'

He gave her his arm and she took it gratefully. They were just making their way across to the loos when they heard Grace's soft timbre over the tannoy. She was just starting to thank people when Amanda reached the toilets, grateful that there was no queue. Ben waited outside, pacing up and down until she knocked on the door to tell him she was finished, and he practically wrenched it open, just to see for his own eyes that she hadn't fallen down the toilet or passed out. Amanda was shocked by the look of worry and relief on his face, and felt her heart leap as they locked eyes.

'Ben,' she said softly as he reached for her. 'I'm fine, OK?'

Ben looked a bit sheepish, realising that she was on to him. 'I'm sorry.' He sighed, placing her hand around the crook of his arm, holding her up with the other. 'I just worry.'

Amanda nodded. 'It's really cute,' she said, not bothering to censor what she was thinking.

On the stage, Agatha was standing next to Grace and Taylor now, holding a large silver envelope and looking rather green. Ben nodded to Amanda, and they both made their way back to the stall, trying to look as innocent and oblivious as they could. Amanda could feel Agatha's eyes on her as she thanked the villagers for the lovely gift of an evening out for her and Taylor. Sebastian Taylor, for his part, looked relaxed, positively laidback next to the uptight Agatha.

As Amanda sat down next to Ben, Hetty and Marlene came closer from their place at the stall. Hetty smiled at Ben, and whispered to Amanda, 'If Agatha flips, claim amnesia. We will hit the Mexican border till the heat lifts.'

Amanda and Ben lost it then, laughing so loud that half the village turned to look at them, distracted by the spectacle of the city girl and the bachelor vet howling with laughter together. When Amanda next looked at the stage, Taylor gave her a wide grin and nodded. She nodded back, pleased that he seemed quite happy with the gift. Daring to look at his employer, Amanda was surprised to see she was smiling. Amanda gave her a wave and Agatha waved back, a little understated gesture that anyone not looking for it might have missed. As Amanda kept watching, she saw Agatha gaze down at the envelope and do something she never expected to see. Agatha Mayweather, cool, calm, elegant, poised Agatha, hugged the envelope tight to her chest, and squeezed.

Had Amanda not recently had a huge jolt to the cranium, she might have thought that Mrs Mayweather was ever so slightly the giddy kipper at the prospect of a night with Taylor.

* * *

Later that evening, Amanda and Ben pulled up to Ben's house. What remained of Amanda's stall was packed neatly into the back of the jeep and they figured it was safe till morning, given that the crime rate in Westfield consisted of a few speedy drivers and Mr Jenkins' goose, aptly named Goose, nipping a few heels now and then. Amanda felt bone tired. She hadn't done a thing for herself all day, but she felt as though she had run a marathon. Ben killed the engine and stepped out into the cool August night air. He appeared seconds later at her door.

Amanda smiled at him, awkward at what was to come. 'I can go to a hotel, you know, I really don't want to put you out.'

Ben shook his head, lifting her out as though she weighed nothing. She didn't protest, instead laid her head on his shoulder and enjoyed the scent of his aftershave, mixed with the smell of the country air. Ben always smelled so fresh, so outdoorsy. He barely wore any cologne and he still smelled scrumptious. He sat her down gently in the porch swing he had near his front door, unlocked the house, picked her up again and took her inside. The house was tidy, and warm from the summer sun and Amanda smiled as she looked around. The house was so Ben, it already felt homely to her. He settled her on the sofa, wrapping a clean blanket around her from the back of the settee, and handing her the remote. He scurried off, and Amanda caught the waft of cooking food as he entered the kitchen. He came back minutes later, a glass of water and tablets in hand, to find the TV still off and Amanda asleep. The kittens, Pinky and Perky, having been asleep in the kitchen, jumped up to her and settled in on her lap. Ben gently laid her down, making her more comfortable, and left her to sleep, placing the tablets and water on the coffee table next to her. Returning to the kitchen, he grabbed some stew from the slow cooker, Dotty's creation, and ate.

As he settled in later that night, on the settee opposite Amanda, he smiled. He thought it would feel awkward, having Amanda here, even if it was just on the settee tonight, but it wasn't. The fact was, he hadn't even considered what it would entail when the doctor asked if she had anywhere to stay, anyone to look after her. He had cut down everyone around him, although the ladies didn't seem that eager to fight the point, and declared that she would stay with him, he would have time off work to look after her. The words had flown out of his mouth before they had fully formed in his own mind, but he found he didn't want to take them back either. Now, as he drifted off to sleep watching Amanda and the kittens slumbering across the room, he congratulated himself on speaking up.

He just hoped that, when the time came for Amanda to go back to Baker Street, he would be able to let her go. Because one thing was for sure, while she was here, Ben's house felt more like a home than ever before.

Twenty

Agatha scoffed at Taylor's words the next morning. The clean-up crew could be heard outside her open bedroom window, taking down the marquees, returning the lawns to their original unaltered glory. 'I really don't see why they did it, Taylor, and we can't go, obviously!'

Taylor shook his head, bemused, as he held her breakfast tray. She looked lovely this morning, her hair immaculate, lips glossy. She looked as though she had done her hair and make-up, but Taylor knew he had just awoken her with his knock at her door. 'Mrs Mayweather, they have made the booking, and it's all paid for. For tonight, and we are going. Your calendar is free, I checked.'

Agatha frowned, taking the cup and saucer from the tray. She took a sip of tea contemplatively. What Taylor didn't realise was that the gesture was Agatha's way of buying time. She was terrified at the prospect of going out for dinner with him, and she didn't quite know what to make of her feelings. Taylor, however, took her awkward silence as something else entirely.

'Are you ashamed to be seen out with me?' he asked boldly, his chin jutting out in a manly way. Agatha nearly choked on her Earl Grey.

'What?' she said, incensed. 'Taylor, don't be so absurd! We are always together!'

Taylor shook his head, his jaw tensing as he sat down on her bed. Agatha flinched at his proximity.

'Yes, but not as dinner dates, as employer and employee,' he said, poking himself in the chest at the word 'employee'.

Agatha's eyes grew wide, and she gently replaced the cup onto the saucer. The small chinking noise was the only sound in the room as they stared at each other. Agatha sat up and, spotting his hand resting on the eiderdown, she shakily placed her hand over his.

'Taylor,' she said softly. His eyes flashed and his nostrils flared, but he didn't take his eyes from their hands. 'Sebastian,' she said, the word sounding foreign in her own mouth. He looked at her then, and his hand clenched beneath hers. 'I am not, nor ever have been, ashamed to be seen with you. We are friends, not just work colleagues. You know that as well as I do. It's just a little strange, that's all. I haven't been out to dinner with a man since...'

Taylor's eyes crinkled at the edges, and his fist relaxed. He moved their hands until his was entwined in hers, and he brought it up to his mouth, planting a kiss on the back. 'I know, I am sorry. I should have realised.' She nodded then, not trusting herself to speak further. He squeezed her hand again. 'Agatha,' he said, voice above a whisper, just barely. Agatha could hear the low rumble behind it and realised that he was nervous, his voice thick with something she couldn't quite put her finger on. She looked at him. 'Agatha, you have annoyed me since primary school, since the day we met, in fact.' He smirked. She pulled a face at him, sticking her tongue out, making his rumble deeper, more pronounced in his chest as he continued. 'You annoy me every day, and I have had a blast the entire time. Now, Agatha, will you please come to dinner with me this evening?'

Agatha nodded once. 'I will, thank you,' she said quietly.

Taylor grinned then, whisking himself off the bed and out of the room, whistling as he walked down the stairs to feed the children breakfast. As the door closed behind him, Agatha lay back against the pillows, absentmindedly checking her lip gloss was still in place. She was just getting out of bed when she realised that for the first time since they were five, they had called each other by their first names. The fact that it felt so natural was the thing that surprised her the most.

* * *

Amanda awoke to a voice yelling, 'Darcy, don't be a dick! Share!' She frowned, wincing at the dull ache that resulted with the movement. The voice laughed then, and she heard the meow of Pinky, much closer to her proximity. She opened her mouth to speak and got a mouthful of hair and whiskers as her cat ecstatically greeted her. She giggled as she stroked her little pet. She heard a door go and then Ben came into view, carrying a small basket of eggs.

'Morning, sunshine! How are you feeling?'

Amanda was mortified. She felt, and probably looked, disgusting. She still had dried blood in her hair as she had to wait to heal more before she could wash it, she was in yesterday's clothes and she *knew* she would have dire morning breath. She smiled tightly, hiding her teeth, and nodded. 'Fine thanks,' she said, lying. Ben sat on the coffee table, leaning in, with her cats either side of him, and showed her the dish. It was full of eggs, all fresh and covered in bits of straw, and she grinned. 'Wow, the Bennet sisters have been busy,' she laughed.

Ben grinned. 'Yep, and these beauties are breakfast. Lovely with some toast and bacon, you up for it?'

Amanda's stomach growled at the thought. She was starving. 'That sounds amazing, but I need to get dressed.' Ben jumped up, nearly dropping the eggs in the process.

'Oh God, sorry!' He put the eggs down and motioned

to help her up. 'I have put your things in the guest room, the ladies packed you some bits, and there is an en suite ready to go with towels and everything.' He looked nervous for a second. 'Will you…er…be okay undressing? Want me to call someone?'

Amanda was desperate to get a bath and change of clothes. She was so concerned about feeling and looking so grotty that she didn't care if she had to strip wash with a baby wipe. 'I'll be fine, don't worry,' she soothed. 'I am used to looking after myself, remember?'

Ben, arms wrapped around her protectively as he guided her up the stairs, stilled. He looked her straight in the eye, with a determined look. 'I know that,' he said eventually, leading her to the door of the guest room. 'But it doesn't mean that you have to all the time.'

Amanda regretted being so bullishly independent then, and wanted to bite her own tongue off. She allowed him to fuss over her, suddenly feeling very contrite as he started running the bath after settling her down on the double bed. The guest room was lovely, all fresh, bright colours and understated ornaments. Very much how a woman would decorate a room. She was still gazing around the room when Ben came back in from the en suite, a large cream bath towel in hand. He must have guessed what she was thinking. 'My mum decorated it, just before… She had nice taste, not the chintzy sort, you see.'

Amanda smiled at him. 'It's lovely.'

He nodded, looking around. 'I haven't changed much since they died. I redecorated the master bedroom, and sorted the garden out for the chickens, but other than that, it's pretty much the same.' Amanda felt comforted somehow that he had taken the time to explain how little an effect his ex had had on the shaping of his current home. Weird thought to have, but there she was, thinking it. He came over and, leaning over her, he took in her bandages. 'Doc says you have to leave this on another day, but then you can wash your hair, so I got you this.' He passed her a plastic shower cap. 'To protect you,' he said.

She was still melting from his thoughtfulness when he dropped a kiss on her forehead and left. She sat there a minute, listening to the water running in the next room. She felt like she had really gone through the wars, and she felt vulnerable once more, even more vulnerable than she had all those months ago. This felt different though, she reasoned, as she heard Ben downstairs, humming to himself over the sound of the radio, banging pots and pans. This time, she was scared because she was beginning to like her new surroundings, her new friends, and the thought of starting again, alone, scared her more than anything.

* * *

Ben was dancing around the kitchen when Amanda padded into the room. She had scrubbed herself pink in the bath, brushed her teeth and run a comb through her hair the best she could, before giving it up as a bad job and pinning it back off her face with a piece of ribbon. She had almost rang Dotty when she had opened her cases, to give the women a sound ticking-off, but she resisted. They had packed her case as though she were going on honeymoon, with all her best underwear and skimpy nightwear at the top. She was just ridiculously grateful that Ben hadn't seen any of it. She had eventually settled on a pair of boyfriend jeans and a loose pink sweater that she could pull over her head without scraping her wound. She stopped dead in the doorway, watching Ben dancing about the kitchen as he made breakfast. The kitchen smelled gorgeous, and Duran Duran was banging out on the radio airwaves. She loitered at the door, watching Ben's hips wriggle as he placed fried mushrooms and bacon on two plates. The toaster popped up and Ben shimmied across the lino, stopping with a horrified look on his face as he spied her. He immediately dropped the leg that he was kung-fu kicking out, and laughed. Amanda burst out laughing too, or as well as she could with the pains in her head.

'Busted,' he said, chuckling. He looked her up and down. 'You look great,' he said.

Amanda blushed. 'I look like I have roadkill on my head,' she said, pointing at her matted hair.

Ben pulled out a chair. 'Don't be ridiculous,' he said, motioning for her to come sit. 'Dotty is coming soon to open the practice and the locum is on the way in, so we have the whole day. What do you fancy doing?'

Amanda looked at him as he finished preparing the food for breakfast. His jeans were pulled tight with a belt, and his white cotton shirt was open at the neck and rolled up at the sleeves, drawing her eyes to his tanned skin. *I could think of a couple of things we could do*, she thought to herself. 'I should go see the shop, really, and I have the stock and stall stuff to sort out from yesterday.'

Ben sat down at the table with her, passing a steaming plate full of mouth-watering breakfast to her. 'OK, the stall stuff is in my car, but the shop is definitely out of bounds today. Hetty and Marlene are there, making sure the insurance company and the builders are all on the ball. Trust me, it is better that you don't exert yourself dealing with that today.'

Amanda nodded, grateful that the decision had been made for her for once. She didn't feel up to much anyway.

Ben smiled at her, his eyebrow raised in query. 'You have gone again, where are you now?'

Amanda looked at him, a sheepish look coming across her face as she realised he was on to her. 'Nothing,' she said. 'Just weird to be told what to do, been a while.'

Ben shrugged, taking a bite of sausage. 'Well, for the next week or so, you had better get used to it.'

'Week?' Amanda said, incredulous. 'It will be that long?'

Ben nodded. 'Yep. Sorry to disappoint you, but you are stuck here for at least that long, till you recover, and Baker Street is back up and running.'

Amanda took a bite from her fork. 'I am sure I will survive,' she said.

He smiled at her then, and they ate breakfast in companionable silence.

* * *

Later that same day, Agatha was just finishing off getting ready, sat at her dressing table fumbling with a bracelet that matched her dress, when she heard a knock at the door.

She looked across at the dogs, sleeping at her feet. 'Now, who can that be?' she asked them, only generating a fart in response from Buster.

Wrinkling her nose, she headed to the stairway, still struggling with the clasp on her bracelet.

'Taylor?' she called down the stairs. No answer. 'Taylor?' she tried again.

Tutting, she clicked down the stairs in her heels, looking around doors and corners as she went. The door knocked again and Agatha looked at the dogs, who had managed to get themselves down the stairs before flobbing down again at the bottom.

'Humph,' she said. 'Some guard dogs you are. What would you do, chase the burglars away with your stench?'

Maisie snuffed in reply, obviously agreeing.

Agatha opened the door to see a man standing there, resplendent in a grey suit and light blue tie. She was about to apologise for her tardiness in answering the door, when she realised just who the man was.

'Good evening, madam, pleased to meet you.'

Agatha stood there, stunned. 'Taylor, what are you doing?'

The man held out a hand. 'Sebastian Taylor, pleased to meet you. Are you ready?'

Agatha stood and looked at him, bemused. She went to hold her hand out to him, being the polite woman she was, and realised that she had no hands free. Taylor, seeing this, deftly stepped into the room, took hold of her bracelet and swiftly closed the clasp.

She nodded her thanks, blushing.

'So,' he began again, a wry smile on his face. 'Are you ready for our dinner?'

Agatha cottoned on. He was winding her up. *Game on, Sebastian Taylor, game on.*

'Ah,' she said. 'How lovely to meet you, Sebastian. Won't you come in?'

Taylor shook his hand. 'Nope, your carriage awaits, my dear. We have reservations at nine.'

Agatha grinned at him devilishly. 'OK, shall we call a cab? I gave my driver the evening off.'

Taylor didn't miss a beat. 'Not a problem, I have my car.'

Agatha nodded, reaching for her bag. She tried not to

look at the dogs as she locked up, but if dogs could roll their eyes, Maisie and Buster would have.

Walking down the steps, Agatha looked at a midnight blue Mercedes that was parked on the drive. 'Did you rent a car?'

Taylor shook his head. 'No, this is my car.'

Agatha looked puzzled. 'Your car?'

'Yes, Agatha,' Taylor said, pointedly. 'I do have my own car, you know.'

Agatha nodded. 'Fair enough, sorry.'

He opened the door for her without being asked as normal, but this time it felt different. Agatha settled into the passenger seat, not the back, and could feel the close proximity of him as he took his seat next to her. She looked at him momentarily, blushing as she turned to look out of the window. Taylor grinned to himself as he pulled away smoothly. *Tonight is going to be fun*, he thought to himself.

* * *

The meal was lovely. They couldn't have gone to a nicer place. The Harrogate night air was warm and sweet and, as they sat out on the terrace waiting for their coffees, the pair were giggling together at something that had tickled them.

'I did not!' Agatha protested. 'You say this all the time, and there is just no truth to the tale!'

Taylor made an appalled face, clutching his chest as though she had aimed the barb directly at his heart.

'Madam! I do not lie!' he said, and they collapsed into laughter again. 'You did cheat at the egg and spoon race, and poor Harold never recovered!' he said, recalling their primary school sports day.

Agatha wiped a tear from her cheek, clutching for breath as she shook with laughter.

'You are wicked, Sebastian, you really are!'

Taylor stopped laughing a little then, and his eyes grew dark and serious. 'It's a long time since you called me that, Agatha.'

Agatha turned to look at him, sensing his change in mood.

'Well, it has been a long time coming,' she admitted.

Taylor beamed at her. 'A good night had by all then,' he said happily.

As they sat, their coffees arrived. Taylor placed his hand over hers as she reached for the sugar bowl. Instead of stopping him, she covered it with her own.

'It has been nice, Taylor.' She smiled.

Taylor squeezed her hand. Noticing her frown, he wondered what she was thinking.

'Penny for them?'

Agatha squeezed his hand back, and Taylor nearly fell off his chair when she pulled it to her lips to drop a kiss onto it.

'My problem, my dear, is that I fear now I can't kill the meddling buggers that arranged this.'

Taylor's laughs carried through the night air, as the other diners looked on, amused to look at this couple, best friends and in love.

Twenty-One

Four days had passed since the fair, and Amanda was feeling more comfortable day by day at Ben's house. The kittens, Pinky and Perky, were already masters of their realm, having picked out their own sleeping posts around the house, and enjoying far too many rich treats at the hands of Dotty, who came in every day to clean, cook and generally make a fuss of the pair. Ben had started to go back to work a little, but was never gone long, and had taken to working on his paperwork and client files from the kitchen table, whilst Amanda sat propped on the sofa, or at the other end of the table, putting together an order from the fair. She was feeling better every day, the headaches were gone, and this morning she even managed to wash her hair. The downside to her wound however was that she couldn't yet towel dry or hairdryer her hair, so whilst her hair was now very clean, and no longer matted with blood, it was still very much in the Worzel Gummidge realm of hairdos. Not that Ben said a word, he was a perfect gent. Much to the surprising disappointment of Amanda.

They had agreed to stay away from each other, but were all bets off whilst they stayed in the same house? Amanda was as confused as ever, and she was aware that she was getting as comfortable as the cats were, the furry little Judases. They even got on with the chickens, and other than a couple of warning pecks from Darcy, they had pretty much lived in accord, with the kittens even going out for a wander in Ben's garden. It was lovely to see them dashing about on the grass, and Amanda suddenly felt very guilty that she had no garden at home for them to play in. She just hoped that when the time came to sojourn back to Baker Street, the cats would come with her, and not just wave her goodbye from their new home.

This morning had consisted of Ben making them a good breakfast, before he settled her on the couch with her order boxes and dashed off to help set up the surgery. He was due to call into the dog groomer's too, and said he would pop his head into New Lease, to see how the women were getting along. Amanda was just ensconced on the sofa, when there was a knock at the door. Opening it, she was surprised to see Marlene and Grace standing there, with Hetty locking up her car.

They had boxes and bags with them, and they all came bundling in, all lavender smells and bustle of cardigans.

'Hi!' Amanda said, surprised. 'What's all this?'

Marlene covered her in kisses as the women bandied her back onto the sofa. Grace eyed her project, a half-finished duck for a customer from Leeds, who had come to the fair. 'Looking good this, Amanda dear, you are getting better all the time.'

Amanda smiled, pleased with the endorsement. 'Thanks, but how come…?'

Grace grinned at her. 'We have our club, remember? Ben said that we could use his house, till your shop is done. That way you don't lose any money, and we don't miss out on our gathering.'

Amanda couldn't believe it. She flushed as she thought of Ben; he had literally turned his life upside down for her this week, and she was moaning because he wasn't throwing her over his shoulder and racing her upstairs. She made a mental note to thank him that night. The ladies were all chatting away, getting themselves set up, so Amanda settled back onto the sofa, and let the chatter wash over her. She had missed their company, and was so glad they came.

* * *

It was getting dark by the time Ben arrived home, and he mentally scolded himself for leaving Amanda alone so long. The truth was that he was so busy playing catch-up at work that he had lost track of the time, and he knew that the girls would have kept her company earlier in the day for their group. By the time he had called in at the market for some groceries and wine, it was after six and the mid-August sky was beginning to dim—a sure sign that the September change was on its way. Turning off his engine, Ben looked at his house, all lit up and looking homely, and grinned. It was so nice to come home to company, especially since that company was Amanda. In truth, Ben was getting very comfortable with her being there, and he was secretly pleased when the builders at Baker Street had said that the work would take another week. He was in no hurry for her to move back home, and he saw no problem in her working from his house in the meantime.

Opening the door, he was greeted by the smell of tomatoes and garlic, and he took a deep sniff. Walking through the house, he saw that every room was immaculate, all of Amanda's work had been put into neat boxes at the side of the kitchen table, and candles were lighting up various surfaces in the rooms. Soft music was playing in the kitchen, and he walked through, bags in hand, to see Amanda stirring something on the stove. Her hair was pinned up neatly to her head, and she was wearing a simple black shift dress, together with black flats. He smiled as she turned to look at him, wooden spoon in hand.

'Hi!' she said, grinning. 'Here, taste this!' She thrust the spoon into his mouth before he could protest, and his taste buds were assaulted by a gorgeous Bolognese sauce.

'Um, yum,' he said, licking his lips. 'Dotty does it again!' He winced as she swatted at him with the spoon.

'Cheeky, I made this myself!'

Ben laughed, passing her the wine. 'Good job I got this then, eh?'

Amanda opened the wine and started to dish up. Turning to the table, Ben saw that she had set it for two, complete with candles and napkins, and his heart did a little jump. *I could definitely get used to this*, he thought as he ran upstairs for a quick shower and change.

* * *

The meal was a success, even if Amanda did say so herself. Even the kittens ate the leftovers, which Ben said was the true test of a good cook. 'If the pets don't eat it, run,' he said, laughing.

Amanda sniggered, taking a gulp of wine. 'Hey, I am not the best cook, but I wanted to do something to thank you for everything you have done.'

Ben shrugged her off. 'Any time, it's been lovely having you here,' he said honestly.

Amanda winced. 'Another week though. You will be dumping me out of the jeep doors in another seven days, mark my words.'

Ben shook his head, putting his hand over hers as he leaned in closer to the table. 'I mean it, I am in no hurry for you to leave, just make yourself at home.'

Amanda opened her mouth to speak again, but fell silent when Ben reached up his hand and ran his thumb along her lower lip. 'Sauce,' he said, answering the question she didn't ask. He put his thumb into his mouth then, sucking off the offending blob. Her breath caught in her throat, and she could do nothing but look into his gorgeous grey eyes.

'What can I say,' she breathed. 'I'm a mess lately.'

Ben put his hands on either side of her face. 'You seem pretty perfect to me,' he said, his eyes boring into hers.

Amanda's heart flip-flopped in her chest at his words, and she couldn't hold back any more. She couldn't keep living like this; she knew what she wanted. She had to know if she was kidding herself, once and for all.

'What are we doing, Ben?' she asked in a breathless whisper. 'I don't really trust my head at the moment, so I kinda need you to tell me. Do you want this?'

She couldn't hold back any longer, she moved to stand and brazenly went to sit on his lap at the table, her hands shaking as they wrapped around his thick muscular shoulders. Ben pushed back his chair and caught her in his arms, pushing her body onto his. She straddled him on the chair and felt his hands run up and down her back as she lowered her lips onto his. She could taste the remnants of their meal on his lips, with an undertone of mint, and she settled into the kiss, flicking out her tongue to meet his. They kissed for what felt like forever, entwined in each other's arms, both of them reluctant to let go. It was some time later, when her lips were swollen and tender, that they finally pulled away.

'Wow,' she said, suddenly feeling like a crazy teenager.

'Wow indeed,' Ben echoed, as he looked at her, daft grin emblazoned on his face.

He leaned in again, and Amanda felt the heat building deep in her belly, her face flushed and red hot. She needed to keep her head, she didn't want to rush this, but one more minute and she would be lost forever in his arms. *Too soon, take it slow*, she thought sadly, maddeningly. This was too special to be rushed. She broke off the kiss, using every inch of her willpower, and smiled at him ruefully, before planting a soft peck on the tip of his nose.

'I had better turn in,' she said reluctantly. In truth, she was tired, but it was more to do with not jumping his bones like a polecat than getting a good night's kip. She had been here before, and wasn't in any rush to get hurt again. She sensed that Ben had the same hesitation, which only made her want to pull back all the more. She wouldn't be able to take hurting him too, not after getting to know him. They had already agreed that this shouldn't happen, and now they were here. It needed to be right, for both of them. The thought of not having Ben in her life chilled her to the core.

Ben dropped a kiss on her lips, grabbed her hands

and helped her to stand up away from him. 'I have a suggestion, if you don't think I am being too forward?' His voice trembled as he spoke, and Amanda was suddenly afraid of what he was going to say. *Would he ask her to sleep with him? She longed for him to ask, but silently hoped that he wouldn't. She knew, if he asked, she couldn't tell him no, but telling him yes would open up a whole other can of worms.*

'Would you stay with me tonight?' he asked, and her heart sank. 'Look at me,' he asked, and she looked into his eyes. 'I meant to sleep, nothing else. Truth is, I have been wanting to do that all week, but I didn't want to hurt you, after your knock.'

Her heart skipped as she looked at him, asking her to sleep beside him in the same bed. She smiled. 'I would love to, Ben.'

He grinned then, his teeth catching his lip a little as he smooched her again.

They turned out the lights and headed for Ben's room, arm in arm. 'One thing though,' Ben said, whirling around to face her, a serious look playing across his features.

'Yes?' she asked hesitantly.

Ben kissed the back of her hand as he opened the door. 'I wear Batman pyjamas, so no mickey-taking, OK?'

Amanda giggled and let him lead the way. If that was the only thing she had to worry about discovering, she could live with that.

* * *

The next morning, Amanda woke up in Ben's bed and reached across the sheets for his form. She felt nothing but pillow, and realised that he wasn't there with her. She flipped onto her back, nuzzling into the warm space he had left, remembering the night. They had spent the night locked in each other's arms, and despite her thinking it would be awkward, like a teenage sleepover, it wasn't. It felt as natural as breathing, and she had slept like a rock when she had drifted off. In fact, she realised, she hadn't had one nightmare since she had been staying here. She stretched, enjoying the comfort of the bed.

The room was neat, painted in muted blues and creams, and the sheets still carried the scent of his aftershave. She resisted the urge to bury her head into them and inhale the smell. Hearing movement in the kitchen downstairs, she quickly brushed her teeth, ran a brush through the bits of hair she could get to and went downstairs, still wearing her wrinkled PJs. Rounding the corner into the kitchen, she spied Ben and her blood ran cold. She stopped dead, watching him. This Ben wasn't a Ben that she had seen in a while, and this imposter was light years apart from the kind, gorgeous man she had shared a bed with last night.

He had his back to her, dressed in tracksuit bottoms that showed off his sculptured behind, and a tight white running top. His hair glistened with sweat at the nape of his neck, and he was studying a piece of post intently.

His gait was different though, and Amanda doubted it was just from the run he had obviously just been on. His shoulders were set square, and he looked coiled up, the opposite of the dancing, cooking man of the days before. A whole night away from the giggling, snuggly man of just hours before. *He regrets it*, she thought in horror, suddenly very glad that they hadn't done more than sleep and steal a few kisses. *He is mortified, obviously. He got up, panicked, and ran. Literally.* Amanda's heart dropped through the soles of her feet. She had used enough energy forcing herself to open up to the possibility of a future with him, but if he had doubts still, after everything, then that was a different matter.

She wasn't about to convince a man to go out with her. She turned to go back upstairs, but the squeak of the floorboard beneath her foot betrayed her location. He turned to look at her, and she nearly turned to stone from his gaze. A tortured expression shrouded his features, and then it was gone, hidden behind an unresponsive mask. Amanda was right; he was gone.

'Hi,' he said, a faint smile playing on his lips, never reaching his eyes. It was more like a grimace.

'Hi,' she said, not trusting herself to speak more.

'You sleep OK?' he asked, as though he had deleted forever the memory of her in his arms from his memory banks.

'Err, yes, thanks,' she replied, playing along.

'Good,' he said, throwing the post into the kitchen bin

beside him. Her heart broke when he looked back at her. He looked stricken, pale, and she couldn't believe that this man was the same one she had slept beside the night before. *I knew it*, she chided herself. *Nothing good would come from any of this, and you still jumped in feet first. What are you going to do, genius, move again? This is his town, his friends. You have nothing here.*

'I thought I would move back to Baker Street today,' Amanda ventured. She had to get out, lick her wounds in peace. She felt like her face was on fire, she couldn't bear to linger there if he didn't want her to be. She wondered what had changed, and wished things had been easier, cleaner, like they felt last night.

Ben turned fully then, frown lines scarring his face.

'Why?' he said softly.

She looked away from him. 'I have been here a while, disturbing your life, the shop won't be far off being finished now. I can cope, and you need to go back to work.'

'What about last night? Amanda, I...' He stopped dead, running his hands through his hair in agitation.

He opened his mouth to speak again, taking a step towards her, but she cut him off.

'Ben, it's fine. I don't really want to talk about this. I think we will both be glad of our own space. I'll go pack,' she said, and she ran up the stairs. Shutting the spare room door behind her, she sank to the floor, putting her head in her hands. She tried to stop the flow of hot tears that threatened to pebble-dash her flaming cheeks like hail, but in the end, she let them come.

* * *

Ben looked at the stairway, willing Amanda to come back down, to tell him she didn't want to go, but all he heard was the sound of the guest room door closing. Why had everything changed in the space of a few hours? This morning, when he woke up in his bed with her snuggled up to him, their pyjama-clad limbs entwined together, he was so happy. He watched her sleep. She was the most beautiful thing he had ever seen, and he finally felt like he was strong enough to take a chance. Her accident had woken him up, shocked him, made him realise he didn't want to have a life without her in it. He had realised that he had been sleeping through his life, going through the motions for everyone around him, but not really living for himself. In truth, he hadn't been living his own life for years.

When he left the village for university, he was so excited, full of plans of big city life. The reality was that he missed home. He had tried his best to carve out a life though, and before long he had almost forgotten that he was faking it.

He even had a group of friends to hang out with, who had no idea of his background. Tanya, his high-maintenance girlfriend, was far from the type of girl that he would ever go for, but somehow they worked. Yin and yang, she brought him out of his shell and he

kept her grounded. It was never a big love affair, but
the pair of them got on well enough, and with Adam, a
plastic surgeon and Ben's student roommate, they had
a laugh. Till the day that Ben got the call about his parents. That meant the party was over, and when Ben
emerged from his grief bubble a few months later, he
found himself married, living in his parents' house, running his father's business, with a wife who suddenly
hated him and everything about their new life. The only
thing they had in common any more was Adam. They
both ranted and vented to him about their marital problems, and with Ben's hours and commitments, he was
grateful when Adam offered to look after Tanya while
she had a break in the city. Ben never saw it coming, till
the day she turned up, Adam in tow, to get her things.
Their marriage was over, and Ben wasn't convinced it
had really ever begun.

Sighing deeply, he fished the gilded envelope out of
the bin, eyeing the calligraphy as though the letters were
serpents, ready to strike. Sitting down at the kitchen
table, he read the wedding invitation again, noting that
Tanya had reverted to her maiden name for the invite.
Classy as always, he thought to himself. It had eaten him
up when he got back from his run that morning, ready to
cook Amanda breakfast, to find it lying on the mat with
the normal junk mail. He had been so happy, waking
up with Amanda in his arms, and getting the news had
felt like a huge punch in the gut. His ex-wife, marry-

ing his ex–best friend, in London. God knows why they felt like they had to invite him. He had no intention of going—the shock and sheer brazenness of the pair had just enraged him. He had stared at it for ten minutes before he could even unclench his jaw enough to swallow. And now Amanda was leaving, and the perfect night he thought they had shared was tainted. She looked like she couldn't get away fast enough. He ripped the invitation into tiny pieces and scattered them back into the bin. Not for the first time, he wondered why everyone in his life left, and why he was always the one sat alone at the end of it.

* * *

An hour later, Amanda was showered, dressed and packed. She felt cheeky using Ben's hospitality, but she wasn't entirely sure what she would be walking into when she got home, or if she had any hot water. She started to pull her case to the top of the stairs, when Ben appeared, freshly showered and dressed himself. He looked awful, and Amanda wondered why he would look so drawn.

'I can help,' he said.

Amanda shrugged, pushing the handle to him.

'I'll bring the kittens later, when you are settled.'

Amanda nodded, grateful. She had been worried about taking the little guys back to a potentially dangerous place, especially for a couple of curious cats. She walked out of the house with Ben, deliberately not looking behind her for a last glance of the house. Ben followed behind, putting her bags into the back of the jeep and locking up. She opened the passenger door and got in before he had a chance to open the door for her, and she mentally congratulated herself on the petty show of stubborn independence. He got into the driver's seat next to her, and she turned in her seat to focus out of the window. The atmosphere was tense in the small space, and Amanda went to open the window, enjoying the breeze on her face as he drove towards Baker Street. They drove slowly through the village, and Amanda wondered whether she was imagining the slow pace. Did it just feel that way to her because she was dreading the journey's end? She rubbed at her temple, trying to dispel the headache that was developing.

'Are you OK? You shouldn't be alone, you know.'

Amanda looked at Ben, who was driving whilst watching her from the corner of his eye. 'I'm fine, Ben. I need to get home.'

Ben sighed then, a harsh sigh that came out like more of a huff. 'Amanda, your flat isn't finished, you are not well enough to work yet, the kittens are still at mine, you should have just stayed with me.'

Amanda frowned, wondering where this was coming from. 'I'm a big girl, I can look after myself.'

Ben snorted. 'It's not about looking after yourself, Manda,' he retorted, arms flexing on the steering wheel. 'It's about letting people help you.'

'I don't need your help,' she spat.

Ben's head whipped around in shock at her tone. 'Manda, what's the matter? What did I do?'

She shook her head at him, anger rising in her own hurt feelings. 'I don't need your help, Ben, or your pity. Let's just leave it at that.'

Ben recoiled as though she had slapped him. 'What are you talking about? I don't pity you, I—'

'Oh pur-lease!' Amanda shouted, throwing her hands up in frustration. 'Just leave it, Ben. I get it, OK? Game over.'

Ben said nothing as Baker Street came into view. Manoeuvring around a dark car parked outside A New Lease of Life, he slammed on the handbrake. 'Amanda...'

She didn't wait around for him to explain why he didn't want her. She jumped out of the car, heading for the front door, her hand jabbing wildly into her handbag for her keys. Ben slammed his door and followed her, catching up with her as she reached the front door. They collided together, and Amanda's bag fell to the floor. Kneeling down, she tried not to cry as she fumbled for her keys.

'Amanda!' he said again, touching her arm. She flinched and pulled away, feeling wretched now. Ben's face fell and she cringed at the hurt look he gave her, his grey eyes moist with emotion. 'Please, Amanda, I don't know what you think, but please, we need to talk.'

Amanda spied her keys on the step and grabbed for

them. Scrabbling to her feet, she looked down at him, sniffling already.

'Ben, it's fine, I—'

'Mandy?' A voice startled them both.

Looking to the sound of the voice, Amanda stared, floored with shock. Ben jumped to his feet and looked from the man to Amanda, and back again.

'Marcus?' she said.

He nodded, looking from Ben to Amanda, and back again, a confused look on his face. He was about to say something when the car door opened again, and Celine stepped out. She looked at Ben with a look that dripped pure disdain, and then levelled her gaze at her only child.

'Amanda Perry, what in God's name are you doing here?'

Twenty-Two

A New Lease of Life was positively buzzing. The builders were absolutely terrified, having to work under the eyes of such intimidating women, and they were pulling out all the stops to finish the job well, and finish it early. Agatha was pacing the shop floor, muttering things under her breath. Taylor sat in a chair nearby, nursing a coffee and watching the women plot and plan. Hetty and Marlene were cleaning up after the builders, much to their chagrin, and Grace was furiously knitting in a corner.

'What the hell are we going to do?' Agatha asked, swinging her arms wildly.

Taylor sighed. 'Agatha, there isn't much we *can* do. She has gone, we can't just drag her back.'

'Of course we can,' she scoffed. 'She has a life here now, friends, a business, a…a…Ben! And what about the community centre, she helped to save it. Mr Beecham is coming personally to reopen it once the roof is fixed. She needs to be here to look the beady-eyed buffoon in the eye like the rest of us!' She was turning purple now, gesticulating wildly.

Hetty's brows rose at Taylor's use of her first name, and Marlene sniggered, covering it up with a fake cough before Agatha noticed. Grace, still knitting away, huffed loudly.

'I just don't understand them, they are so good together. How can she flit off back to London with that flash git, and why didn't Benjamin even try to stop her! He was right there! In my day, those two would be on their way to their first wedding anniversary by now, instead of flitting from county to county willy-nilly.' She tutted as she dropped a stitch, and picked it back up with a determined flourish of her needles.

'Where is Ben anyway?' Taylor asked.

Agatha sat down next to him, exhausted from stomping up and down. He placed his hand over hers on her lap, and Marlene made a kissy-kissy face at Hetty, who snorted with laughter, belatedly disguising it as a sneeze. Taylor looked at the two and grinned, giving them a look that told them he was on to them. Agatha, holding his hand tight, was oblivious, very upset about the previous day's events.

'He is home, we think,' Agatha said, frowning. 'Dotty is on her way there now, to try to talk to him, and

Amanda's phone is switched off. If I hadn't seen her leave with my own eyes last night, I never would have believed it! I didn't like who she was with either, his eyes were too close together, and that suit, well,' she said, puffing her hair up with her hand as she spoke, 'it just wasn't classy. And why did he bring her mother? Something does not sit right with me, not at all.' Agatha remembered the look in the woman's eyes as they had briefly glanced at each other. Amanda was her double, but younger, softer, kinder. This woman was all airs and graces, hard edges to her face. Was Amanda in trouble?

Taylor looked at the women. 'We only saw her get into the car with them as we drove past, it could be for any reason, but I must admit, she didn't look her usual self, and Ben nearly took us out on the road. He must have been coming from there.'

The ladies nodded, and Agatha frowned at him.

'I just said all that, didn't I?' Taylor waggled his brows at her, which made her start to giggle, but she squashed it down to a ladylike clearing of the throat.

'What about the shop?' Hetty said. 'It will be ready to open again soon, what is she going to do, sell up?'

Taylor patted her hand. 'Hey, she will have to come back at some point, it's not over yet. We don't know what happened, and I can't see that she is the flighty type.'

The ladies all nodded, seeing the truth in what Taylor said.

'You are right, Sebastian, it's not lost yet.'

Dotty flounced through the door at that moment, causing Fred, the plasterer, to drop his trowel. The plaster splattered to the floor, just missing her clothes. She gave him a stare that could curdle milk, making him step away from her, before she flew over to the group.

'Ben's a mess, but he is not letting on, of course. He is a stubborn mule, just like his father.' She rolled up her sleeves, spooning coffee into the machine. 'He won't talk about it. He is locked in his office. He has even asked the locum to stay on a while, says there is nothing wrong, he is just behind on paperwork. He practically shoved me out of the door.'

'I told you, Sebastian, it's not good. How are we supposed to get them to talk when they are not even speaking to us?'

Taylor stood up. 'We make them talk to us. We don't give up. We keep trying.'

The girls all nodded, Grace even pausing the super stellar click of her needles to show her agreement.

'Right, plan of action then,' he said, wiping the blackboard on one wall of the shop clean and brandishing a piece of chalk.

'I have a question,' Dotty said. 'Who the heck is Sebastian?'

* * *

Amanda felt like she was playing dress up in her mother's clothes, as she hobbled down to the hotel reception in her high heels. They felt alien to her after so many months in flats and walking boots, and the skirt suit she was wearing felt like a body bag, suffocating her. As she reached the foyer, she saw Marcus there waiting for her.

He jumped out of his seat as she neared him, quickly sweeping his hair back in a distracted move. 'Good morning, sleep well?'

Amanda nodded. She hadn't, in fact. After fielding questions and admonishments from her mother for over two hours, finally getting her to shut up long enough to escape, she was exhausted. She was so relieved that her mother hadn't insisted she stay with them, but apparently her father was 'too disappointed' to see her right now. Amanda couldn't have cared less. What did they think she had been doing all this time, running a meth lab in the Yorkshire Dales?

They had dragged her back her to sort out her mistake, and sort it she would before, as her mother put it, 'she put great shame on the great name of Perry'. Not once had her mother or father asked whether she was OK, or happy. Marcus was there the whole time, simpering to her parents. They obviously had no idea of what had gone on between them, and Amanda wasn't about to add fuel to their indignation.

The hotel room had been stuffy, and when she managed to open the window a crack for ventilation, the noise of the streets below had shocked her with its volume, so she had spent a night tossing and turning. She couldn't get the image of Ben out of her mind, his face when he realised that the man before them was part of her past. By the time Marcus had slipped and slid around her like the snake he was, telling her the firm needed her back, that the Kamimura contract was going south, and Amanda had managed to take the information in, she was numb. She had turned to see Ben looking at her. He had been standing behind Marcus the whole time, listening to the conversation, not saying a word, all the time having Celine glare at him like he was the Antichrist. Before she had even had a chance to process, Ben had made his apologies for intruding and left. He was as polite as ever, of course, being Ben, and Marcus and her mother sneering at him didn't even seem to register, but Amanda couldn't stop picturing the look on his face when he left.

'Good, good, well, we have a busy morning, so if you are ready?'

She smoothed down her skirt, eyeing him coolly.

'Fine, Marcus, but I don't see why they would want me back, they fired me, remember? How can I help sort the account, when I was the one who screwed it up? And what have you been saying to my mother? Why the hell did you get her involved in all this?'

'Did I tell you how glad I am to see you?' he said, shifting from one foot to the other as he walked beside her, struggling to keep up with the determined pace she kept as she strode out onto the street.

'A few times,' she said tersely, putting her hand up

to call a taxi. 'And I told you, I'm only here to set right what I did wrong, nothing more.'

Marcus nodded, practically falling over himself to stop the taxi that drove past, whilst agreeing with her like a nodding dog.

'I know, I know, that's fair enough,' he said contritely, and Amanda itched her palm, trying to ease the tingle she felt with the urge to slap him across the chops.

'You look great by the way, really different from last time I saw you.'

Amanda snorted at the clumsy compliment. 'Well, I am different, and you look different too.' She pointedly looked him up and down. He did look different, she decided, and not in a good way. He had gone downhill fast, like a politician once elected to office. His suit gaped at the bottom, the buttons struggling to keep his expanding belly within its confines, and he was so pale and clammy he looked positively green. He was looking at her like she had the power to end his world, and she wondered again how bad things must be at work for them to have called her back, especially after how things had ended.

'How's Angela?' she asked tartly, as a taxi saw her gesticulating and pulled in.

'Err,' he said, fumbling with his collar, which seemed to be constricting his neck, 'we are done.'

'Oh,' she said, oddly feeling a little bit sad for Angela, who had obviously harboured desires to be the first Mrs Marcus Beresford. She marvelled at how little she felt at all when she looked at Marcus, when he had been invading her dreams for weeks. Amanda thought back to the night the dreams stopped, and remembered Ben, his warm, protective, arms around her in bed as they slept, and her heart seized violently. Gliding into the cab, she looked across at the pudgy, shiny man before her and, once again, wondered why the hell she was here, and not with Ben. If only he had wanted her then the urge to run to London to put her ghosts to rest wouldn't have mattered a jot. She would have found the strength to fight against her mother, to stay with him, stand her ground. She leaned her head against the window, wishing the day ahead of her away.

* * *

Ben whanged his biro across the room, startling the kittens in their basket. He had brought them across from home to keep him company as he worked, or pretended to, and they had been unsettled all morning. Sighing heavily, he sat down next to their basket, which was on the comfy chair in his office. Sitting with his back against the wall, he sagged down into himself and smiled as the furry pair jumped onto him, purring instantly.

'At least you guys are pleased to see me, eh?' Pinky rubbed her nose against his hand, and he stroked her affectionately. 'Well, if your mummy moves to London, you might have some adjustments to make, girls.' Perky miaowed at him, as if she understood. 'I sure hope that doesn't happen though, I kinda got used to having you ladies around.'

He stroked both cats, thinking of the last time he saw Amanda. Something had happened that night, or that morning, to make her pull away from him, but he couldn't think of anything that could account for that, other than the fact that she just didn't like him as much as she did, and she regretted getting close to him. God knows, he had been waiting for the alarm bells to ring that night, but it had felt so perfect to just be with her that he had found himself happy. Happy, and falling for her. Hard. Something had happened, but when he had got that invite, he had been distracted, probably too distracted to notice how she was feeling. He wished to God he could have spoken to her for longer, sorted things out, but then the smarmy git and the ice queen from London had shown up, and things had fallen apart. He had got out of there, even though what he had wanted to do was knock the guy flat on his ass and bundle Amanda back into his jeep, away from him, back to his home. He had driven home like a lunatic, and spent the night obsessively checking his phone and drinking enough Jack Daniel's to give him the hangover from hell this morning.

He had gone straight back this morning, under the pretence of taking supplies to the dog groomer's, only to see a sign on the shop door of New Lease, stating that the shop would be closed for a few days as the owner was away. It was in Amanda's cute swirly handwriting, and he had known then. She had gone to London with them, with him, Marcus. He had been holed up in his office ever since, maintaining radio silence from the ladies in the village, who had taken to ringing him every ten minutes since dawn. He knew that they knew she had gone, but he didn't care to hear the details, or speak about the reasons behind them. He had lost, again, and was left with the animals as usual. Dr Doolittle had nothing on him. He could see himself now, fifty years on, grey-haired, alone, living with a menagerie of abandoned animals. A modern-day masculine twist on the old woman who lived in a shoe. The thought depressed him to his core.

He picked up the phone from his desk, viewing all the missed calls from the village women. None from Amanda, he noticed. He opened the text screen, scrolling the names, and stared at the blank screen. *What would he write? Hello? Are you OK? Come back?* He remembered what she had said when she was on drugs in the hospital. About her dreams, about him. Was it Marcus she was talking about? She had never really told him why she came here; maybe it was something bad. Maybe she was afraid of him. He shook his head. What an idiot. He had just driven off and left her with that man. Maybe he should have punched him after all. Steeling his resolve, he typed out a message and hit the 'send' button before he could second-guess his decision.

It was time to do something, and Ben had just decided that today would be the day to do it.

* * *

Amanda walked into the foyer of Stokes Partners at Law and marvelled at how little had changed. Smiling at the receptionist, she headed to the elevator, Marcus in tow.

They hadn't spoken in the taxi, and that suited her just fine. She was still feeling groggy, weak, and the travelling and lack of sleep had definitely taken its toll. She was relieved when Marcus took her straight to one of the large meeting rooms, which was empty, and shuffled off to get the Kamimura files. The contract was on deadline, and whatever work needed to be done, it was obviously important if they had called her in to sort out her failures, although she still didn't get why. Marcus had been in charge of the contract from day one. Her error had been helping him in the first place, and she had more than paid for that. What could she do now that Marcus couldn't?

She walked over to the window, taking in the London skyline. She remembered how much she used to love the views from these windows, watching the heart of England live and breathe below her as she worked away, day after day. Now she found herself feeling lost, longing for the view she had from her little flat on Baker Street, that looked down on the street below, and the fields, hills and meadows beyond. Marcus broke the silence as he bounded through the double doors, files and pens bundled in his arms. He dumped the lot on the table and headed over to the phone, ordering coffee and sandwiches from reception. Amanda said nothing, turning away from the window to look at him questioningly.

'No one else coming?' she said, as she registered that he had asked not to be disturbed for the day.

Marcus replaced the receiver and avoided her gaze. 'Er, no, we can do this together.'

'Marcus,' she said sternly. 'If you think that spending the day with you like old times is going to change my mind about you being a colossal sleazebag, you are in for a big disappointment.'

Marcus nodded, taking a seat in front of the files. Pulling out a chair for her, he looked at her earnestly.

'Mandy,' he started.

'My name is A-M-A-N-D-A,' she said, cringing at the name he used for addressing her. She flashed to a memory of Ben calling her Manda, and ignored the way her heart squeezed with pain. That nickname she didn't mind, and she didn't think that she would hear it again. 'I hate Mandy. Especially when you say it.'

Marcus sighed, pushing his hair back from his face with a tight fist. 'Sorry, sorry,' he said. 'I am trying, Amanda. Once this contract is done, I really think I can have a word with Stokes, get you back in. I hated the way you left, and I want to help.' He looked sincere for once. 'It's the least I can do.'

Amanda nodded then, walking over to take the seat

next to him, pulling it away slightly before she sat down. 'Fair enough. I suppose we can call a truce, till this is done at least.' Marcus smiled pitifully at her, and she gave him a sly look. 'Just try not to sleep with anyone in the meantime, OK?'

* * *

Several hours and a few curled tuna sandwiches later, Amanda was exhausted. She couldn't believe the mess that the files were in. Marcus had not done a thing since she had left, as far as she could see, and if the transfer and completion were going to take place on time, it would take a hell of a lot of work and a whole lot of faith too.

'Marcus, how can you have left it like this, to get this bad?'

Marcus reached for the coffee pot, pulling a face when he saw that it was long cold. 'I just got overwhelmed, my caseload as new partner is massive, and I was just blind to how bad things were, I suppose.'

'I feel sorry for you, really,' she said sarcastically. 'People would kill to be partner, and you are moaning. I don't even know how you got it anyway! You work part-time, if that!'

Marcus jumped up, coffee pot in hand. 'I'll go get some more coffee, shall I?'

Amanda rolled her eyes. 'Fine, make yourself useful, but we are not done here. Something doesn't add up, and unless you have been sleeping with Mr Stokes to get to the top, then you are up to something.'

Marcus made a weird squeak deep in his throat, and scuttled through the door. 'Don't go anywhere,' he pleaded with her as he went out. 'A lot of folk don't know you are back, and the questions will just waste precious time.'

Amanda sighed heavily. Great, stuck in this room with that weasel till the job was done. She suddenly longed for her chic little boutique and its freedom.

She rummaged in her handbag, reaching for her mobile phone. She had better check in with home, see how the shop and the cats were. She would be worrying everyone by now, and leaving Ben to look after her cats wasn't her finest hour. She hoped that Dotty would take them in till she could get home. She wondered what Ben was doing, and pictured him sitting at his desk at the practice, working away. She felt a pang as she remembered how she had lain in his embrace only days before, wrapped in his muscular tanned arms, smothered by his sweet, bristly kisses, and felt a tear drip onto her cheek. She missed him so much it hurt. She had never felt so herself as she had with him, and now, sitting here, firmly back in her old life, she felt trapped, and she didn't like it one bit. She put the phone, still switched off, back into her bag. She would wait till she knew when she would be coming back before speaking to anyone. She was desperate to know whether or not Ben had contacted her too, but she feared that if he hadn't her concentration would be lost for the day. Hope was a wonderful thing, until it was lost, and she wanted to cling on to it a little longer.

Getting up, she felt the pops and clicks in her back as she stretched, and she yawned loudly. *Where was Marcus with that coffee?* She decided to venture out of the meeting room, slyly dash to the kitchen to grab a cup. Walking into the corridor, she didn't see anyone. Glancing at the clock, she saw it was just after eleven— everyone would be firmly attached to their desks till lunch. She was just at the door to the kitchen when a voice halted her.

'Miss Perry?!' a surprised voice said. Whirling around, Amanda saw her old secretary Elaine standing there.

'Elaine! Hi!' she said, rushing to hug her. Elaine stiffened in her arms, and she realised that Elaine wasn't accustomed to this new, warmer, huggier version of herself. She giggled. 'Sorry, I didn't mean to startle you.'

Elaine shook her head, looking Amanda up and down as she grasped her hands. 'No, no, it's fine! You look amazing! Where are you working now? I tried to call, and I went to your flat, but you had left.'

Amanda nodded. 'I sold up, I needed a change.'

Elaine grinned. 'Well you look great, and listen, I tried to get in touch, I have something to tell you, something really—'

'Elaine!' Marcus said, coming out of the kitchen with a coffee pot in hand. 'Have you no work to do?'

Elaine scowled at him, and Amanda could have kissed her former secretary for her show of loyalty. 'It's OK, Elaine, Marcus is actually helping me sort things out with the firm.'

'Yes, yes, that's right,' Marcus said hurriedly. 'Hopefully Amanda will be coming back with us very soon,' he said, gripping Amanda's elbow and steering her back to the meeting room.

Amanda brushed him away, smiling at Elaine. 'Well no, we don't know that. I am not even sure I want to come back, but I want to make things right.'

Elaine opened her mouth to speak but Marcus grabbed Amanda again and pushed her to the door. 'Yes, well, we can work out the details later, but right now we have some work to do, and I am sure Elaine does too.'

Amanda glanced apologetically back at Elaine as Marcus practically catapulted her through the double doors. 'Sorry, Elaine, he is right, more's the pity, but we can catch up soon, yeah?'

Elaine nodded, looking through Amanda straight to Marcus. 'Oh you can bet on that, Amanda.' And with one last glare, she walked off.

Amanda frowned, reaching for the coffee pot that Marcus seemed to be trying to absorb through his skin with his tight grip. 'Marcus, let go!'

He released his grip, and looked at her as though he

was about to say something, but then thought better of it. He sat at the desk, and buried his head in a file. Amanda took a grateful glug, eyeing him over her coffee cup. *Men*, she thought to herself, *she would never understand them or their mood swings.* As the caffeine started to buzz through her system, she picked up a file. The sooner she closed this deal and finalised the contract, the sooner she could get out of here.

* * *

Dotty was just making coffee for a customer at the practice, something she often did when anxious owners were sat waiting for news, when her phone buzzed in the pocket of her trousers. Serving the customers, she waited till they were seated till she sat back at her desk and opened the message. It was from Agatha, with details of their train times listed. At their meeting, they had gone back and forth with suggestions and ideas, Grace's idea of a shotgun wedding complete with real shotgun being the worst, until they decided that if Mohammed wouldn't come to the mountain, then the mountain would saddle up and get on a train to London. Hetty had tracked Amanda's old firm down after scouring the internet, and had been put through to a woman called Elaine, who confirmed that Amanda was working there for the next few days. Everything was in place, they would be back within the day, and New Lease, being worked on by the builders, could stand without them for a while. Hetty suspected that the builders would actually be glad to be shot of them for a little bit.

The only thing that they needed to work on now was Ben, but Dotty hadn't been able to speak two words to him on anything apart from work, and he had planned his clinics so tight that he was working before she arrived and long after she left. She had tried to get his attention, but Ben had rebutted her at every turn, and time was running out. She was off for the day tomorrow, the day of the London plan, and she needed to make him see sense. She was still staring at the text, contemplating her next attempt, when Ben appeared next to her. 'Dotty, can you do me a favour tomorrow? I am going to London overnight, and I need someone to take the cats while I am gone.'

Dotty looked at him open-mouthed. 'You? You're going to London? Tomorrow?'

Ben raised a brow, frowning. 'Yes. Me. I am going to London for the night, and I need someone to look after the kittens.'

Dotty wanted to jump up and down on the spot with glee. *He must be going to get Amanda!* Composing herself mentally, she shook her head, trying not to grin. 'Sorry, Ben, but I can't, the girls and I have something planned. Going anywhere special?' she enquired as innocently as she could.

Ben wasn't listening though, he was dialling a number on his mobile phone. 'Mr Jenkins?' he said into the handset. 'I need a favour, if you could, please. I need someone to watch the kittens, as I am going away for a couple of days.' He nodded as Alf replied to him, and a flash of pain struck his face like a lightning bolt. 'Er yes, Mr Jenkins, Amanda will be away too.'

Dotty tried to concentrate on the computer screen in front of her as she heard the booming voice of Alf Jenkins through the phone, congratulating him on 'getting it together' with Amanda. Ben stood silent, and eventually thanked Alf and ended the call.

'Ben?' Dotty said lightly. He turned to her and Dotty could have broken her own heart for him. He looked devastated, and she knew it must have been hard to hear, when the truth was so much more uncertain. 'You OK, duck?'

Ben nodded slowly. 'I'm fine, Dotty. He is going to look after the cats. I better get back to work.'

He went back to his examination room before she could formulate a reply. Whatever Ben's plan was, she hoped it would work. She picked up her phone and fired off a group text, telling the others that Ben would be going there under his own steam. The ladies' excited replies all came back thick and fast, with a shotgun emoji from Grace, and she smiled at their enthusiasm. They decided that they would go to London all the same. They wanted to see Amanda too, and they had to be sure that she would come home. After all, leaving things to a man was never a sure thing.

* * *

The London sky hung like a drape outside the huge glass windows of the meeting room. Amanda was tucking into some pad thai, feet propped up on the table. Energy drink cans and empty cups of coffee littered the mahogany surface. It was well after 9 p.m., and Amanda was starting to long for her hotel room bed. Marcus was clueless, she knew that now. There was no way he would have been able to pull off this contract, and even though she had messed the paperwork up, filing the wrong forms, she had *still* done a better job than he had. She had no idea how he had been made partner, but she knew it wouldn't last long. It couldn't, the man had less legal knowledge than his ex-secretary, the boobalicious Angela, and that was saying something, given that the average pot plant had a higher IQ than her.

He was sat staring at her over a legal pad, chewing on a hangnail. She eyed him and sighed. 'I think we are about done. It's tight but it should be good to go before the board tomorrow for final checking.' Marcus huffed out a huge puff of air like a deflating balloon. She half expected him to whizz off around the room.

'That's great,' he said, smiling, relief obvious on his features. 'I can't thank you enough, I really can't. I will speak to Mr Stokes tomorrow after the meeting, tell him you helped on this, get him to think about taking you back. It will be great working with you again.'

Amanda flashed to a future with the firm, watching Marcus take all the glory as usual for her work behind the scenes, now as a partner of the firm, whilst she spent long hours working at her desk, making the faceless rich even richer with every transaction, every billable hour another hour lost of her own life.

'I don't think I want to come back,' she said before the thought had even formed fully in her head.

Marcus looked at her in horror. 'Not come back? But why? You love your job!'

'Loved,' Amanda retorted. 'Loved the job, till I made one mistake, albeit on a big account. I made one mistake after years of hard work, missed birthdays, weekends, holidays, and they bin me off. Just like that. Out the door.'

Marcus hung his head, not saying a word.

'I just can't forget that, Marcus. That's why I came. To put things right. Put this to bed and get my parents off my back. Once the account goes through, I can look Mr Stokes in the face, draw a line under the whole thing and move on.'

Marcus's jaw dropped. 'You want to talk to Stokes?'

'Yes, Marcus, of course I do. I will have to face him sometime, whether they want to take me back or not.'

Marcus paled. 'Sure, sure,' he muttered. 'Never thought of that.'

Amanda nodded. 'Yes, this needs closure. I can hold my head up high—I came, I fixed, I left.'

Marcus nodded weakly. 'I suppose. Let's just talk after the meeting, OK? You might change your mind yet.'

Amanda started to pack the files away, ready for the morning. 'I doubt it, Marcus, I actually have a life now, and I am not in a hurry to give it back to the rat race.'

* * *

The commuters on the Westfield to London King's Cross train might be forgiven for believing that they had stepped into Narnia the morning they encountered the Knit and Knatters of Westfield group. Taking over a corner of business class, the ladies were dressed in all their finery, ready to do battle in London. Grace, resplendent in cream and rose, was knitting away, the strand of wool coming as if from nowhere from a large bag at her feet. Hetty and Marlene were both embroidering, and Dotty was on the laptop, using the free Wi-Fi to plan the reopening of the community centre with Agatha. Mrs Mayweather, complete with bluetooth headset and Clarks leather shoes, was patrolling the aisles, talking to the caterers, clipboard in hand. Taylor was sat reading the morning paper, occasionally looking over the pages at Agatha and the girls, chuckling at the bemused looks of the passengers on the morning commute. The announcer signalled their imminent arrival at King's Cross, and the carriage heaved a mechanical sigh of relief. The girls hurriedly decamped, applied fresh lippie, aside from

Taylor, of course, and charged out of the carriage doors, ready to get to Stokes Partners at Law.

* * *

Amanda had had no sleep again, once again stuck in the stifling heat of the hotel room, and unable to bear the noise from the window outside. She had dreamed the night before too, but this dream was new. She dreamed that she was under the water again, and Marcus was still chasing her under the waves, but this time he was trying to apologise, begging her to stop and listen. Once again she charged through the blue depths, trying to hit the surface, when she started to see something above the water, hovering over the top of the ocean water she was immersed in. She kicked on, ignoring Marcus, paddling and thrashing to hit the surface, lungs burning, but the surface never seemed any closer. As she started to slow down, spent, she spied something coming through the water, reaching for her. As her eyes closed, she heard someone shout for her. She prised open her tired eyes and, with her last ounce of strength, she forced her arm up. Her fingers just touched the hand, her slender digits brushing against it as it grasped hers, when she woke up.

She sprang out of the uncomfy bed and wrestled against the scratchy sheets wrapped around her, throwing them to the floor and stamping on them.

'For God's sake, just leave me alone!' she said to the empty room. Scowling at the room, she gave the duvet another swift kick before heading to the shower.

Today was the day that the contract would be put to bed, and then maybe she could get back to her own, and put this whole thing behind her. She missed everyone, but it was the thought of Ben that made her stomach flip. She wanted to see him again, just one more time. At least then she could get some sign, some sort of peace, and who knows? Sometime, in the future, they could be friends. Amanda frowned at the thought, seeing Ben date, fall in love, marry? She couldn't bear it. She had to get sorted, no more living with a foot in two lives, she had to put those feet together and jump right in.

* * *

The atmosphere in the offices of Stokes Partners at Law was thick with tension. Vince Stokes was coiled like a cobra, and had been pacing the offices all morning. When Amanda arrived in the foyer, she could sense how on edge people were. Sadie, the head receptionist, was quietly crying in a corner whilst a work experience student, together with college name badge and terrified smile, was doing her very best to man the phones. Amanda was on her way over to see what was going on, when Marcus appeared in front of her. 'Amanda!' he said, grabbing her. 'What are you doing out here? We need to get you into the meeting room.' He started to push her to the stairs.

'Marcus, what are you doing? Why can't we take the lift?'

Marcus froze. 'Er, it's out of order, now come on, we need to get ready, the Kamimura meeting is soon.'

Amanda barely got time to put her hands up to open the door as he bundled her through it, before taking the steps two at a time up to their floor. She scarcely had a chance to draw breath before she found herself in the meeting room. Marcus shut the door behind him, hurrying to straighten up the files, which were lying haphazardly on the desk. Amanda looked over at him and scowled. 'Marcus, what the hell is wrong with you? You damn near broke my neck on those stairs, why are you trying to hide me?'

Marcus stuttered, and Amanda once again felt a 'what were you thinking' moment as she looked him over. Shaking her head, she brushed an errant strand of hair back into her bun and bit down the anger she felt. *After the meeting*, she told herself. *After the meeting, she could have it out with Stokes, clear the air, and go.*

Marcus was hovering over her now, jumping from one foot to the other nervously as she took a seat and double-checked all the paperwork. Amanda's nose wrinkled as a waft of stale sweat and bad aftershave slapped her in the nostrils. 'God, Marcus, you are a wreck! Will you bugger off! Go and get changed before the meeting, you can't see the other partners like that!'

Marcus sniffed his armpit, pulling a face. 'Sorry, I didn't sleep much last night. I won't be long. Stay here, OK?' he pleaded.

Amanda waved a hand behind her, eyes firmly planted on the account files.

Minutes later, the door went again. Amanda huffed impatiently.

'Marcus, there is no way you have showered, go sort yourself—'

'Amanda,' a hushed voice said.

She turned to see Elaine standing there.

'Hi!' She smiled, happy to see a friendly face.

Elaine came to sit next to her, putting a hand gently over hers.

'Amanda, I have been trying to speak to you for ages, since you left in fact. We haven't got long, he will be back soon, but here.' Elaine passed her a large brown envelope, furtively glancing at the door as she did so. She turned back to look at her former boss and smiled kindly. 'Read it quickly.' And with a quick squeeze of her hand, she was gone. *What was all that about?* Amanda thought to herself. Checking through the Kamimura files for the fiftieth time, she put them in a neat pile and stared at the envelope that Elaine had left. She somehow got the feeling that the contents of this envelope were important, and she braced herself.

Twenty-Three

Vince Stokes was in dire need of a holiday. The strong coffee he was mainlining that morning was making his stomach ulcer sizzle, and his long-suffering wife had told him, in no uncertain terms, that morning, that he had better book them a holiday abroad; an expensive, exotic holiday. When Vince had started to grumble about taking time away from the office, and the expense of jetting off, his wife had pointed out that wherever the holiday might be, it would be a darn sight cheaper than a divorce. Vince had stopped arguing right then and there, and told his wife to go to the travel agent's, and tell his secretary the dates. So this morning's meeting had to go well if he had any hope of getting any sleep or peace at all. Marcus, the new junior partner, had been prattling on for the past half-hour about the Kamimura account, and he hadn't spoken a word of sense in all that time. Vince was just about to tell him to cut to the chase, when the door flew open.

A smartly dressed woman stood there, a sheaf of papers in her hand. She took a breath and walked to the table. Stokes' face dropped when he registered who she was.

'Er, Miss Perry, you no longer work here, and we are in a meeting. If you need to discuss something with payroll, go and see them.'

* * *

Amanda ignored him, staring intently at Marcus, who looked like a terrified little rabbit, trapped on a moonlit road in the headlights of a truck. She wished for a second that she was a truck, a huge freight-carrying transporter, that could squish him under her wheels like the miserable little piece of roadkill he was.

Stokes stood up. 'Miss Perry, leave. Now, please, before I call security.'

She waved him away with her hand. 'I am not here to cause trouble, sir, I just wanted to show you and the other partners this. I have been here for the past two days, working with Marcus to get the Kamimura account ready for today.'

Vince exploded, banging on the desk with his fist. 'Marcus! What the hell are you doing? We can't have fired employees working on important accounts! Especially those who screwed them up in the ruddy first place!' He punctuated this sentence with a hearty jab of the finger in Amanda's direction. Amanda did not flinch, she kept her eyes trained on Marcus. 'And why the hell do you need her help anyway, you made partner!'

Marcus was looking from the partners to Amanda, back and forth, back and forth. Amanda took the opportunity to walk up to the table, thrusting the papers into Vince's hand.

'This, sir, is the paperwork that *I* did *for* Marcus, whilst he was on the golf course. You will see that the paperwork is done correctly, but these aren't the papers that were filed. The ones at the back are the ones that Marcus mistakenly filed, the ones *he* did. The ones with the errors on them.'

Stokes looked at the papers, a frown deepening the lines on his face as he flicked through the paperwork.

'You will see, sir, the mistake was his, not mine.'

She turned to glare at Marcus, who was now sunk into a chair, head in his hands. 'The truth is,' she said, addressing all the partners now, who were flipping through the papers with Stokes, 'I was doing a lot of work for your new partner, because he is, at best, a shitty solicitor and, at the worst, a coward and a liar.'

Stokes looked up at her, loosening his tie as he sat down. 'Why didn't you speak up sooner?'

Amanda sighed. 'Because, sir, I made mistakes myself. One being getting personally involved with this

Rachel Dove

snake,' she said, pointing at Marcus, 'and wanting to help him. I didn't realise until now what he truly was.'

Stokes formed a peak with his fingers, resting them on his nose, and was about to speak when they heard a commotion outside, and a well-to-do voice cutting through the others.

Amanda couldn't believe her ears. *Was that Agatha's voice? No*, she thought, *can't be.* The door flung open, and in walked the ladies, Taylor in tow. Amanda scanned the faces open-mouthed, before she realised that the one face she was looking for wasn't there.

Agatha strode across the room, taking in the scene. Seeing Amanda, she walked over to her. 'Sorry to interrupt, Amanda darling, but we wanted to have a chat with you.' She came close and whispered to her, 'Close your mouth, my dear, you are not catching flies.'

The women all stood behind her, waving and looking around the room. Amanda couldn't quite believe the sight, her two worlds had collided in more ways than one. She was about to apologise for the intrusion when Mr Stokes spoke again. 'I have no idea what is going on here, but we have a contract to close, and I need my meeting room back in some semblence of order. Ladies, if you don't mind.'

Amanda went to follow the girls out, together with a very amused Taylor and a very put out Agatha, who was biting her tongue so much it was nearly hanging off, when Marcus whined at her side. 'I'm sorry, Mandy, I really am.'

She froze, setting her shoulders tight. Turning to look at him, she clenched her teeth, drew her fist back and punched him square on the nose. The room exploded. The partners were shouting for security, Taylor was bent in half on the floor, slapping his thigh with shaking laughter, and Marcus screamed. The man actually screamed as he hit the deck. There he lay, a crumpled, sweaty, stinky wreck of a man, bawling like a baby and clutching his bloody nose. The ladies all laughed and left the room.

Agatha tapped Amanda on the shoulder and whispered, 'Well done, dear, nice right hook too, I must say.' She grabbed Taylor's arm with a good-natured tut and stood by the open door.

Amanda took one last look at the man who had haunted her dreams, and squashed down the laugh that bubbled deep inside her. Instead, she smiled at him. He looked even more terrified as he registered the fact that his attacker was now grinning down at him like a maniac.

'I just want to say, Marcus,' she said, smoothing her hair back, ignoring the pain in her hand as she did so, 'thanks.'

Marcus whimpered. 'Thanks?' he echoed, confused.

'Yes,' she said, smiling serenely now. 'I owe you thanks. If you hadn't tanked my career to further your own, or cheated on me with that stick insect airhead of a secretary of yours, then I never would have left. I never would have left London, started a new life and made these friends.' She pointed with her good hand at the people watching over her at the door, and they all smiled supportively back. Marlene gave Marcus a sarcastic wave; Dotty and Hetty ignored him. Grace gave him the finger, which made Amanda giggle. 'These people are more genuine and caring than I ever thought possible, and I thank you for being such a git that I left, and met them.' Her smile faded a little now, thinking of Ben.

Unseen by her, Dotty moved away from the group and pulled out her mobile.

Amanda turned to the room. 'I thank you, gentlemen, for the opportunity you gave me working here. Goodbye,' she said, closing the door behind her.

'Well done!' Taylor said as soon as the wood connected. 'That was bloody brilliant!' He grabbed her arms and did a little jig with her.

The women all spoke at once, asking questions, messing with her hair (Hetty), and telling her how much they had missed her. Amanda laughed, trying to take in all the voices and excitement. The door opened again and suddenly Vince was in front of her. Amanda grimaced as security also came from the lift, and she prepared herself for the embarrassing walk of shame to the foyer. At least this time she had no desk to clear, she thought to herself.

'Miss Perry, I feel I owe you an apology,' Vince said, putting a hand out to the security guards to halt their progress. Amanda's jaw dropped, and Agatha quickly pointed a slender finger and closed it again, chiding her with her eyes. 'We were misled with our choice, and we won't be making that mistake again.'

He motioned again for security to come, and after a whisper in their ear, they were dragging a bloody, snot crusted, snivelling Marcus to the stairs. Marcus didn't even resist, he just sobbed, so loud he could still be heard several flights down. Stokes focused his eyes back on Amanda. 'We have a deal to finish, Miss Perry, and the clock is ticking. Help us finish what we started? I will pay you, of course.'

Amanda nodded. 'Yes, Mr Stokes, I will be in shortly.'

Mr Stokes nodded, glancing at the women behind her and giving a barely perceptible nod. 'Excellent swing by the way,' he muttered, as he closed the door.

Amanda fist bumped the air. 'Yes! Did you hear that, girls? I get to finish this whole thing, put things right!'

She grinned at the women, who grinned back weakly. Agatha, never one to beat around the bush, asked what the group was all thinking. 'Is this what you want, Amanda dear, to come back and live here?'

Amanda thought for a moment, and took a seat on one of the chairs nearby. The women all moved in close, eager to hear. *Did I want all this back*, she thought to herself. *I could work in law again, now my name is not mud. I could just come back, slot right into my old life. My parents would be over the moon.*

She looked at the faces of the people she now considered family, and shook her head. 'No.' The girls all looked so relieved, it tugged at her heart strings to think they cared whether she stayed in their lives. Taylor whooped for joy, grabbing Agatha by the shoulders and kissing her passionately. Agatha swiped and batted at him a couple of times, but then kissed him right back, just as passionately, raising one leg behind her demurely.

Amanda motioned to Hetty, astonished. 'What have I missed!?' she said.

Hetty rolled her eyes and put a finger to her lips. 'Secret, remember?' she whispered as the couple smooched on unawares.

Amanda laughed out loud, till she caught sight of Dotty, who was lingering in the back.

'Dotty,' she said, cuddling her. 'Er...how is Ben?'

Taylor and Agatha stopped puckering up abruptly. Dotty smiled thinly, and Amanda suddenly had a bad feeling.

'Has he not been in touch?' Grace asked. 'Have you not seen him in London?'

'In London?' Amanda echoed. 'No, I haven't spoken to him, why would he be here? Did he...?' *Had he come to London to find her, bring her home?* She wished that were true. Dotty took her arm, sitting in the next chair to her.

'We thought he was coming to London to see you, but I just spoke with him on the phone.' Dotty smiled sadly. 'He is in London, but he isn't coming here. He didn't mention it, and he doesn't know that we were coming. He is at a veterinary conference somewhere.'

Amanda's heart dropped through her feet. That was it then, she admitted.

She couldn't blame him really, he was pretty clear the morning after the night they spent together, he wasn't interested. This shouldn't even come as a surprise to her, but it still felt like a sucker punch to the gut. She had hotfooted it to London with another man, and instead of being fit to be tied in a jealous rage, riding his horse—or jeep—to London and staking his claim on his true love, Ben had gone to a convention for vets, a work event. Amanda nodded to herself, and stood up.

'I have to go. I have the Kamimura account to finalise, and Stokes will be back out in a minute to chivvy me along.' She looked at the carpet, willing her cheeks to stop flaming with the hurt and embarrassment she felt. She was not going to cry, not here. She had a job to do. Heading for the doors, she waved behind her. 'I'll see you soon, OK?'

Agatha stepped forward from the others, looking as forlorn as Amanda felt. 'We are due on the six o'clock train back to Westfield. Are you coming with us?'

Amanda nodded. 'Yes, Agatha, I am coming home.'

* * *

Ben felt just about as comfortable as a canker sore on a donkey's bottom. He was miserable, and having to put on a happy smile for a room full of people all day and all night was stretching the limits of his easy-going country manners. He stuck his finger discreetly into the neck of his silk tie, pulling it looser. He looked at the huge crowd of people, who were mostly unfamiliar faces in the great hall of the hotel, and asked himself for the fiftieth time why he was even there. A waiter passed and he grabbed at a glass of champagne, tipping most of the contents down his throat in one gulp. He adjusted his cuff for something to do, and was just debating whether to slip out when he saw them. Or rather he saw her first. She was hard to miss, with her Day-Glo fake tan and over-the-top white dress. She was sashaying around the room, talking to small groups of people, one hand resting on the forearm of her companion. Steeling himself, he drank the rest of his glass before dumping it on a side table and walked over. She saw him then, and whispered into her partner's ear.

He walked up to the duo and smiled. 'Hello, Tanya.'

Tanya grinned at him nervously, and he noticed how she squeezed her hand tight around her companion's arm. 'Hello, Ben, we are so glad you could make it.'

He nodded, noticing that their exchange was attracting some attention. 'I wouldn't miss it. You look lovely, by the way,' he said, nodding at her over-the-top pouffy wedding dress. She actually looked like one of the knitted dolls his mother used to make from old Barbies, the ones that sat on toilet rolls as decoration, but he kept that thought to himself. He reached out a hand and offered it to the man beside her.

'Adam,' he said, shaking the hand of his ex–best friend, the one who his wife had left him for. 'Congratulations to both of you.'

Adam looked shocked, and took his hand, shaking it eagerly. 'Er, thanks, thanks a lot,' he said, still shaking his hand fervently. Ben laughed and pulled his hand away. 'Thanks for coming, Ben, it really means a lot that you came.'

Ben shrugged. 'Hey, water under the bridge, right?'

Tanya and Adam looked at each other. 'We are sorry, we want you to know that,' Tanya said, looking a little green, although it could have been the effect of the heavy tan under the lighting.

Ben nodded again, and smiled. 'I came here to tell you it's all forgotten, and to wish you all the best.'

Tanya welled up. 'Thanks, Ben,' she whispered.

The master of ceremonies stopped the music then, and announced the start of the speeches.

Ben flicked his gaze to the stage. 'You are both wanted.'

Tanya smiled, touching Ben's arm. 'Stay for some cake, OK? There are people here who will be glad to see you.'

Ben shook his head. 'I am not staying. I have to get back to Westfield. Work is busy, but enjoy yourselves, OK?' He put his hand on his old friend's shoulder, giving it a quick pat and then turned away.

Walking towards the door, Ben felt eyes on him and grinned. This had been a brilliant idea, he realised. When he had got the wedding invitation that morning, and Amanda had rebuffed him, he had been devastated, but he realised that he couldn't live with ghosts any more. He had come today to exorcise a few, and it felt great. He finally had some closure and the weight lifted from his shoulders was immense. He just wanted to get back to Westfield now, and talk to Amanda. If she was willing to listen. Dotty had texted him earlier, saying that she was coming home with them that evening, and he just hoped it was for good. Heading to the foyer, he decided to ring her, to see if she had plans for the evening. Noticing his phone was still on silent, he was just flicking to the call screen when he saw a Google alert on his screen. He had put Amanda's old firm on one, just in case the douchebag she left with had stepped out of line, and a notification pinged onto his screen. Standing outside the hotel, he clicked on it and waited for the page to load. It was about Marcus, but not what he had expected. Stokes Partners at Law had issued a press release, stating that Marcus Beresford had been fired for immoral dealings within the company, and they had announced a possible replacement. Ben froze when he read further.

Marcus Beresford is now no longer working for the law firm, and the legal world is abuzz to find out who will take the coveted partner position. A close source to the senior partner, Vincent Stokes, has stated that Amanda Perry, former employee of the firm, has today finalised the Kamimura six-figure deal and is the front-runner to return to London to take the spot. Mr Stokes declined to comment on Mr Beresford, other than to state that Miss Perry was a valued asset to the firm, and they hoped to make an imminent announcement.

Ben thrust his phone back into his pocket, motioning for the valet to bring his vehicle. That was that then. She had got her life back, got rid of Marcus, and come out the other side. He was happy that she wouldn't have to deal with Beresford again; the thought of him being near her made him feel sick, but now she would leave anyway. What was there to keep her in Westfield, after all, if she had a high-flying job to go back to? Ben took the keys from the valet and slumped into his seat. As usual, the woman in Ben's life was leaving, and he was left behind. Firing the ignition up, he winced as Kings of Leon started to play through the CD-player. He clicked it off and pounded his fists on the steering wheel. He pulled out his phone and dialled a number. A male voice answered after two rings.

'Nigel?' Ben asked. 'It's me, Nige, Ben Evans. Hi, yeah, mate, I'm fine. Listen, you know what you were saying the other day, about needing a new partner for your practice? I might have a proposal for you.' Ben listened to the voice on the phone, swallowing to try to dislodge the huge slab of pain that sat on his chest and choked his voice. 'I am here actually, in London. I can meet you in twenty minutes.' He tapped a postcode into his satnav as the voice spoke on. 'Got it,' Ben said, his voice monotone. 'I'm on my way.'

* * *

Amanda nodded to the builders as they pulled away from A New Lease of Life. She didn't know who was more relieved, her or them. When she had arrived back from London late last night, it was all she could do to keep her eyes open on the drive from the station to Agatha's mansion.

The train journey had been sombre at best, the ladies all seemed deflated and lacklustre. Taylor and Agatha had sat quietly to one side, whispering to each other animatedly as they sat arm in arm. Amanda, sitting across from them, next to Dotty, couldn't help but stare at the pair. They looked so natural with each other, so happy and comfortable in each other's company it made her want to sob. She was happy for them, finding each other finally, and she was glad more than ever that she and the girls had done their matchmaking. She knew that the women were all quiet because of the other match-making project that they had tried, and the failure of it hung around the carriage like a shroud. Even Grace's knitting speed had decreased, and every time she looked across at her, she was focused on her needles, a deter-mined look on her face. Dotty had clung to her side since they set off, and she now sat next to her, one of Amanda's hands clasped into her own as though she feared Amanda would disappear or bolt from the train window if she let go. She said nothing though, enjoying the comfort and reassuring warmth it provided.

Dotty kept checking her phone discreetly from time to time, slipping one of her hands into her pocket, the other still clinging to her travel companion. Every time she checked, Amanda had to look out of the train win-dow to avoid the questioning looks from the women as they searched Dotty's face for an answer to a ques-tion not put into words. And every time, Dotty gave a tut, a sigh, or a shake of the head. Looking at the trees and buildings whizzing by her window, Amanda tried to ignore the stabbing pain in her heart, knowing what those gestures meant. Ben wasn't interested. He wasn't tearing up the motorway to get to her, risking a ticket to speed through the lanes to claim her love. He was at a conference, mingling with fellow professionals, quaff-ing drinks and appetisers as they discussed the cost of medicine nowadays and the latest *Supervet* episode on TV. She was suddenly acutely glad she had left her phone switched off.

Once back at Agatha's mansion, Amanda showered and dressed in a nightgown she had borrowed from Agatha. The Westfield dowager had brooked no refusal at her offer to stay over, and Amanda had taken one look at Taylor's kind face and nodded. A New Lease of Life was all but finished, but she found she was in no hurry to return to an empty flat. She lay in a four-poster bed in one of the guest rooms, watching the shifting light change through the thick embroidered curtains at the window. She reached for her phone and turned it on, looking at the screen as it powered up. The blank notifications screen mocked her, and she finally turned it off petulantly and stuffed it to the bottom of her case. Her parents had obviously heard then, she was betting that their cold shoulder would last a while yet, and there was no word from Ben. Throwing herself back onto the bed like a sulky teenager, she pounded the pillow a little, taking out her frustrations, before sleep finally claimed her.

* * *

It felt like she had just closed her dry, gritty eyes when Taylor knocked at the door with a steaming pot of coffee, and now here she stood, cases beside her, back at A New Lease of Life. She looked around the place she had built and smiled at the warmth and security she had felt when walking in that morning. The builders had finished early, and had done an amazing job. The fresh paint smell was a comfort, and she loved how good it felt to be home.

When Vince Stokes had offered her the partnership, after they put the Kamimura account to bed, she had turned it down, and it wasn't until this moment that she was utterly sure she wouldn't regret her decision down the line. Being here though, back in Westfield, was the happiest she had felt in a long time. She just wished she could tell Ben, thank him for helping her, for being there, for making her New Lease of Life truly special. Sighing, she went to put the coffee machine on, taking her bulging order book with her. The girls would arrive soon, and she had a lot of work to do.

* * *

Dotty Arbuckle was one of the most determined, stoic and kind women that anyone should ever encounter, and today was no different. Walking into the practice that morning, she strode around the building, flicking on lights and computer screens, opening blinds, preparing for the day ahead. She had noticed that Ben's jeep was in the drive as she walked in to work, and the relief she had felt at seeing that hunk of metal had been indescribable. Ben was home, and her relief and happiness had been immense.

Those emotions were now replaced though, she realised as she flicked on the kettle. She looked on Ben like the son she never got to have, and she was one surrogate mother who was mightily ticked off. She was heading for the consulting room when she heard muffled voices, and realised that Ben was already at work. She heard the locum's voice in reply to something Ben had asked, and she huffed at the thought of having to wait till they had a lengthy handover before she could rip into him.

She walked into his office and opened the curtains, frowning at the sea of junk food wrappers and dirty coffee cups that littered his normally clean and tidy desk. *What a pig!* she thought to herself, thinking of the locum, sitting in Ben's working space, stuffing his face with sugar and caffeine. She was just clearing the cups when she saw some papers on his desk, and froze. She jumped back in shock, dropping one of the cups on the floor, and winced as she saw a brown stain appear on the carpet, complete with mouldy skin.

Ben's voice called out from the next room. 'Dotty, that you?'

Dotty grabbed the papers, stuffing them into her pocket before she ran from the room. She heard the consulting room door open, and she dashed past, racing past reception, grabbing her bag on the way.

'Er, yes, it's me, dear. I am just nipping out, I need some carpet cleaner. Shan't be long, kettle's boiled!' She dashed out of the practice before he could answer, and she power-walked up the road.

* * *

Amanda was sitting with the girls in the shop, coffee cup in hand, Pinky and Perky on her lap, when Dotty collapsed through the shop door. The kittens, who had not left her lap since Alf Jenkins had dropped them off, turned to the door in unison before stretching and re-curling up, accustomed now to the drama of the group.

Agatha, who had just arrived with Taylor, looked up from her secret talk with Hetty astonished at Dotty's dishevelled and rather sweaty appearance. 'Good God, Dotty, whatever is the matter? You look like you ran here!'

Dotty, bent over the back of Grace's chair, huffed and puffed, clutching her side at a painful stitch.

Grace tried to push her off, poking at her with a knitting needle. 'Dotty, gerrof! You are dripping sweat on my knitting!'

Dotty fought for breath, and Amanda, after carefully extricating the cats from her lap and putting their disgruntled furry bodies into their basket, went to get her a drink of water. Dotty was trying to get her words out, rather unsuccessfully, waving a bundle of papers in her hand.

'Meeting…today…soon…practice…Ben…'

Amanda brought her water, her face now a picture of concern as she heard Ben's name. 'Ben? Is he OK? Is he home?'

Dotty nodded, glugging at the water like it was a desert oasis. She took the hanky that Hetty offered her and wiped her brow frantically.

'Is he OK?' Amanda tried again, starting to panic now.

Dotty shook her head, sharp breaths pushing out of her. 'Practice... Ben...leaving!' She threw her hands up, glad to get a relevant word out at last.

Taylor stood and took the papers from her hand. 'He's leaving? He can't be.' Taylor's face changed from confusion to realisation as he scanned the pages. 'I don't believe it. He *is* leaving. Today.'

'What!?' the women all said in unison.

Dotty threw her hands up in a 'that's what I was trying to tell you' pose, before flopping down into a nearby chair.

The only person who didn't react was Amanda. She was stood at the cats' basket, stroking their fur softly, delicately, with her back to them. The ladies all looked at each other, unsure of what to say. This was the polar opposite of what they had dreamed of. Agatha nodded to them all, accepting silently the role of leader once more. She walked over to Amanda, putting a hand on her shoulder.

'Are you OK, dear?'

Amanda turned to her, and Agatha realised that she was holding back tears. Her eyes were glassy and moist, and she was blinking rapidly. She swallowed the lump in her throat and nodded. 'I am fine, don't worry. It's nothing to do with me, is it? We were just friends really, and I am not even sure we are that any more.'

She walked over to Taylor, taking the papers from him and reading them herself. It was true, he was leaving. The papers were a printout of an email, confirming a place as partner in a new state-of-the-art veterinary facility in London, and the contract started that day. She couldn't believe it. She thought she knew Ben, and this didn't suit him. It was out of character. She never thought he would want to leave Westfield, let alone live in London. She realised that the Ben she knew might not have existed at all.

Dotty had caught her breath now, and was shaking her head. 'He doesn't want to go, I know it. London isn't for him. He lived there before, and he came home. I think he is running away.'

Amanda turned to her. 'Running from what?'

'You, my dear,' said Grace, who for once had stopped her ever-moving needles. 'You.'

Amanda's shoulders sagged. 'It isn't me, Grace. He isn't interested, trust me.'

Dotty made a funny noise from her chair, and the others looked at her, goggle-eyed. She made the noise again and, for a moment, Amanda wondered if she had done herself an injury on her mad dash. The noise came again, much louder this time, and it was then that she realised: Dotty was crying. She started to walk over to her, grabbing an embroidered tissue box on her way, when

Dotty broke down, railing loud sobs and snorts. Agatha looked uncomfortable at the very emotional display, and nudged Taylor closer, as though he was the bomb squad sent in to defuse the wailing woman.

'It's just so sad,' Dotty said. 'I thought you were perfect for each other, and Ben has been so happy lately. Happier than I have ever seen him in fact.' She sniffed loudly, taking a tissue from the box and blowing her nose, producing a large trumpeting noise.

Agatha gurned and nudged Taylor closer still, hiding behind his broad back.

Taylor looked over his shoulder, rolling his eyes at her, and she poked him in the ribs, making him smile.

Amanda knelt by Dotty. 'Dotty, he obviously wants to do this, he is not the type of man to make a decision like this on a whim.'

She sniffed again, wiping at her eyes. 'You must hate us, pushing you towards a man you didn't even like.'

Amanda shook her head. 'I did like Ben, I do like him. I could never hate you.'

Hetty moved closer. 'But you didn't fancy him, did you? I mean, you didn't want to be with him—we got it so wrong.'

Amanda folded her legs under her on the floor, her legs aching from kneeling. 'No, that's not true,' she countered. 'I did fancy him, of course! Who wouldn't, he is gorgeous,' she said sadly, thinking of the way he smelled when she lay in his bed, wrapped in the scent of him. 'And he is strong, and kind, and when he smiles, he gets this little dimple in his cheeks, which is adorable, and—'

'Yes,' Grace said, cutting her off. 'But liking the cut of one's jib isn't enough. You have to get on, don't you?'

'But we did get on,' she replied, her voice getting higher. 'Not at first, granted, but we get on great now. He is so funny, he always make me laugh. He is clever too, so smart, and we like the same things and...'

'Ah yes,' Taylor said, moving closer, Agatha's head perched over his left shoulder. 'That's all well and good, but then the arguments start, and the things that annoy you, and then it's all downhill. Before you know it, you are bickering and *being poked*—' he looked at Agatha when he said this, who blushed '—and then it's all tears before bedtime.'

Amanda got to her feet. 'No! You are wrong, it wouldn't be like that with Ben, I mean, we bicker now, but it's all part of it, right? I can honestly say that being with Ben would be great. I know we would be happy.' The words tumbled out of her mouth before she even knew what she was saying, and she realised she was up on her feet, arms waving wildly, defending a relationship that didn't exist. She glanced at Marlene who was smirking at her.

'If all that's true, duck,' she said, grabbing her cardigan from the back of the chair, 'then what are we doing stood here?'

Amanda looked round the room, realising that she had been played into showing her hand. She raced to the counter, kissing the sleeping kittens on the way, and grabbed her keys. 'Come on then!' she shouted. 'Let's go!'

The women all shrieked and hollered, racing for the door. Amanda locked up, flipping the closed sign and throwing her keys into her pocket. Taylor ran for the car, opened the doors for the women and jumped into the driver seat. Within minutes, they were speeding off, Amanda in the front, willing Taylor to go faster as he sped through the country lanes.

'My phone!' Amanda exclaimed. 'I left it behind! Someone, call Ben quick!'

The women all looked around in panic. 'We left our stuff at the shop!'

Taylor felt his pockets and shook his head. Amanda groaned.

'Get us there, quick!'

Taylor shifted up a gear. All five women were squashed in the back, and the car lurched awkwardly through the corners, unaccustomed to the heavy weight. Marlene and Hetty were clawing and huffing at each other, as they fought for space, the occasional 'oof' and 'gerrof' coming out from the wall of bodies.

Amanda turned to check on them distractedly and was stunned to see them all, stuffed like sardines in the back. Agatha's face was slammed into the side window, and she was trying her very best to look ladylike and poised, which wasn't working out well. They spied some people from the village, setting up the banners and stalls at the community centre, and she gave them a regal wave as they sped past, leaving them open-mouthed. Dotty was curled in a ball, crocodile tears long gone, staring determinedly out of the front windscreen, and Grace was at the other side. She was doing her best to ignore the jostling women, and Taylor chuckled under his breath as Hetty admonished her for knitting. 'Grace, you loon, who brings knitting on a high-speed car chase? You poked me in the eye with your needle!' Grace shrugged, still focused.

'Oh wind your neck in, Hetty. I am doing a neckline, if I drop a stitch I am buggered!'

They turned the corner to Ben's street, and the car fell silent. All eyes fell on the driveway, and Taylor slowed to a stop outside his house. The driveway was empty, and Ben's jeep was gone.

* * *

Maisie and Buster jumped at their mother as she came through the door, looking decidedly wretched. Her normally pristine look was long gone. Her hair, normally coiffed to perfection, resembled a bird's nest, and her outfit was rumpled and askew from her cramped car ride. She sat down in the large room, cuddling her babies and lighting the already stacked fire. The dogs came to lie in front of it, in between the pair. Taylor came in after her, taking a seat in the chair opposite. 'Do you think she'll be OK? She was headed for the fell, I think, it can be a bit nasty out there when the weather turns.'

Agatha sighed.

'I don't know, dear,' she said honestly. 'I will call her later, see if she got home OK. I am sure that she just wanted some time alone.' She started to sort out her hair, pushing strands back into the clip she had worn that day, but in the end she gave up, pulling it out altogether and shaking her hair free.

Taylor looked at her. Framed by the firelight, hair a mess, heartbroken look on her face—she had never looked so hauntingly beautiful. He rubbed his hand down his jawline, feeling the stubble coming through, and felt for something in his jacket pocket.

'Agatha?' he said, smiling at her kindly when she looked at him questioningly. 'Whatever happens with Amanda and Ben, I want you to know, I love what you did for them both.'

Agatha snorted slightly, shaking her head. 'What? Breaking her heart? Pushing Ben out of the village? I should have left well alone, there is nothing worse than a silly old fool meddling in things she doesn't understand.'

Taylor stood and crossed the room to her. 'Hey, we'll have less of that talk, thanks. I happen to think highly of that silly old fool.' She smiled at him, reaching for his hand. He knelt beside her, and she ran her fingers through his hair, brushing his fringe back so that she could get a better look at his beautiful eyes. He looked different tonight though, and she recognised an unfamiliar emotion in his face. Fear.

He cleared his throat. 'In fact, I have grown rather fond of that fool. I love her, and I think I always have, ever since I was a boy, chasing a girl around a fountain.'

Agatha looked into his eyes, her own wide with surprise, and she saw the love burning behind them. She put her hands on either side of his face, dropping a slow, tender kiss onto his lips, which were as soft as always, and warmed slightly by the fire.

'I love you too, Sebastian Taylor,' she whispered. His expression said it all, and he claimed her lips for another kiss. Drawing back, he shifted slightly in his kneeling position. 'Get up,' she said, laughing. 'You will do yourself an injury sat down there.'

Taylor shook his head. 'I have something to ask you first.'

Agatha gasped as she saw he had moved onto one knee, and in his hand was a box. An open box, with the most elegant and understatedly pretty ring nestled within it.

'It was my mother's,' he said, pulling it out of the box. 'She always told me to save it for the girl I loved, and so I did.'

Agatha teared up then, and a single tear ran down her cheek. 'Oh, Taylor,' she said.

He tapped his finger on her nose delicately. 'I have told you a million times, Agatha, call me Sebastian.'

She laughed then, and more tears spilled out. 'Well, *Sebastian*,' she said, showing him her bare ring finger, where she had taken off the rings she once wore there some weeks ago, when she had realised she loved the man before her. 'I guess you had better call me Mrs Taylor then.'

Twenty-Four

Amanda headed back to Baker Street at a slow pace, walking like a condemned prisoner to their fate. The sun was setting and the air was crisp, the slight change in the air noticeable as the season started to change. September was approaching, and Amanda groaned inwardly as she thought of the dark nights that were coming. Summer would be a distant memory, and so would Ben. She had spent the day on the fell, remembering the day they had spent together there. When the sky had changed, and the rain had started coming down, she had considered lying there, waiting for a Willoughby lookalike on a horse to ride up and save her, but then she remembered how that had ended, and headed home to feed the cats. Now the rain was slowing down to a light drizzle and, as she turned onto Baker Street, she marvelled again to herself about how pretty it was. Heading to her front door, she remembered that her mobile phone was still switched off and languishing at the bottom of her bag, and made a mental note to check in with the girls, who would no doubt be worried by now. She reached for her keys, frowning when she saw the A-board had been left out again for next door. She was just picking it up to take into her shop for safekeeping from the elements, when she heard a voice behind her.

'Hi.'

The deep voice startled her, and she dropped the advertising board. It fell with a clatter to the floor, and Amanda cursed under her breath, her heart pounding with surprise. She knelt down to pick it up, flustered, and promptly banged heads with something hard. 'Ouch!' she said, her recovering injury smarting from the impact. Touching her head and rubbing at the healing cut gingerly, she looked up, ready to give a tongue-lashing to the stranger. The scolding dried up in her throat when she looked across, straight into a familiar steely grey pair of eyes.

'Ben,' she whispered.

'You're still here.' The question came out more like an astonished statement.

'What are you doing here?' she said, not registering his words.

Rubbing his own head, he stood up and offered her his hand palm up. She took it and immediately felt that all too comforting jolt of lightning run up her arm. She shivered despite herself.

'Sorry,' he said, as they stood across from each other. He didn't move to drop her hand, and she left it there, wrapped in his. He was so close that she could see the tiredness around his eyes. He had stubble on his chin, and, as he turned his head to her, she caught a waft of his aftershave. 'Are you OK? Your head, I mean.'

She nodded, ignoring the dull ache it produced. 'I'm OK. I didn't hear you come.' She looked behind him and noticed his car wasn't there. 'Where's the jeep?'

She locked eyes with him again, and his expression was confusing. He was looking at her so intensely it made her flush, as though he were trying to commit her features to memory. He glanced at her lips, and she licked them unconsciously, making his eyes widen.

He cleared his throat. 'I left it in the village. I was walking, and somehow I ended up here.'

She nodded. *What does that mean?* she wondered to herself.

'Oh, right.'

They stood in awkward silence, hands still linked.

'When—'

'Are—'

They spoke together, their words coming out all at once, and they laughed awkwardly. His eyes crinkled at the corners, and she resisted the urge to reach up and smooth them out with her fingers. The effort made her hands squeeze, and the hand around hers squeezed her back. She smiled at him, and his thumb started moving, tracing small circles on the skin on the back of her hand.

'You start,' she said.

He looked at her, a sad smile playing on his lips. ' I guess I just wanted to come here, I don't really know why. I didn't expect you to be here.'

Amanda frowned. 'Why, where would I be?'

Ben face was a picture of confusion, and his thumb stilled. 'I thought you would have left for London by now. When does the job start?'

Amanda realised then he must have heard about the offer from Stokes. She shook her head, marvelling at her own pig-headed determination not to call him. 'I didn't take the job. I am staying here.'

Ben exhaled loudly, as though he had been holding in his breath the whole time. His thumb started again, and he reached for her other hand. She let him, and took a hesitant step closer to him. She could feel the heat from his body now, and her own body responded, sending shivers up from the tips of her toes. Steam rose up between them, as the warmth radiating from them interacted with the cool rain around them.

'I thought you were gone,' he said, his eyes boring into hers. 'I have been trying to ring you all day. I wanted to talk to you, to say goodbye.'

Amanda's heart, which had been fizzing and bounding out of her chest, flatlined at his words. Her body went cold, the shivers turning into ice water. She looked away from him, down at the pavement, and pulling her hands from his, she folded them across her chest.

'Well, you can say goodbye now.'

Ben's face dropped, and an emotion she couldn't quite place passed over his features, and then it was gone. His jaw clenched, and she could see the muscles flex. They stood there silent for what felt like an age, the only sound to be heard was the crickets in the bushes nearby.

'Is that what you want?' he croaked finally.

She tightened her arms, hugging them close to her and stared at him. She could feel her cheeks burn, with anger and pain. *Don't cry*, she commanded herself. *Don't you dare cry.*

'It's not about what I want, is it, Ben,' she snapped. 'You made your decision.'

He flipped then, his face a mask of pain and frustration. He threw his hands into the air, and ran them through his hair aggressively.

'I just don't get you!' he boomed. 'What the hell do you want from me!'

She jumped at the volume of his voice. She had never seen him so angry, and his reaction fuelled her own outrage.

'Nothing! I don't want anything from you! Just go to London with your fancy new job, and leave me alone!'

Ben reared his head back as though she had slapped him. She clenched her fists by her sides, breathing hard.

Ben took a step towards her, his voice softer now. 'Amanda, I don't know how you know about that.' He scratched his head. 'I have a fair idea though,' he said, realisation dawning on him. 'But I am not leaving. My locum, however, left for London this morning. I recommended him for the post. It's not me with the job offer from the smoke.'

He reached for her hand again, and she snatched it back, still angry. He sighed and grabbed it forcefully, trapping it between his own. 'Look at me, Manda.'

She blinked back her tears, and forced her head, which felt as though it was weighed down, to look at him. He was shaking, she could feel the vibrations from his hands reverberate through her own, and she wondered if it was the light rain that was making him shiver, or something else.

'Manda, the morning after the night we spent together, I got a letter. An invitation actually.' He resumed circling his thumbs on the back of her hands, the rhythm sending little shocks round her body. 'My ex-wife got married. I was mad, and I don't think I handled it well that day.'

Relief coursed through Amanda, as she realised the reason for his behaviour that morning. *We are just as stubborn as each other*, she thought to herself.

'Then you left for London, and I thought that I had lost you. I went to the wedding, to get some closure.' Amanda raised her eyebrows at him. He nodded at her.

'It was good, actually. I have put it all behind me now. I actually feel better. I wished them well.'

Amanda squeezed his hand, and he squeezed hers back, taking another step closer to her. She felt his minty breath on her cheek, and she sighed audibly.

'I am staying here, Ben, this is my home now, and I can honestly say I feel happy for the first time in a long time.'

He chuckled. 'I hear you gave them hell in London. I read all about Marcus.'

She giggled herself then, remembering Marcus's face as he sat sniffling on the floor.

'I punched him,' she said, laughing.

Ben cracked out then, laughing with her with his low rumble, and Amanda felt elated to hear the sound again. He dropped one of her hands, and wrapped his arm around her waist, drawing her closer. She took her free hand and cupped his cheek with it, and he nuzzled into her, tickling her palm with his stubble.

'You look tired,' she whispered.

He nodded, his grey eyes gazing into her own. 'I haven't been sleeping well. You see, my bed used to smell of you, but that smell has gone now, and I want it back.'

She put her other hand up to match the other, and he smiled, wrapping both arms around her tight. The rain was getting heavier now, and a drop dripped from his hair down his cheek and over her hand.

'I missed you too,' she said to him breathily. 'The kittens do as well.'

'Well,' he said cheekily, 'I don't blame them, Dotty is a better cook than you.'

She swatted at him with an open palm, and he dodged her deftly, wrapping her arms around his back before pulling her close.

'I love you, Amanda,' he murmured. 'I want to wake up with that smell in my bed every day. I don't want to spend another day apart. I beg you, please give us a chance.'

'I love you too, Ben,' she answered, dropping a soft kiss onto the stubble on his chin. 'I think I always have.'

He broke into a grin, and brought his lips to hers. 'Be mine then,' he said, the rumble in his voice travelling through her whole body. She brushed her lips over his gently, looking into the eyes she loved so much. 'Stay with me, be my wife, love me forever.'

'Always,' she replied. 'I would marry you tomorrow.'

They kissed then. Soft, passionate kisses, kisses that defied time and obstacle, kisses that held a person to the earth itself, and spun it into a frenzy. The rain fell down around them, and neither even noticed.

* * *

When Amanda had said that she would marry Ben tomorrow, she didn't expect him to take her so much at her word, but here she was, less than two months on, sat in a wedding dress that the girls had designed and made especially for her. To say that they had outdone themselves would be an understatement, because the dress was exquisite. The shimmering ivory fabric pooled at her feet, swishing when she moved, and the heart-shaped neckline and fitted lace bodice flowed into long sleeves, making her arms look so long and elegant she felt like a runway model. She never wanted to take it off.

She sat at the lavish head table, watching the guests dance to the band, thanking the British weather once more for getting them this rare and beautiful October night. The rain had held off, the sun had shone and now the night was mild, warm even. She spied Mr Beecham, enjoying a sandwich with Hetty, and she wondered whether they had misjudged him too. The community centre was back open now, new roof and all, and was busier than ever. Looking out across the grounds of the Mayweather estate, she saw people milling around under the huge marquee, drinking, dancing, and having fun. Even Agatha was dancing, looking as regal and elegant as always in a light cream suit. Taylor was holding her in his arms, spinning her around the room. Their wedding was such a shock to the village that the after-effects were still being felt. Two weeks before, at the party they had thrown to celebrate saving the centre, Agatha had waited till the evening was in full flow before announcing that the night was actually a dual celebration. They were so in love it was a joy to see, and they suited each other so well it was hard for Amanda to think of them as anything other than a happy couple. Ben had given Agatha away, and she still smiled at the memory. Taylor had been best man that morning, and she was ridiculously grateful to have two such good people in her life, like the second mother and father she never knew she needed, the guardians of Ben, and the instigators of their happiness. Even her parents had come today, and her mother had even shed a tear at the ceremony, and seemed to like her choice of husband, especially since the events of recent months had come to light.

Ben came to sit next to her then, having danced with Dotty, who was like the proud preening mother, beaming from ear to ear. He sat next to her, kissing her till her toes curled. 'Are you OK, Mrs Evans?'

Amanda giggled, pulling him in for another huge kiss. 'I,' she said between kisses, 'am the happiest woman alive, Mr Evans.' He kissed her back, before he offered her a glass of champagne. They both took a sip, surveying their wedding reception.

'I have to say,' Ben said, grinning. 'These women of Westfield, they can do anything they put their minds to. This is stunning.'

Amanda nodded, looking across at Hetty and Marlene, who were sitting at a table nearby, giggling and guffawing at Mr Jenkins and some of the other men, who were doing their best to dance to a Rihanna song. Grace was sitting next to them, knitting as per usual.

She had even made a discreet knitting bag out of the same material as the chair covers, so it blended in. She caught Amanda's eye and held up her knitting, beaming. She pointed between the two of them, and then tapping her watch, tittered to herself and went back to staring at her needles. Amanda was confused for a moment, till she realised what she was knitting. They were only small, but the yellow booties were unmistakable as they took shape on her needles. She nudged Ben. 'Did you see that? I think Grace is knitting...'

'Booties?' Ben said, smirking and rolling his eyes. 'You don't know the half of it.' He took her hand into his and kissed it. 'My darling, they have been at it for weeks. I caught Dotty knitting a baby blanket at the kitchen table the other day, and she tried to tell me it was for the cats, and I caught Taylor in our spare room the other week. He said that Dotty had called him in because she smelled gas, but he was measuring up!'

Amanda's mouth dropped open. 'Oh my God!' she said, stunned.

Ben flashed a cheeky grin at her. 'Well, what do you expect, my darling wife? We are married now, we are expected to reproduce. They will be on our backs till we give them what they want, you know that, right?'

Amanda shook her head, laughing at the truth of the situation. 'They are incorrigible!' she said, pretending to be mad.

Ben pulled her close, peppering kisses all over her

face. 'Well,' he said, breathing into her ear. 'We can always practice. In fact, I am all in favour of plenty of practice.' He nibbled her ear lobe, giving her a little growl.

Amanda laughed, nuzzling into him. 'Well, at least we will save money on clothes,' she said, wrapping her arms around him.

'Exactly,' said Ben. 'Be nice to have a playmate for Pinky and Perky too. The chickens have been ruling the roost for far too long.'

Elaine strode up to the top table, and turned on her heel as she saw the embracing pair.

'Hey you,' Amanda called, spying her from the corner of her eye. She swatted at Ben as he nipped her bottom before going to talk to the band.

He dodged her and shouted, 'Better luck next time, Mrs Evans' as he walked away.

Elaine came and sat in Ben's chair, looking sheepish. 'Sorry,' she said.

Amanda giggled, giving her a hug.

'Don't be silly,' she said. 'So, settling in OK?'

Elaine looked gorgeous in her bridesmaid dress, and Amanda was once again thanking her lucky stars that Elaine, her friend from work, and loyal ally, had taken her job offer and come to live in Westfield. Amanda and the kittens lived with Ben now, and Elaine had moved into the flat above A New Lease of Life. With business being so busy, and Dotty retiring, there was more than enough work for her to do in the businesses, and she had taken to village life like a duck to water.

Elaine nodded, casting a shy smile to someone across the room. Amanda followed her gaze and spied a handsome man that she had not seen before, looking back at Elaine with the same puppy dog expression. She nudged Elaine discreetly. 'He is gorgeous, who is he?'

Elaine flushed. 'He is the greengrocer's son, Simon. He just moved back here. He's an architect and is going to set up round here.'

'Oh really, get his life story, did you?' Amanda teased and Elaine flushed a deeper shade of red.

'Nooo! I was just making conversation, that's all. He is new here too, or kind of.'

'Single?' Amanda asked, smirking at her friend's discomfort.

'Oh yes,' Elaine rushed. 'Er, I think so, anyway, didn't really ask,' she said, trying and failing to shrug non-committally. 'Er, anyway, I am going for a drink.' She motioned to the refreshments tent, which Simon just happened to be standing in. 'You want one?'

Amanda shook her head. 'No thanks, I don't want to be blotto for my wedding night!'

Elaine kissed her on the cheek and practically ran off towards the bar. Agatha came over with Taylor then, taking their seats at the top table. Agatha air-kissed her, and Taylor threw his arms around her, giving her a sloppy cheek kiss, to annoy Agatha obviously. Agatha shot him a look that said 'wait till I get you home' and Taylor whooped and gave her one to match, much to her chagrin. She tried and failed to look unamused.

'You do look truly wonderful, my dear,' she said to her for the fiftieth time.

Amanda's face lit up at her praise. 'Thanks, Agatha, and thank you both for everything. Today is amazing.'

Agatha brushed her off with a flick of her manicured hand. 'No need to thank us, dear, you are family.'

Amanda squeezed her hand tight, feeling happy tears sting at her eyes.

'Now,' Agatha said, back to business. 'Elaine and Simon, do you think we could help there?'

Taylor groaned loudly as he realised what she was up to, and Amanda choked on her champagne.

'Not again, woman! Not again,' Taylor said, dragging her to her feet. 'Come on, Mrs Taylor, let's work some of that matchmaking energy off on the dance floor!' Agatha allowed herself to be dragged away, surreptitiously giving a wink to Hetty, who in turn nodded to Dotty. *They are at it again*, Amanda thought to herself as Ben appeared before her, offering her his hand.

'Come on, Mrs Evans, they are playing our song.'

Amanda took his hand and marvelled as their wedding rings kissed each other with a click. 'Uptown Girl' struck up with the band, and Ben waggled his eyebrows at her devilishly. She groaned, trying and failing again to tap him on the arm as he folded her into his arms.

Agatha and Taylor flashed past, and her parents nodded at them both as they swished past. Dotty, Hetty, Marlene and Grace, for once knitting-free, danced close by. Elaine and Simon were dancing too, eyes for no one but each other, and Ben kept dropping kisses on her lips with his own warm soft ones as they moved on the dance floor. They began to twirl around, and everyone else joined in, till the dance floor was full. As she was dancing away with her new husband, family and friends around her having fun, she cherished the moment in her heart. Amanda Perry truly had found A New Lease of Life, and she was going to enjoy every single moment of it.

* * * * *

Acknowledgements

This book is a magical dream come true for me, and it wouldn't have happened without help. First of all, can I thank the amazing judges and staff involved with Prima Magazine and the Flirty Fiction competition. I enjoyed every minute, so thank you. Also, huge thanks to Anna Baggaley, my lovely editor who has been with me for every word, turning the jumble in my head to a book I am proud of, and the lovely people at Mills & Boon for being fabulous in general.

The writing and book blogging community on Facebook and Twitter have been amazing too, and without their support, encouragement and general nuttiness, I would be in a corner somewhere dribbling, so thank you all.

MILLS & BOON®

Mills & Boon have been at the heart of romance since 1908... and while the fashions may have changed, one thing remains the same: from pulse-pounding passion to the gentlest caress, we're always known how to bring romance alive.

Now, we're delighted to present you with these irresistible illustrations, inspired by the vintage glamour of our covers. So indulge your wildest dreams and unleash your imagination as we present the most iconic Mills & Boon moments of the last century.

Visit **www.millsandboon.co.uk/ArtofRomance** to order yours!

FREE EBOOKS

If you enjoyed this book why not try another? From historical heroes to hotel scandals, there is something for everyone in this collection of FREE ebooks from Mills & Boon®

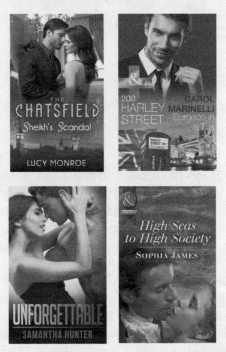

Just visit **www.millsandboon.co.uk/free-ebooks**
for more details

MILLS & BOON®